Calling a Dead Man

They used John's dental records to identify the body, and afterwards they cremated it . . . A week later Hayley saw him for the first time.

Hayley can't believe that John got himself blown up. Not on one of his own demolition jobs. He was an expert. That was why he'd gone to Siberia in the first place. So when Annie, John's fiancée, decides to fly to Russia and find out the truth, and asks Hayley to go with her to help her with her wheelchair, Hayley agrees to go, despite her parents' objections.

But she and Annie aren't prepared for the dangers that await them in Russia. What links John with the *mafiya*, the gangs that seem to control everything and everybody there? Why does Hayley still see John's face wherever they go? And why is everyone so anxious to keep them in Moscow? Hayley and Annie have to undergo a long and hazardous journey, deep into the Siberian forests, before they can find the answers.

Gillian Cross has been writing children's books for over twenty years. Before that, she took English degrees at Oxford and Sussex Universities, and she has had various jobs including working in a village bakery and being an assistant to a Member of Parliament. She is married with four children and lives in Warwickshire. Her hobbies include orienteering and playing the piano. She won the Carnegie Medal for *Wolf* and the Smarties Prize and the Whitbread Children's Novel Award for *The Great Elephant Chase*.

Other books by Gillian Cross

The Iron Way
Revolt at Ratcliffe's Rags
A Whisper of Lace
The Dark Behind the Curtain
Born of the Sun
On the Edge
Chartbreak
Roscoe's Leap
A Map of Nowhere
Wolf
The Great Elephant Chase
New World
Pictures in the Dark
Tightrope

For younger readers

Twin and Super-Twin
The Demon Headmaster
The Prime Minister's Brain
The Revenge of the Demon Headmaster
The Demon Headmaster Strikes Again
The Demon Headmaster Takes Over

Calling a Dead Man

Gillian Cross

OXFORD
UNIVERSITY PRESS

This book is dedicated to
Roma Gill, Steve Pazderski, and Jim Riordan,
with grateful thanks for all the help they gave
me while I was writing it.

OXFORD
UNIVERSITY PRESS

Great Clarendon Street, Oxford OX2 6DP

Oxford University Press is a department of the University of Oxford.
It furthers the University's objective of excellence in research, scholarship,
and education by publishing worldwide in

Oxford New York

Athens Auckland Bangkok Bogotá Buenos Aires Cape Town
Chennai Dar es Salaam Delhi Florence Hong Kong Istanbul Karachi
Kolkata Kuala Lumpur Madrid Melbourne Mexico City Mumbai
Nairobi Paris São Paulo Shanghai Singapore Taipei Tokyo Toronto Warsaw

and associated companies in Berlin Ibadan

Oxford is a registered trade mark of Oxford University Press
in the UK and in certain other countries

Database right Oxford University Press (maker)

First published 2001

British Library Cataloguing in Publication Data available

ISBN 0 19 271827 4

1 3 5 7 9 10 8 6 4 2

Typeset by AFS Image Setters Ltd, Glasgow

Printed and bound in Great Britain by Biddles Ltd

www.biddles.co.uk

1

They used John's dental records to identify the body, and afterwards they cremated it. Trevor went to Novosibirsk on his own and came back with an urn full of ashes, a folder of official papers and a few belongings, parcelled up in a suitcase.

On a windy day in September, the three of them drove to the South Downs together. Trevor, Chris, and Hayley— John's father, his mother, and his sister. Standing on top of Firle Beacon, they took turns to dip their hands into the urn, opening them slowly and watching the ashes blow away.

A week later, Hayley saw him for the first time.

He was sitting under the railway arches, in the rain. She didn't recognize him to begin with, as she walked by on the other side of the car park. He was hunched over, with his head on his knees and his coat collar turned up. She heard him cough and saw him shiver, leaning back against the dirty wall for support.

It was only after she was past that she looked round suddenly and saw his face, with all the colour gone out of it and the eyes sunken and staring.

She turned back and ran, calling his name out loud and splashing through muddy puddles, to try and get to him. But when she reached the arch there was no one there. Only the wind, blowing through empty space.

* * *

They burnt all his things. Emptied his bedroom and tipped out the suitcase that had come back from Russia.

Send them to Oxfam, people said. *Do something useful with them.* But Chris gathered everything into a great heap at the bottom of the garden. Books and clothes. The CDs and the CD player. School reports and photographs and newspaper cuttings. His rock-climbing magazines and the black, hardbacked notebooks that he'd used for work. Everything went straight on to the bonfire.

They set fire to it on a Thursday evening, when the sun was going down. Standing shoulder to shoulder, the three of them watched the flames eat everything. In front of them, John's face fizzled and twisted a hundred times over. Baby and toddler. Schoolboy and student. In his best clothes at a party and in a hard hat on a building site. Certificates glowed and blazed up, newsprint charred and disintegrated. *BRITON DIES IN SIBERIA . . . EXPLOSION DISASTER . . .* Blackened flakes fluttered and broke free, floating up into the dark sky.

They watched until the last red spark turned grey. Until their faces blurred and their shadows disappeared, so that they stood like three great stones in the darkness. Tall and solid and powerless.

'That's it, then,' Trevor said. And Chris turned and walked away from him, and away from Hayley. She went up the garden and into the house, shutting the door behind her.

'She'll be all right now,' Trevor said, looking at the closed door.

They both knew he was wrong. Hayley fetched the rake and began to rake out the embers, spreading them so that they cooled down. Tatters of paper, bits of twisted metal, unrecognizable dust.

Trevor stared, following her movements. When she stopped, he leaned forward and stirred the ashes with his shoe. Something had hitched itself on to one of the rake's teeth. Hayley peered at it.

'What's that, then?'

Trevor shrugged. 'Looks like a ring.'

Hayley hooked the object out of the debris. It was small and plain. The heat had distorted it without melting it completely, and it was black with soot.

'It's nothing,' Trevor said. 'Just something he picked up and put in his pocket. You know what he was like for hoarding.'

Hayley closed her eyes. That brought John back, sharp and fresh. The way he would bend over suddenly on a site full of rubbish to pick out a medieval nail or a hand-painted tile. *Look, Halo* . . .

Trevor remembered too. 'No point in hanging around,' he said abruptly. 'Put that rake away and come on in.'

Hayley waited until he was halfway to the house before she tipped the ring on to the grass. She pushed it backwards and forwards with the rake, cooling it down and rubbing off the soot. When she picked it up, one edge gleamed gold—or brass. John would have known the difference, but she couldn't tell. She looked at it for a moment and then dropped it into the pocket of her coat.

When she went inside, Trevor was playing back messages on the answerphone. Hayley stood in the sitting room doorway and heard Annie's voice, quick and insistent.

Why have you always got the answerphone on? I'm sick of leaving messages. You never call me back and I need to talk to you. Do you want me to come down and see you—?

Trevor put his finger down hard on the ERASE button. 'Not that,' he said heavily. He looked over his shoulder at Hayley. 'You'd better ring her.'

'Me?'

3

'Tell her she can't come. Mum's not ready for that sort of thing yet.'

He went past Hayley, into the kitchen, and she heard him fill the kettle and plug it in. Overhead, her mother was moving about in John's room, making strange noises that Hayley couldn't identify. Bumping. Dragging. Tearing.

Trevor came out of the kitchen carrying two mugs of tea. MUM and DAD they said. He caught Hayley's eye and nodded at the phone. Then he went on upstairs with the tea. A moment later, Hayley heard him tapping on John's door, with his foot. When the door opened, there was a silence and then a low mumble of voices.

Hayley looked at the phone. Then she picked it up and dialled.

It hardly had time to ring before Annie answered. She kept her phone in a little pocket on the arm of her chair.

'Annie Glasgow.'

'It's me,' Hayley said. 'Hayley.'

'Life at last!' Annie said. Hayley imagined her leaning forward, her thin shoulders poking, her small, sharp face keen and attentive. 'What's going on down there? Why hasn't anyone called me?'

'We've been—' Hayley couldn't think how to explain what they'd been. She left the words hanging.

'Oh come on!' Annie said. 'It's been like talking into a fog. I've phoned half a dozen times. Left messages. Written letters. Why hasn't anyone answered? I want to know how you are, all of you. I need to talk to you.'

Hayley shuffled her feet. 'Mum's not very—she needs to forget all that stuff for a bit.'

'Stuff?' Annie's voice sharpened slightly. 'What do you mean *stuff*?'

'I mean—' Hayley swallowed.

'You mean John? She's saying she wants to forget *him*?'

4

'She won't even say his name.'

There was a long pause. When Annie spoke again, she sounded different. Cautious and questioning. 'And what about you?'

'Me? I—' Words vibrated in Hayley's brain. *I saw him under the railway arches. It was him, I know it was, because I saw his face. But when I went to him, he wasn't there. Of course.* 'I'm OK,' she said out loud.

'You don't sound OK. You sound like hell. Oh come on, Hayley, don't buy this forgetting nonsense. You *need* to talk about him. He's your brother.'

'Was,' Hayley said. And then wished she hadn't, because the sound of her voice gave her away.

'You *see*?' Annie said. 'You've *got* to talk. I'm going to come down and see you tomorrow.'

'You can't! You mustn't! Dad said—'

'OK, OK, don't go bananas. I'm not going to come to the house. We can meet somewhere in the town. How about lunch?'

'We're not supposed to go out of school at lunchtime.'

'Don't be such a wimp.' Annie sounded firm now. 'Just walk out of the place. No one's going to notice. And if they do, just tell them where you're going.'

'I don't think—'

'If you don't come, I *will* turn up at the house. And I'll ask Trevor and Chris what they think they're doing to you.'

'No!' Hayley said. She heard the door open overhead. Feet on the landing. 'Look, I'll meet you at—' Her mind went blank.

'We can go to McDonald's,' Annie said. 'They're usually all right for me to get into. I'll park in that car park across the road and wait for you. Half past twelve?'

'Just after. Look, I've got to go now—'

'OK,' Annie said. 'But you'd better be there.'

5

Hayley was shaking as she put the phone down. Her parents came into the room and she jumped up.

'I'd better do some homework.'

It was an excuse to get away, but she needn't have bothered. They hardly looked at her. Chris's face was blank and Trevor was holding on to her elbow, carrying the two mugs of tea in his other hand as he steered her across the room.

'We'll have our tea in here. Come on, Chris. Sit in the chair.'

Hayley escaped upstairs. She meant to immerse herself in homework straight away, but as she passed John's room the light caught her eye, through the half-open door. She stopped and looked in.

The room was stripped. The window gaped black and cold, with no curtains. The naked light bulb glared down on to bare boards. The walls were a mess of tattered paper and bald plaster.

All the furniture had been piled into the centre of the room, with the carpet and curtains on top and the lampshade thrown into the heap. The wallpaper was mostly there too, ripped off and screwed into ragged balls. On the far wall, a long strip of paper hung down, showing where the destruction had been interrupted.

Hayley looked at it and felt sick and afraid. Closing her eyes, she pushed the door shut and went on into her bedroom.

2

I t was Frosya who found the stranger in the forest.
She was always the one who found things.
Mushrooms. The lost cow. Small wood for kindling
when the stoves went out. If Baba Yaga's chicken house
had strutted into a clearing and squatted there, it would
have been Frosya who stumped through the trees to stare
at it with her mouth open and her head on one side.

She was the only one who could go into the forest
now. The rest of them were too old. Only Frosya was
steady on her feet, strong enough to plough through the
sludge and jump across the worst wet places. Until the
winter came to freeze it solid, there was nothing under the
trees but mud and water, water and mud. Frosya plodded
between the birch trees, squelching and splashing,
enjoying the last of the warm weather and the smell of the
wet green air.

On that particular day, she was chasing Yelena's goat.
Long before anyone was awake, it had pulled its stake out
of the ground and trotted into the forest. When Yelena
opened her door and saw the hoof marks, she yelled for
Frosya. Frosya peered at the marks, following them to the
edge of the trees. Then she went to see the Komendant.

He was sitting in the cottage doorway, dozing while
his wife laid out his breakfast. His clothes were old and
patched, but he sat upright, with his walking sticks
hooked over the arm of the chair. Frosya stood in front of
his chair, mumbling at him.

A snore gurgled in his throat and his thin eyelids

7

fluttered. Irina Petrovna, his wife, came across and touched his shoulder. He opened pale eyes, smiling and rubbing at the stubble on his chin.

Frosya mumbled again, waving her hands and pointing to show what she meant. Irina Petrovna looked past her, at the hoof prints.

'It's Yelena's goat again,' she said. 'It's wandered off.'

The Komendant nodded and scratched his head. Unfolding his long bent legs, he took the walking sticks and shuffled into the cabin. Frosya stood with her red hands folded, waiting.

The Komendant stubbed his toe on the stove, swore under his breath and came back carrying a lump of hard, stale bread. He pressed it into Frosya's hand, closing her fingers round it.

'Go into the forest and find the goat,' he said. His hand shook, but his voice was steady, giving orders. 'Look for other things if you like, but get hold of the goat first. And watch the light. You must be back before dark.'

Frosya stared solemnly, waiting for the nod that would mean he had finished. When it came, she beamed and lumbered off at a trot, chewing on a corner of the bread. By the time she had crossed the clearing and reached the trees, she was out of breath. She pushed the bread into her apron pocket and slowed to a walk.

Under the trees, tiny black flies buzzed at her, whining in her ears and settling at the corners of her eyes. She brushed them off and pulled out her old bee-net, tying it over her whole head to keep them away. The dappled light flickered over her as she stepped from tree to tree, her old felt boots squelching in the mud.

She saw the man and the goat almost at once.

The man was lying across the path in the second clearing. The goat was by his ankles, chewing at the tuft of grass that had tripped him up.

8

Frosya stopped at the edge of the clearing and frowned, wondering what to do. She nearly went back for instructions, but then the goat lifted its head. Once it had seen her, there was no holding back. Now it had been disturbed, it would probably go deeper into the forest. Frosya held out the lump of bread and moved forward, clicking her tongue. Watching the sprawled body in case the man leapt up at her.

But even when she was right beside him, with the toes of her boots against his head, he didn't move. He didn't stir an inch, even though the goat put its two front hooves on his chest, reaching for the bread in Frosya's hand.

Frosya crooned to the goat, scratching the side of its head and running her fingers along its hairy cheek. Aiming for the rope round its neck. *Get hold of the goat first*, the Komendant had said. *Then you can look round if you want to*. When she had tightened her fingers on the rope, she bent down to look at the man.

His flesh was burning hot. She reached out to touch him and snatched her hand away. When she prodded at his face he stirred faintly, making a weak sound that was not quite a moan.

Frosya looked at him. She looked at the goat which glared back with its angry, square eyes. She looked at the sky. Then she pulled the dangling end of the goat's rope through her belt. She knotted it hard, three times, to leave both hands free for pulling at the stranger's arm.

She pulled for a long time. The goat had finished the bread and was butting angrily at her before the man opened his eyes. He stared over Frosya's shoulder, without focusing.

Frosya tugged at the arm again, shouting to make him get up.

He shrank back, trying to pull his arm away from her. But he was too weak to break her grip.

9

Frosya yelled louder, shaking his shoulder and heaving awkwardly at his body.

Muttering and sobbing under his breath, the man began to haul himself to his feet, scrabbling at the ground with his knees and his free hand. His clothes were wet and foul and the smell when he moved was stronger than the goat, but Frosya didn't let go of him. When he was on his feet, she moved her hand, slipping her arm round his waist so that he could lean against her. He was a head taller, but she was square and solid and used to carrying heavy weights. She pointed back towards the houses and pulled him to make him move.

The goat was tugging at her belt and butting her other side, but she battled forward, putting her head down and taking one step after another. Gasping for breath, the man slumped against her and began to walk, planting his feet blindly. Every time he fell into the mud, Frosya hauled him up, bracing herself against the goat, which alternated between butting her and trying to pull her over.

By the time they came out of the trees, all three of them were covered in mud and coated with tiny flies. The moment the goat saw the cottages, it bolted up the slope towards them. Frosya was dragged on to her knees and she scrabbled up like that, yelling at the top of her voice and towing the stranger after her.

She was halfway up the slope when Irina Petrovna hobbled out of the nearest cottage, carrying another piece of bread. The goat changed direction to meet her and she dropped the bread on the ground, to distract it, while she untied the rope from Frosya's belt.

With the goat gone, Frosya heaved herself off the ground, tugging the stranger up too. She pulled him towards the Komendant's cottage and the Komendant came out to meet them, leaning on his sticks.

Frosya loosened her grip, babbling and pointing at the stranger. He slipped away from her and collapsed with a groan, sprawling at the Komendant's feet.

Slowly the old man walked round him, examining his filthy clothes and his feverish, distracted face. Watching him shiver and twitch and stare into the distance.

'Heat some water,' he said at last. 'And bring my knife.'

Frosya lumbered into the cottage. When she came out again, most of the others had gathered. Not her father—he never left his bed now—but Yelena in her ancient fur coat, and Piotr, and old Nikolai on his crutches. They were standing in a huddle by the stranger's head, muttering darkly to each other.

The Komendant ignored them, concentrating on what needed to be done.

'Cut his laces. Take off his boots.'

Frosya was the only one who could kneel down. She dragged the knife blade across the tight, knotted laces and began to pull at the boots. The stranger yelled once and passed out.

'Socks off,' the Komendant said. 'And those disgusting clothes.'

Now the stranger was unconscious, it was easy to strip off his things. Every time Frosya hesitated, the Komendant urged her on.

'Everything! Take them all off and burn them!'

Voices buzzed above Frosya's head, but she was too busy to take in what they said. As the Komendant directed her, she cut fabric and undid buttons, easing off the clothes in sections.

The stranger was a young man, with square shoulders and strong muscles. His skin was dirty and mud-stained, scarred by dark bruises and swellings and hundreds of insect bites. Frosya knew that he was ill, because of the heat under her hands—and the way the old people were shaking their heads. Nikolai mumbled under his breath and Irina Petrovna clicked her tongue as she leaned closer.

'We need the water now, Frosya. And a clean rag. I think he has brain fever, from tick bites.'

It took them over an hour to find all the ticks. Frosya rubbed and scrubbed at the unconscious body, wringing out stinking cloths and running up and down the slope for more water. And as she washed the stranger, the others stood round scanning his skin.

There were five ticks, striped black and white and embedded deep in the swollen flesh. The Komendant made Frosya cut out every trace of the heads and swab the wounds with vodka. Once or twice she heard Irina Petrovna mutter and catch her breath, but the Komendant's voice went on steadily, giving orders. Frosya did what he told her to. The way she always did.

When she had dealt with the last tick, he made her check again. But he was beginning to tire, leaning heavily on his sticks. Piotr had already given up and gone back to his cabin and Yelena and Nikolai were moaning and grumbling, peering down at the stranger's body.

'What's he going to eat?' That was Yelena, of course.

'And who is he?' Nikolai prodded with his foot. 'Maybe the whole thing's a trap. If we take him into our houses, he'll steal everything we have.'

Irina Petrovna shook her head scornfully, but Yelena screeched and headed back to her cabin, hobbling as fast as she could move. The door slammed shut and they heard the bolt slide across.

'So many treasures,' the Komendant said, sarcastic and weary. 'This is such a rich place for robbers to come to.'

Irina Petrovna walked forward, painfully. Her arthritis

was always worst in the wet autumn weather. The stranger was still now and she stared down at his flushed face and the raw places where the ticks had been.

'He has nothing,' she said. 'And he is getting cold. What can we do but take him in?'

He is falling through nothing, exploding into a chaos of pain and dust and destruction. If he opens his eyes, light crashes over him like tumbling blocks of concrete, blasts through his head, blowing his brains apart.

Voices pound into his ears at a million decibels, throbbing in his skull. Every touch on his burning skin scorches it with agony. His mouth is as dry as rubble, as dry as crumbling mortar in a desert wall, and his lips split open when he tries to speak.

There is no chance to think. No chance to wonder who he is, or where he is and how he got there. There's nothing except the pain, taking him from moment to moment. Drowning out everything else.

3

'*E*verything?' Annie put down her carton of fries and stared at Hayley. 'She burnt the whole lot?'

Hayley nodded.

'All the photos? All his notebooks?'

'Everything. She'd have burnt the furniture and the wallpaper if Dad hadn't stopped her.' Hayley looked down at the cheeseburger and wondered how she was going to eat it.

'I don't believe it.' Annie leaned back in her wheelchair, gazing at the posters round them. CYBERMEAL FOR KIDS FREE WITH EVERY . . . She shook her head. 'I didn't even *see* the stuff Trevor brought back from Russia.'

Hayley picked up her cheeseburger and took a small, difficult bite, wishing she hadn't come. Annie always made her feel big and clumsy and awkward.

'Chris is trying to wipe him out, isn't she?' Annie said. Her face was like a weasel's, sharp and fine-boned, and her eyes were fierce. 'She's trying to pretend he never existed. That's why she won't answer any of my messages.'

'It's not like that—'

'Yes it is! She's blotting him out. Everything to do with him. His own family's forgetting him.'

'Not all of us,' Hayley said. 'It's only Mum. That's the only way she can bear it. *I* don't want to forget him.' *No chance of that. Not if I see his face in the rain under the railway arches.*

'But how are you going to remember?' Annie said. 'If everything's burnt?'

14

'I don't need things to remind me.'

'So what *are* you going to do? If Trevor and Chris won't talk about him, what's left? What kind of remembering is that?' Annie was getting angry now, smacking her hand down on to the table. 'John was the most fantastic person I've ever met. Strong and honest and beautiful. If you were dead, he wouldn't forget *you*!'

'It's not my fault!' Hayley said, getting angry herself. '*I'm* not an adult. If I were—if I could do anything I wanted, then I'd—'

She stopped abruptly. Annie looked at her across the empty cartons and the crumpled paper napkins.

'Yes?' she said softly. 'What would you do?'

'I'd go to Russia.' Hayley hadn't known what she wanted until that moment. The idea sprang up in her mind as she spoke, so sharp and painful that she had to look down, away from Annie's probing eyes. 'I want to see the place where he died.'

There was an odd silence. A long silence.

Then Annie said, 'That's what I want too. Shall we go together?'

'What?' Hayley blinked at her.

Annie said it again. 'We can go together. I couldn't possibly manage on my own, but it'll be fine if you come as well. We can go for a week—or even two. And see everywhere he went.'

'But it would cost a fortune,' Hayley said. 'Dad flew straight into Novosibirsk and out again the next day, and that was bad enough, but a week—'

Annie shrugged. 'What else am I going to spend the money on?'

'Money?' Hayley looked at her cautiously. Was this something she was supposed to know about?

'The money John and I saved up together,' Annie said. 'So we could get married.'

'You were going to get *married?*'

Hayley was caught off guard. She said it without thinking, and the moment the words were out, she cringed inside.

John's poor little friend in a wheelchair. That was what Chris always called Annie. *He's very good to her, taking her round the way he does, but they can't really have much in common. I mean—Annie's hardly going to go rock-climbing, is she?* (As if Annie must be boring, just because she was small and frail.)

Had *she* sounded like that too? Crass and patronizing?

Annie gave her a shrewd look, but she didn't comment. She just said, 'We had enough to put down on a house— with the money John was getting from the Russian job. And it's all sitting there in the bank. We can go to Siberia tomorrow if we want to.'

She stopped. Waiting for Hayley to say something.

Hayley thought of all the difficulties. Persuading her parents. Spending two weeks on her own with Annie. Coping with the foreignness of Russia and the vastness of Siberia.

Then she thought of John's face, under the railway arch.

'Well?' Annie said.

'There's no way, love.' Trevor sat down on the edge of Hayley's bed. 'You know what Mum's like. It would be crazy to suggest it.'

'But Annie would pay.'

'It's not the money, Hay. Have a bit of sense. It's Mum. She just can't cope with anything else. She needs some peace and quiet.'

'Maybe *I* need to go to Siberia,' Hayley said. 'Or doesn't that matter?'

Her father rubbed a hand across his eyes and smiled,

wearily. 'It won't make any difference, you know. Going to Russia won't bring John back. Any more than burning his things did. He's dead—and we've got to accept it.'

Hayley nodded and slid down in the bed. That was the last word, wasn't it? *John's dead.* Nothing left to say after that.

But when Trevor had gone, she lay awake in the dark, staring up at the ceiling. Watching the headlights of the passing cars sweep across the empty space.

Once, when she was very small, John had taken her to see a blowdown. It was one of the first jobs he'd worked on and they were on the edge of the site, she and Trevor and Chris. He'd found them a place with the owners and the visitors who had come along to watch.

Just before the explosion, John walked across in his hard hat and held out his arms to Hayley. 'Up you come, Halo. Get a good view.'

Hoisted on to his shoulders, she could feel the pace of his breath, steady and regular, as he walked across to where his team-mates were waiting to blow the charges.

'There it is then.' He pointed at the tower block across the open space. His voice was casual, but Hayley could remember how his breathing speeded up as the engineer in charge began the count.

'Five, four, three . . . '

The voice was flat and unemotional, but Hayley caught John's mood, twisting her hands into his hair until he reached up to pull them down.

' . . . two, one, blow.'

The sound of the blast thudded across at them. Dust billowed out between the floors of the tall, empty block. It shivered from top to bottom.

And then—nothing happened.

For a couple of seconds, the whole building hung motionless, blown to pieces but not displaced, every brick hovering in its own position. No one spoke. John's breathing stopped completely.

Then, in bizarre slow motion, the block collapsed down and outwards, sprawling on to the waste ground in front of them. For one dreamlike instant, with everything loose in midair, there was no sound at all. Then the debris rained on to the ground in a thunder of grinding concrete.

A week later, she came in from school and heard voices in the sitting room. Her mother was muttering something fast and angry and it was Annie who answered.

'Why don't we *ask* Hayley? She's just come in, hasn't she?'

Hayley pushed open the sitting room door. Trevor and Chris were side by side on the sofa and Annie was facing them, with her wheelchair squeezed in between the armchair and the fireplace. She looked tiny and very fierce.

'Ask her!' she said, the moment Hayley stepped into the room. 'Go on. She's here now. Give her the chance to say what *she* wants to do.'

'Why does she have to be involved?' Chris said. Her mouth was tight and ugly. 'You don't need Hayley to go with you. If you've got all that money, you can *hire* someone to be your minder.'

'But I want Hayley,' Annie said.

Some instinct in Hayley said *That's it. That's too much.* For a breathless instant, she stared at her mother's stiff, icy face and knew that the politeness was a lie, that it was already collapsing, already destroyed.

Then Chris was on her feet with her mouth wide open, yelling at Annie. 'You want, you want, you want! You wanted John, didn't you? So he had to go to Russia and kill himself with that stupid consultancy! Now you want Hayley! And after that it'll be Trevor, won't it? Why have we got to let you have everything, just because—just because—'

Whatever it was, she couldn't say it. Instead, she started across the room towards the wheelchair, with a violence that brought Trevor hurtling to his feet. For an instant, Hayley was terrified. Then her father put his arms round Chris.

The hopeless, powerless gesture collapsed. Chris caught her breath with a sob and ran out of the room and away upstairs. There was a long, terrible silence.

'She needs a break,' Trevor said at last. 'That's all. I ought to take her away for a while. Just the two of us.'

'Why don't you do that?' Annie said. Challenging him. 'Take her away for a fortnight—and Hayley can come to Russia with me.'

Trevor met her eyes for a second—and then he smiled, wryly. 'Very neat. But it wouldn't be much of a break for us. We'd just spend two weeks worrying ourselves sick about you both. How would you get by in a place like that?'

'*You* managed all right,' Hayley said.

Trevor shook his head. 'That was different. Frank Walsh sorted things out for me.'

'So I should think,' Annie said. 'He was the one who got John out there in the first place.'

'He could take care of us too,' said Hayley. 'We wouldn't need much. Just a bit of advice.'

Trevor looked from her to Annie and back again.

'Oh, go on, Dad! I'm not a baby. And we only want to go to Russia—not the moon.'

Trevor glanced up at the ceiling. Over their heads, Chris was moving about in John's room. They heard her feet, pacing backwards and forwards—and then the sound of tearing. Sudden and abrupt.

Hayley reached for the phone and held it out. 'Ring Frank Walsh now. Go on.'

For another second, Trevor hesitated. Then he looked at his watch. 'It's coming up to eight in the evening in Moscow.'

'A great time to phone,' Annie said.

Slowly, Trevor nodded. And took out his diary to find the phone number.

From that moment on, the trip was settled. The only question was how fast it could be arranged.

While Annie was sorting out visas and bookings, Hayley tried to get Chris to take an interest in what was happening. She found a map of Russia on the school computer and printed it out, marking their route with coloured pens.

'We fly into Moscow—that's that red dot. But we're not staying there long. When we've talked to Frank Walsh, we're flying on east, into Siberia. Look how far it is. A thousand miles? More . . . ?'

The distance was daunting and exciting. The place names made Hayley's heart thump: Moscow, Novosibirsk, Tomsk . . . But Chris didn't even look at the map. She sat by the window, staring out into the dim October evening and picking at the edge of the curtain.

It was like that all the time, until the night before they went, when Hayley was packing her case. Her bed was covered with piles of clothes and she was trying to decide which suitcase to use, the little black one (a bit of a squash, but neat and smart) or the shabby red one with its handle held on with string.

She turned round and found her mother standing behind her, in stockinged feet.

'Mum! You made me jump.'

Chris's eyes drifted dully over the bed. 'You haven't got enough clothes there. You'll be cold.'

'It's all the warm clothes I've got. Look.' Hayley pushed open the wardrobe door, to show what was left.

'You ought to have had some new things,' Chris said, still in the same listless voice.

Pity you didn't think of that before. But there was no point in saying it. 'Don't fuss, Mum. I'll be fine.'

'No you won't. Wait a minute.'

Chris padded out of the room and down the stairs. A moment later, she was back with something heavy and dark looped over her arm.

Hayley pulled a face. 'That's my *gardening* coat. It's ancient. And it smells of smoke.'

'Better than freezing to death. Go on.' Chris pushed the coat at her. When Hayley didn't take it, she rolled it up and put it on top of the other clothes.

It didn't seem like a good idea to argue. Hayley resigned herself to taking the red suitcase. Lifting it on to the bed, she began to pack the clothes. Her mother watched until everything was in, including the old coat.

Then she said, 'You have to be serious about keeping warm in a place like that. It's much more important than what you look like.'

But there was no force behind the words. She sounded like someone reading a notice. Hayley wanted to hug her, but it was already too late. Chris was backing away, heading for the stairs, and when Hayley struggled down with the suitcase, she was in her usual place on the sofa. Staring out at the black mark on the grass, where the bonfire had been.

'You're not coming to the airport, then?' Trevor said, looking into the room.

Chris shook her head without looking round. 'I'll be all right. Don't worry about me.'

'Come on then, Hay.' Trevor looked tired too, as he picked up the case. 'I bet Annie's waiting for us when we get there.'

She wasn't just waiting. She was at the check-in, with everything organized round her. An airport wheelchair. Her own light, folding wheelchair, ready to put on to the plane at the last moment. A sheaf of documents in her hand. And two porters ready to wheel her through to the departure lounge.

Trevor looked down the concourse and stopped for a moment. 'Are you sure you can cope with this, Hay? Two weeks with Annie, on your own—it could be hard work.'

'What's the big deal? Look at her. I'm twice the size she is.'

'I don't mean *that*,' Trevor said, impatiently. 'I know you can wheel her around. I'm talking about the mental stuff. Annie's very demanding. She—'

'I know what she's like,' said Hayley, cutting him short. She looked down the concourse, watching Annie give directions about labelling her luggage. No doubt about who was in charge there.

'You've still got time to change your mind,' Trevor murmured.

Hayley didn't even bother to answer. She just started walking again, waving to attract Annie's attention.

4

Frosya was impatient for the stranger to wake up.

Five or six times a day, she went up to the Komendant's cabin, to peer at his unconscious face, leaning close in the dim light and touching his cheek with her fingers. The fever had gone down and sometimes he stirred, shifting in the big double bed, but he didn't open his eyes. And when Frosya shook his shoulder, Irina Petrovna hobbled over and pulled her hands away.

'Leave him alone. He'll wake when it's time. Now let's turn him again.'

They did it together. Irina Petrovna stood over the bed and gave instructions, and Frosya obeyed, heaving the stranger over with her big red hands and then bending his arms and legs and working his fingers to keep them supple.

Three times a day they stripped the covers back and washed him. Then Frosya hauled him up, propping him on pillows so that Irina Petrovna could try to give him some thin soup. That meant holding the cup to his slack mouth and tipping it until his lips moved and he swallowed by reflex.

It took hours. Frosya went away to milk Yelena's goat, or weed Piotr's vegetable patch, or cook Nikolai's potatoes, and when she came back the feeding was still going on. If Irina Petrovna grew too tired to sit by the bed any more, the Komendant took over, gravely holding the cup and dabbing at the dribbled soup on the stranger's chin.

And all the time he talked.

'That's good. That will do you good. Swallow some more, and I'll tell you about the village . . . '

Frosya went in and out, day after day, catching snippets of the story she knew and did not know.

' . . . it was never a large village. They call me Komendant, for a joke, but even when all the cottages were full we were just twenty or thirty people living together in the forest. Hunting for meat for the *kolkhoz* down the river . . . '

The stranger's head stayed slumped and his eyes were closed. But every now and again his eyelids flickered and his lips moved, swallowing. Patiently, the Komendant went on holding the cup and talking.

' . . . you'll ask, of course, how Stalin left a place like this. It's true that he wanted to do away with the little villages. He wanted to draw people close together, to live in big *kolkhozes*. And maybe collective farming is a noble idea. But people must have food. After the War, some of us drifted back to the village and started hunting again. No point in wasting what the forest gives. And now things are different, and the *kolkhoz* has forgotten us . . . '

Frosya went out and came in with the last cabbages and a pail of milk.

' . . . sometimes we have fish,' the Komendant was saying wistfully, looking down into the cup of potato soup. 'But there aren't as many as there used to be. Maybe Nikolai is getting too old for fishing. Maybe it's true that the river is poisoned . . . '

Irina Petrovna smiled. Frosya brought her a bowl and a knife for chopping the cabbage. Then she bobbed her head and went out again, to dig some potatoes for Yelena.

On the seventh day it happened, quite simply and with no fuss. As Frosya was hauling the stranger up to turn him for the second time, his eyelids flickered and lifted. She was staring into clear grey eyes that looked straight past her, vague and unfocused.

She dropped him, with a squeal, and Irina Petrovna came across the room, leaning on her stick.

'Is he awake?'

Frosya nodded, and bent closer, looking into the stranger's eyes. She smiled as she saw her own broken teeth and broad red cheeks reflected back at her.

The Komendant came over too, moving slowly, from the stove to the bed, shifting two sticks and two feet.

'Good day,' he said gravely, when he reached the bed at last. 'I hope you are comfortable?'

His words floated over the stranger like scum on a pond, not making any change to the distant depths of his eyes.

'Offer him tea,' Irina Petrovna said.

There was a big old-fashioned samovar on the stove. Frosya took a pinch of tea from the battered tin next to it and dropped it into a glass, holding it under the tap of the samovar. When the tea was ready, she took it across the room and offered it to the stranger.

He gazed up at her, neither awake nor asleep, not lifting his hands. Frosya blew across the surface of the tea, to cool it. Then she held the glass to his lips. He opened his mouth and drank steadily, gazing up at her all the time. When the tea was finished, he closed his eyes again.

'Thank you,' he said. The Russian word came awkwardly, with an effort, and Frosya found it hard to understand.

By the next day, he was awake for longer. He stared round the room with wide eyes, taking in every detail. The old tiled stove and the wood stack beside it. The big painted chest. The two hard chairs, where Irina Petrovna and the Komendant had slept every night for the last week.

His eyes reached the Komendant's face. 'Yerofey Zubov,' the Komendant said, bowing slightly. 'My wife, Irina Petrovna. And Efrosinya Feodorovna Zhizhina.'

Frosya frowned for a moment, because no one ever used her full name. Then Irina Petrovna said, 'Frosya. She is Frosya,' and she held out her hand to the stranger.

He took it and she felt the pressure of his fingers. Then he fell asleep again, quite suddenly, still holding on to her hand. Frosya looked down at him, without moving, hardly breathing. Feeling gentle, so gentle.

Irina Petrovna patted her shoulder. 'He feels safe with you, Frosya. But he is very weak. And I don't think he understands Russian. Maybe he will have to learn everything, like a baby. To talk. To walk again. Everything.'

'He may not learn,' the Komendant said heavily. 'He has had tick fever. Maybe he will never move again. Maybe he will die.'

Frosya looked down at the hand holding on to her. She tried to mumble that he mustn't die, that they must keep him safe and heal him. But her tongue was thick and the words stuck and muddled in her mouth.

Irina Petrovna patted her again. 'Time enough,' she said. 'We shall see. But if he's going to learn to walk, we must find him some clothes. Since we've burnt the ones he came in.' She took the big black key from her apron pocket and held it out to Frosya. 'Please look in the chest.'

Frosya worked her fingers out of the stranger's grasp and took the key. Irina Petrovna had never let her open the chest before and her hand was shaking as she unlocked it.

None of them had much furniture. A bed. A table with

chairs or stools. A big plain stove with a heap of wood chopped ready beside it. That was all, and everything was plain and ordinary, the same in every cottage.

Except for Irina Petrovna's trunk. That was different. It was very old and made of heavy wood, panelled all round the sides and on the lid. Every panel was painted with a different story and, even though the colours had dimmed, the characters still rode and danced across the big square panels, in red and blue and green. Vasilissa the Beautiful. Prince Ivan and the Firebird. Boris and Gleb. The Rusalka and Baba Yaga. And Prince Vladimir who threw the pagan idols into the River Dnepr.

Frosya had been told the stories a hundred times, and she told them over again to herself, when she was lying in bed, making the pictures in her mind and saying the words carefully under her breath. The right story for each picture.

Slowly she lifted the lid. She knew what was inside the trunk, but even those ordinary things seemed special. The clothes were folded neatly on top of the quilts. Trousers and shirts and thick padded jackets. Two long skirts and the beautiful embroidered dress that Irina Petrovna had worn when she was married. Frosya had never seen anyone wear the dress, but every summer Irina Petrovna took out all the clothes and hung them on the trees to air.

'Two pairs of trousers,' Irina Petrovna said. 'Two shirts. And that good thick jacket with the collar. If he's not a Russian, he'll feel the cold when he gets up.'

Frosya took the clothes out of the chest and laid them on the bed. Before she locked the chest again, she remembered that there should be socks, too, and boots. She found those as well, and put them beside the stove to warm. Then she leaned over the stranger and shook his shoulder, so that he could see what good care they were taking to keep him warm when he walked again.

He stirred and turned over under the heap of quilts, hunching one shoulder to pull the covers round him.

'That's good,' the Komendant said. 'Maybe he won't die after all.'

When the stranger woke up properly, it was her name he remembered. He called it each time he opened his eyes.

'Frosya!'

It was a thin, carrying cry. Wherever she was in the village, Frosya heard it and abandoned what she was doing. She went straight to him, leaving the cow half milked or the chopped potatoes browning in the bowl. Before he could call again, she was there, ready to heave him up and prop him into a sitting position.

One day, when Irina Petrovna and the Komendant had hobbled up the village to speak to Piotr, she brought the stranger the things she had found in his clothes. *Take them all off and burn them*, the Komendant had said, when she was stripping him. But Frosya had felt the lumps in the pockets. Before she burnt the clothes, she had emptied them carefully, hiding the things away in her own cottage. Money. A notebook. A strange silver thing, the length of her hand, with black buttons and a little window at one end.

The stranger ran his finger over them, as though he had never seen them before. When he pressed at the buttons, a light flashed in the little window, but the symbols that appeared made no sense to Frosya.

And none to him either, it seemed. He pressed again, until the light disappeared, and then laid the thing aside and flicked through the notebook.

It was full of scribbled lines and circles that Frosya couldn't understand. She tried to ask him about them, but he was suddenly tired and fretful, pushing the book away

28

so that it fell on the floor. Frosya picked it up again and put it on the bed.

He shook his head petulantly, like a child, and dabbed at the things to make them go away. Frosya picked up the silver object and the notebook and put them in her apron pocket. The money was different. She stacked that on the post at the end of the bed, because she knew it would be bad to keep it.

Then she leaned over the stranger to lift him up and make him comfortable again, because he had slipped down in the bed. While she was doing it, Irina Petrovna and the Komendant came back.

'His arms are good now,' the Komendant said from the doorway. 'Strong.'

Frosya understood that. When she lifted him now, he put his arms round her neck and hung on. And sometimes she could feel him helping her, pushing against the mattress with his heels. He held his own soup bowl and drank from the cup himself.

'Try his legs,' Irina Petrovna said. 'Fold the quilts back, Frosya.'

With the quilts pulled back to his knees, the stranger's legs looked pale and scarred. He frowned down at them as though he couldn't remember what they were for. Frosya walked up and down the room, pointing at her own legs and nodding to encourage him, but it didn't seem to have any effect. Once he flexed his toes, but he didn't show any sign of jumping out of bed and imitating her.

'Wait,' said the Komendant.

He hauled himself across the room and sat down on the end of the bed. Then he put one hand against the naked sole of the stranger's right foot.

'Push,' he said. '*Push.*' With his other hand, he mimed the action, showing what he wanted. Then he pushed forward himself, so that the stranger's knee reared up into the air as his leg bent.

And—faintly at first, but then harder—the stranger pushed back until his leg was straight again.

'Good,' said the Komendant gently. 'Very good. Now the other.'

As he pushed against the left foot, Frosya looked round at Irina Petrovna and the old woman nodded at her, smiling so hard that her cheeks were two round balls below her bright eyes.

'So—we can see that he's going to walk again. That one won't give up until he does!'

His mind is like water now. Still water in a mountain lake. Images move over the surface like clouds, without his choosing. The old man and the old woman. The shadows on the cottage wall. The light behind the nailed-up shutters, growing pale and dark and pale again where he can see it through the cracks.

When the door opens, the brightness is safe, contained in the small space of the frame. He can see two other cottages, one with a smoking chimney and the other with its roof falling in. Half-rotten. And behind them, trees with needles or bare branches.

Food comes without his asking, before he even knows that he's hungry. Potato soup and eggs. Cabbage and stewed hare. And strong tea in a thick glass. It's always now—always today, with no yesterday or tomorrow. Peaceful and safe.

The only danger comes in the moment just before he wakes. The no man's land between dream and consciousness. In that uncertain moment, a face invades the darkness of his mind. A heavy head, like a bear's, turning this way and that. Small eyes that shift and flicker, never meeting his. And a scornful, growling voice. He doesn't understand the words, but the meaning is in his head somehow, beating at his brain.

Of course you knew what you were doing. Are you a child? You knew all the time what it meant. You knew . . .

But he doesn't know. He doesn't know anything except that there is danger in that ugly, surly face, danger somewhere in the depths of his mind. Even before he opens his eyes, he is shouting into the darkness, throwing a name against the cold stare of those narrow grey eyes.

'Frosya!'

And she comes.

She always comes.

5

By the time they reached Moscow, Hayley was exhausted.

Travelling with Annie used every ounce of concentration she had, because everything had to be arranged in advance. How to get down to the plane. And on. And off—with the precious lightweight wheelchair ready to unfold the minute they needed it. How to find porters and cope with the toilets and choose a taxi which could take the wheelchair *and* the suitcases. How to get into the taxi.

It was bad enough in an English airport, but at least she and Annie were more or less even. Once they touched down in Russia, Hayley felt like an idiot—and Annie went into hyperdrive. Her narrow face sharpened, concentrating. Her mind focused on the next task. And the next. And the one after that. While Hayley was still gazing round the airport, Annie was rapping out instructions.

No, the baggage carousels are over there!

Take me over so I can talk to him.

Oh, for goodness' sake, give me the phrasebook!

She was constantly interrupting and correcting and tugging at Hayley's sleeve. Everyone—porters and officials and taxi drivers—automatically spoke to Hayley, because she was the one on her feet, but Annie wouldn't put up with that. They had to know that she was in charge.

By the time they succeeded in finding a taxi, Hayley ached all over from pushing and carrying and being pulled backwards and forwards. She could have done with some sympathy.

Annie just ignored her. The moment she was in the taxi, she whipped out a map of the city and crouched over it, working out where their hotel was while Hayley and the taxi driver manoeuvred the chair into the boot. And when they set off, she peered through the window, consulting the map all the time, to check where they were and what she could see.

Hayley lay back and closed her eyes. It was dull of her, she knew it was dull, but just at that moment she couldn't cope with a single new sight, or another notice written in Cyrillic letters.

She would have kept her eyes closed all the way to the hotel, if Annie hadn't reached backwards suddenly and tapped on her knee.

'Look at *that*!'

Automatically, Hayley looked. She saw what had been a big, grey apartment block, tumbled down on one side, like a house of cards. It was cordoned off, but not cleared at all. Furniture spilled off the tilted floors, and bedding lay in damp heaps under a thin dusting of snow.

That wasn't how it was supposed to be! If a building had to come down, it should be controlled and orderly. Everything movable went first. Tables and chairs. Curtains and carpets and books. Then the soft strip took out the windows and doors. All the non-supporting walls were hacked away and thrown down chutes to the ground, until there was nothing left except an eyeless shell, ready for the charges.

John had explained it all to Hayley, a dozen times. Once he'd even taken her on site, illegally, when the boss was off for an hour. She'd seen him drill the walls and pack in the explosives, winding the cables round and down. Taping them into place and leading them strand by strand towards a single point. When that was done, one man could finish the whole job with a single movement.

33

But not until everything was ready. No one could set off the charges until they'd made sure the building was empty. They had to count all the people on site, ticking off their names on a list to be certain they were out.

That was how demolition worked. Careful and methodical, with every stage planned in advance. The building they were passing was quite different. It had just been—smashed.

Annie tapped the taxi driver's arm and pointed back at it. 'What happened there?'

He glanced over his shoulder and pulled a face, shrugging. '*Mafiya*,' he said.

Annie and Hayley were sharing a bedroom in the hotel. By the time they had finished unpacking, Hayley felt claustrophobic. Was it going to be like this for two weeks? Were they going to spend the whole time together? Every single minute?

She scrabbled for an excuse to get away. 'I promised Dad I'd phone when we got here. I'll go down to reception and book the call, shall I?'

'It'll take an hour to come through if you do,' Annie said. She was scribbling in a notebook and she didn't even look up. 'Why don't you use my mobile instead? It's not as fancy as the one John had, but it'll work here.' She fished it out of her pocket. 'There you go.'

Hayley sidled away, evasively. 'Maybe I'll go and take a proper look round the hotel first. So I can tell him about it when I phone.'

Annie gave her a sharp glance. 'OK, if that's what you want. But you'd better hurry up. We're due to meet Frank Walsh for dinner at seven o'clock.'

'We're going *out*? But we've only just arrived.'

'So? We haven't come here to hang around in Moscow.

We just need to talk to Frank, to see what he can tell us. Then we can get off to Novosibirsk tomorrow. The flight's booked. I told you.'

That was right. She had. But the idea of getting on another aeroplane in the morning was more than Hayley could bear. She snatched up the phrasebook.

'I'll be back soon.'

She ducked out of the room, just managing not to slam the door, and found herself face to face with the large, forbidding woman who sat guarding their corridor.

'I . . . er . . . hello,' she said stupidly.

The woman stared at her and Hayley couldn't bear the idea of waiting there for the lift. She rattled down the stairs to reception.

It was the best thing she could have done. When she reached the foyer, she went up to the reception desk and mumbled *'Telefon*? Britain?' and the receptionist beamed. The answer came in perfect, fluent American.

'Sure, there's a cabin right there across the hallway. You can buy a token and dial direct.'

Hayley was so grateful she could have cried. With the token in her hand, she flew across to the cabin. Within a minute, she was talking to Trevor.

'So what's it like?' he said. 'Was the journey OK?'

Hayley opened her mouth to tell him about it—and realized she couldn't. She was two weeks and fifteen hundred miles away. There was nothing he could do, and he had enough troubles where he was.

'It was OK,' she said.

'And the hotel?'

'It seems fine. But we're not here for long. We're having dinner with Frank Walsh tonight, and then we're off to Novosibirsk tomorrow.'

There was an odd silence from the other end of the line.

'Dad? Are you there?'

'Yes, I'm here.' Trevor hesitated. 'Annie's really serious about Siberia, then?'

'Of course.' Hayley couldn't understand what he was talking about. 'It's what we came for.'

Trevor hesitated again. Then he said, 'Look, Hay, don't be too disappointed if it doesn't come off. Frank said it was pretty difficult to get around in Russia. Even without a wheelchair.'

'But that's the whole point of the trip—going to Siberia. We're going to go to Novosibirsk and follow the threads from there. Annie *said*.'

'I know she did. And she's a very determined person. But she may just have to give up. It might even be kinder—'

'What are you talking about?' Hayley said.

'She'd be better off staying in Moscow. Take my word for it. There's no point in going to Siberia.'

'She'll go crazy,' Hayley said, 'if she doesn't get there after all.'

'Be nice to her then. Because it's quite likely to happen.'

Hayley closed her eyes and shivered. Two weeks of being nice to Annie.

Frank Walsh was large and loud. And he wasn't alone.

He had chosen the restaurant where they met and when they arrived he was already at the table, with another man. A thin-faced Russian with grey hair and pale, watchful eyes. They each had a drink and a cigarette, and the Russian was talking steadily in a low voice.

The moment he saw the wheelchair, Frank was on his feet, striding towards them with both hands held out.

'Annie! It's brave of you to come all this way! And Hayley!'

He put an arm round Hayley's shoulders and began to push the chair with his other hand, ignoring the fact that Annie was propelling herself. He almost trapped her fingers, but he was so busy talking that he didn't notice.

'I've ordered the meal already, so I hope you like *pelmeni*. And *stroganoff*. We shouldn't have to wait more than an hour. And I've got a good bottle of wine put by. Unless you'd rather have *champagnsky*? That's what John always fancied.'

'Coke,' Annie said crisply. She looked across at the Russian. 'You didn't say there would be someone else.'

'Don't worry about him!' Frank waved a hand, grinning. 'Viktor's a good mate. Doesn't speak a lot of English, but he was crazy to see you. He's really chewed up about Johnny and what happened.'

Hayley thought she'd never seen anyone less chewed up. Viktor's thin face was closed and wary. His mouth hardly moved when Frank introduced Annie. Just twitched a centimetre wider and fell back into place.

'You see?' Frank said. 'Means a lot to him, meeting you. We miss John like hell, you know. It's not the same, going out on the town without him.'

John? Hayley thought. Trying to imagine it.

'We all miss him,' Annie said, in a cool voice. Very polite.

Frank pulled one of the chairs away from the table and slid the wheelchair into its place. 'I bet you do. You don't need me to tell you. There was no one like Johnny for making a party go, was there? Give him a couple of vodkas and he had the boys in stitches.'

Annie was like a block of ice. 'I never saw him drink vodka.'

'Don't let it worry you,' Frank said, unruffled. Patting her arm. 'You know what this business is like as well as I do. All men together. Away from home. Even someone like Johnny's going to loosen up a bit. Especially when he went to Siberia. There's nothing much else you can do there. It's all bog and birch trees. Excuse me a minute.' He signalled to a waiter and ordered two Cokes and a bottle of wine.

Annie waited until her glass was in front of her. Then she said, 'So why did John go to Siberia? If it's so dreadful?'

'You have to go where the work is,' Frank said. 'Isn't that right?'

He looked round at the Russian and translated, and Viktor nodded gravely and murmured a few words. Frank nodded back.

'If you want to know what it's like—where John was—Viktor says he'll show you some photos tomorrow.'

'*Photos*?' Hayley said, before she could stop herself.

Annie picked it up smoothly, smiling at Viktor as though he'd spoken directly to her. 'That's very kind, but we're counting on seeing more than photographs.'

There was a pause. Just too long. 'How's that, then?' Frank said.

Annie stared straight back at him. 'We're going to take a look for ourselves. Aren't we, Hayley?'

Hayley nodded. 'We want to see where—where it happened. We're going to Siberia, to see everything.'

'That's ridiculous,' Frank said abruptly. 'You'd be wasting your money. There's nothing to see. I told your father that.' He rumbled something in Russian and for a moment incomprehensible words flowed backwards and forwards on the other side of the table.

Annie tapped impatiently on the arm of her chair.

'You don't think we came all this way just to talk to you? I told you what we were planning, in my e-mail.'

'I didn't think you were serious.' Frank leaned across the table. 'Look—Siberia's a bloody awful place and the winter's coming. The real hard weather's due to set in any day now. How are you going to survive in that chair of yours when the snow's a foot deep?'

Hayley saw Annie's fingers picking at the edge of the tablecloth, twisting it into a tight little roll.

'You can't make it,' Frank said. 'Come on, now. Admit it. I can tell you anything you need to know.'

Viktor was watching Annie steadily with his grey eyes narrowed, hardly blinking. Hayley felt as if she were suffocating.

The Russian leaned sideways, murmuring under his breath and raising one eyebrow. Frank looked rebellious for a second. Then Viktor whispered something else and Frank relaxed suddenly, looking amused. He shrugged.

'OK, Annie, you win. I can see you're a determined lady. When are you planning to leave Moscow?'

'In a couple of days,' Annie said firmly. 'We're just going to take a quick look at the sights, and then—we're going to Siberia.'

But that's not what you—

Before Hayley could even think it, Annie's hand went round her wrist, under the table. Squeezing a warning.

Shut up. Don't give anything away . . .

Her fingers were small and bony, but they gripped like iron. It was all Hayley could do not to wince. She looked up and saw that Viktor's eyes had turned from Annie to her.

'There are some wonderful things in Moscow, aren't there?' she said. Forcing herself to smile. 'What are the best places to see if we've only got a couple of days?'

39

Frank leaned sideways, translating for Viktor, and under the table Annie's fingers loosened. She patted Hayley's wrist approvingly.

Then they both sat back and listened to Frank as he told them all about the sights of Moscow.

6

Frosya never thought he would leave. He had come out of nowhere, and there was nowhere for him to go.

It took him a week to walk properly. Irina Petrovna prodded him out of bed three or four times a day and made him shuffle up and down with the Komendant's sticks, inside the hut to begin with and then along the track past the other cottages.

He worked at it steadily, going a little further each time. When he stopped using the stick, Irina Petrovna sent Frosya out with him, in case he needed an arm to lean on. But he never did. He plodded round the village—round and round and round—and Frosya plodded along beside him, gazing up at his set, determined face.

Sometimes he smiled at her, but he never spoke. His eyes were always somewhere in the distance. Even when he was eating, his hands moved blindly, spooning up the food while he stared down at the floor or into the crack of light between the nailed-up shutters.

He didn't answer Piotr and Nikolai when they came out and tried to talk as he walked past. He didn't look at Yelena, when she brought him three eggs from her hens. He didn't even react when the boat came up the river, as it did every month or so.

Boris and Aleksandr moored the boat and came up to the village as usual, carrying matches and vodka and soap. They were very curious about the stranger, but he didn't seem to hear their questions. Even when Aleksandr prodded him with a long, impatient finger, he didn't take any notice.

'Tick fever,' Boris said. He tapped his head and rolled his eyes. 'Want us to take him away?'

No! No! Frosya flapped her hands and bumbled words at them.

Irina Petrovna put an arm round her shoulders. 'He's not doing any harm. He can stay here.'

'We'll tell the police when we get to Kargasok. They can come up and sort him out.'

Aleksandr was trying to be helpful, but Irina Petrovna shook her head at him. 'There's no need for the police.'

Boris looked at the blankets draped over the two wooden chairs by the stove. Irina Petrovna and the Komendant had been sleeping in those for two weeks now. He didn't bother to say anything. He just picked up the satchel where he kept his money, and took the list of things he had to bring next time he came. Then he and Aleksandr went back to the boat.

As they walked away, Frosya could see them shaking their heads, talking about the stranger.

'So,' Irina Petrovna said, half to herself. 'We can expect the police, sooner or later.' She sighed.

From that day, the stranger began to change.

The weather was changing, too. The pines looked dark and heavy, and cold winds sliced through the forest, stripping the birches of their yellowed leaves. Under a thin layer of snow, the mud was beginning to freeze. Twice already, Frosya had heard wolves howl.

The Komendant took out his big axe and ground the edge until it was sharp enough to cut his finger. Frosya knew what that meant. Instead of searching the forest for things to eat, she had to chop wood. There was a stack of logs behind Nikolai's hut, close under the eaves. She had to split them, with rags wound round her hands to save her from blisters, and then carry them into the cottages, so that each one had a good supply, ready for when the deep snow came.

After two days of chopping, her shoulders ached and her neck hurt.

On the third day, she had just begun when she felt someone watching her. Looking up, she saw the stranger. He had come round the corner of the hut and he was standing looking at the axe.

Frosya bobbed her head and babbled at him, but he didn't answer. He just watched as she placed a log on the block and brought the axe down to split it longways, neatly and evenly. And then again, to quarter it.

She tossed the quarters on to the heap she had already cut and reached for the next log. But before she could put it on the block, the stranger was at her elbow, with one hand held out. Frosya snatched the axe away, but he beckoned impatiently, reaching out again.

She frowned and backed away, grunting in distress.

'Ah,' the stranger said, very softly. With both his hands he made gentle, soothing movements, smoothing the air. 'Ssh.'

For the first time, he lifted his head and looked straight at her, and his eyes were clear and direct. Safe. Slowly, Frosya held out the axe.

He took it and ran his finger lightly along the edge. Then he picked up a log. He hit the first one slightly off centre, so that it jumped and split unevenly. After that, he had the feel of the axe. The second log fell into perfect quarters.

Frosya stood and watched him. Having been set to chop the logs, she didn't know what else to do. After ten minutes, the stranger paused, rubbing the palms of his

43

hands. Going close to peer, Frosya saw that they were bright red. In danger of blistering. She clicked her tongue and showed him the rags she was wearing and he smiled and stretched out his hands.

Frosya stared at them. The stranger touched the rags and then spread his hands again. Suddenly she understood. He wanted to borrow the rags. He was waiting for her to bind up his hands, just as Irina Petrovna bound hers.

Frosya slipped off the strips and unwound them. Then she took hold of the stranger's right hand. It had to be done properly. Too tight would hurt his fingers. Too loose and the strips would fall off. She concentrated, holding her breath and biting the end of her tongue as she bandaged first the right hand and then the left.

When she had finished, she patted them and the stranger smiled at her and started chopping again, nodding at the quartered logs to show that she could take them away and stack them.

For half an hour they worked like that. He chopped the wood and Frosya went backwards and forwards to Piotr's cottage, piling the logs neatly against the wall. By the end of that time, the stranger was white and shaking and Irina Petrovna came to chase him back into the house.

But he was there again the next day, holding out his hands for the bandages. This time, he lasted almost an hour.

On the third day, it was an hour and a half. Irina Petrovna carried Frosya off, to help with the cooking, and all the time she was chopping potatoes, Frosya could hear the axe thudding against the block.

By the end of the week, it felt like a routine. Every morning, the stranger came to find Frosya, bringing the rags with him. He stood silently while she bandaged his hands and then he took the axe and went off to cut wood. When he had been cutting for a while, Frosya joined him, babbling cheerfully as she went backwards and forwards, stacking the quartered logs. Every day he managed a little longer and chopped a little more.

She thought that was how it would be now, for ever.

Until the morning when she stepped out of her cottage and found a little pile of cloth beside the door.

It was the rag bandages, smoothed and folded. Coming up to put them there, the stranger had left footprints in the thin snow. Frosya scooped up the rags and followed the footprints down the slope, towards the river. Even from halfway down, she could see that they turned along the river bank and disappeared into the trees. Going just one way.

Irina Petrovna came out of her cottage, carrying an armful of quilts. Steadying herself against the doorframe, she began to shake them out vigorously. Frosya stopped dead and started to wail.

'No!' Irina Petrovna said loudly. 'No, Frosya!'

She dropped the quilt she was holding and stretched out her arms, but Frosya would not be comforted like that. She stumbled back up the slope. Pushing past Irina Petrovna, she burst into the cottage and blundered round it, touching all the things they had used to look after the stranger. The bucket for the water to wash him. The knife that had dug out the ticks. The painted chest. Each time she touched something, she made a small, whimpering sound.

Irina Petrovna didn't try to stop her. She stood in the doorway and the Komendant sat in his chair by the stove and they both watched Frosya, silently and kindly.

At last, Frosya came to the bed. The post at the foot of it was empty. The little heap of money had disappeared.

The Komendant nodded. 'Yes, Frosya. He's gone.'

Gone. Frosya tried to get her mouth round the word, but it came out shapeless, in a kind of mooing noise.

Then she bolted, lurching past Irina Petrovna and slithering up the hill to her own cottage with her long, early morning shadow running beside her. As she ran, she clutched the front of her apron, protecting the things inside the bouncing pocket.

When she opened the cottage door, her father hauled himself up in bed and began his usual rambling, senseless whine.

'There you are, you lazy girl, where have you been . . . the stove will go out and it's almost time for dinner . . . I could starve to death before you noticed . . . the train will be here soon . . .'

Frosya ignored him. Kicking off her old felt boots, she clambered on the bed, stretching up. Her father's old hunting rifle was up there, balanced on top of the nailed-up shutters, and she kept all her treasures below it in a secret place. The top of the window frame made a hidden ledge behind the shutters and that was where she hid her painted beads and her little silver brooch.

When she was away, her father sometimes tottered out of his bed and crawled round the cottage, eating any food there was and breaking everything else. But he couldn't climb on to her bed and stretch up without falling over. She knew that, because he would have taken the rifle down if he could.

He was yelling at her now as she felt along the ledge. 'Hands off my Berdanka, you wicked girl . . . that's what you'd like, isn't it, you'd like to shoot me and steal my rifle . . .'

Frosya worked her fingers behind the shutters, pushing the notebook in. Then she turned the silver thing over and over in her hands, examining it before she hid it away. It was neat and smooth. She recognized some of the numbers on the little buttons—3 she knew, and 8—but there were other signs that were completely strange.

'What's that?' her father said sharply, struggling to crawl down his bed towards her. Reaching out with his bony, brown-spotted hands. 'What's that you've got there?'

Frosya shook her head and reached up to slide the silver thing into her hiding place, pushing it along as far as she could.

'Show me, you disobedient girl! You don't deserve a father like me . . . give me my Berdanka and I'll show you I'm still the best hunter in Siberia . . . '

Climbing off the bed, Frosya brushed her hands clean and showed him that they were empty. As she went out of the cottage, she could hear him calling after her.

' . . . selfish, thieving daughter . . . terrible to be a neglected old man . . . you will be punished . . . it's time to eat . . . we've got a train to catch . . . '

It was days before she went back to the hiding place. Her father slept badly, waking up at the slightest sound, and she didn't want him grabbing at the treasures the stranger had left her.

She waited until the Komendant opened his new bottle of vodka. Then, when he was dozing in his chair, she poured a mugful and took it up to her father. That night, he slept very soundly, snoring like a pig.

In the dark, she reached up behind the shutters and took down the strange, silver object, feeling the shape with her hands. As she touched the buttons, she remembered about the light that had come in the little window, and she pressed one button after another, trying to make it happen again.

When it did, it took her by surprise. The whole thing

buzzed faintly, vibrating in her hands, and her father stirred and muttered something indistinct. Then the tiny window lit up with a faint green light, showing signs that Frosya didn't understand.

She waited, staring at it. After a moment the light went out. However much she shook it, nothing else happened. In the end, she put it back behind the cupboard and fell asleep.

Much later, in the middle of the night, she heard a strange sound from high above her head. Music. Notes that rippled in the air, over and over again. She lay with her eyes open, gazing into the darkness, waiting for—something—to appear. But all she saw was darkness and after a while the music stopped.

It wasn't until a week later that she linked the music with the silver thing. The next time her father fell asleep, she climbed up and took it down again. But the little window was dead and empty and even though she pressed all the buttons, one after another, she couldn't get it to light up.

There are no insects in the forest now. He walks in a mixture of mud and snow, keeping in the trees so that no one will see him as he follows the river east. But there are no boats passing. By the time Boris and Aleksandr come that way again, he will be somewhere else, away from the water.

As he walks, he ransacks his brain, trying to find the things he has forgotten. He remembers Frosya. Her red, kind face and the way she pants when she chops the wood. He remembers the tumbledown houses. The chickens and the goat, and the feel of the axe in his hands.

But he can't remember very much else. His mind won't go back past the moment when he opened his eyes and first saw Frosya, beaming down at him. The memories begin with the sight of his own face, reflected in the dark pools of her pupils.

It's only when he sleeps, huddled against a tree, out of the wind, that the other pictures come to dance on the edges of his brain. The threatening, heavy man with the shifting eyes. And a second man, whose steady grey eyes are as cold as steel.

The Bear and the Wolf.

They circle each other, with their eyes gleaming blood-red, with their steel teeth bared. They circle and wait, watching for an opportunity to leap in and strike. They hunt each other through his dreams and when their faces swim up out of the darkness, he shouts in his sleep, a thin, carrying cry.

But now no one comes.

7

Annie and Hayley started before it was light. They left their hotel in a taxi, heading for Domodedevo airport. And Annie was on the alert, all the way there.

'Keep an eye out behind,' she hissed to Hayley. 'We don't want anyone on our tails.'

'Oh, come on!' Hayley couldn't believe it. 'Why would anyone follow us?'

'I don't know, but I'm not taking any chances. Whatever that Viktor man said last night, Frank thought it was pretty funny, didn't he? They reckoned they'd fixed us.'

'But surely they wouldn't—'

'Just watch out. All right?' Annie's voice was sharp and tense. She wasn't discussing ideas. She was giving orders.

It was just as bad at the airport. She was on the alert all the time, until they were actually inside the plane, taxiing down the runway. Then, as they rose into the air, she slumped down in her seat and closed her eyes.

Hayley was tired too, but she didn't feel like sleeping. They were leaving Moscow—and she hadn't seen a thing. She pulled out her guidebook and started to read about all the things she'd missed. Red Square and the Old Circus. The Kremlin. And GUM

  . . . *the Great Soviet Emporium which has been transformed into a wonderland of modern Russian shopping . . .*

50

Annie had robbed her of all that. She hadn't allowed her even a glimpse of the coloured domes of St Basil's

. . . the ultimate cathedral, so beautiful that, according to legend, Ivan the Terrible had the architect blinded, so that he would never be able to design anything to compare with it . . .

Hayley frowned over the pages, staring at the pictures and reading the words slowly. As the plane laboured east, away from Moscow and over the Urals, she took in words and maps and images, trying to construct an idea of the city in her mind.

The journey lasted for four hours. She read and dozed and read a bit more and every now and again—when there was a break in the clouds—she caught a glimpse of the land below.

Once the mountains were past, it stretched on and on endlessly, flat and unchanging. Sometimes there were fields or small settlements. Sometimes lakes glittered among the dark trees. But there was nothing to hold her attention. She glanced out briefly and then went back to her guidebook.

They were almost at Novosibirsk when Annie finally woke up. She peered sideways, to see what Hayley was reading.

'Why are you bothering with that?' she said impatiently. 'It's nothing like Moscow where we're going.'

She snatched the book out of Hayley's hands and flipped through it, hunting for something. When she found it, she thrust a page of pictures under Hayley's nose.

'There you are. *That's* what Novosibirsk is like.'

Factories. Great, grey blocks of flats. A leaden river and a huge railway station sprawling in the centre of a vast empty space. Hayley's mind was jolted away from Moscow. She took the book back and read, struggling to imagine something quite different.

. . . might be called the quintessential Soviet city . . .
developed under Stalin in the 1920s as part of his plan
to exploit and control Siberia . . . the biggest city in
the whole of Siberia . . .

Everything about it was brutally concerned with size and power . . . *the biggest railway station . . . the biggest theatre . . . the biggest library . . .* In Hayley's mind the whole place coalesced into one gigantic apartment building, with every window identical, every robotic inhabitant dressed in the same drab clothes. All of them imprisoned in a sea of concrete, a wilderness of breeze blocks.

She would have read on, hunting for something more human, but Annie wouldn't let her concentrate. The flight was almost over and she was restless and irritable.

'This airport's going to be dreadful! A provincial Russian airport, for heaven's sake. A provincial *Siberian* airport! I don't suppose they've ever had anyone in a wheelchair go through before. The access will be terrible and we'll have to hang around for ever before they get us off the plane.'

Hayley cringed at the idea of scuttling around for a second time, in an even more difficult airport. She knew just how Annie would react. She would snap and hustle and rattle out orders too fast for anyone to keep up with her. It was going to be a nightmare.

They were both wrong. As soon as the plane stopped moving, a steward was at Annie's elbow, leaning forward politely. Speaking in English.

'Please—are you ready to leave the plane? We have had a message to say that they will take you off first. It is all arranged.'

Annie bent her head and hissed at Hayley. 'I'll believe that when I see it.'

They saw it straight away. The plane doors opened, there was a brief announcement in Russian, and all the other passengers settled back into their seats. Three porters appeared with a brand-new wheelchair and lifted Annie into it, quickly and efficiently. For the first time on the whole journey, Hayley had nothing to do except follow.

The porters produced a trolley for the luggage, plucked their cases off the baggage carousel, found Annie's own folding wheelchair, and whisked them straight past all the officials.

'This is brilliant!' Hayley muttered. 'You've got to admit it.'

Annie looked up quizzically. 'You think this is standard service?'

'What do you mean?'

Annie didn't explain. She just waved a hand, dismissively, and stared forward, tapping her fingers on the arm of the chair. She didn't speak again until they came out of the last hall. Then she scanned the people who were waiting to meet passengers. Suddenly, she pointed.

'It'll be *them*! Bet you! They're the ones who've laid all this on.'

'That's silly,' Hayley said. 'How can you possibly know?'

'It's got to be them.'

Hayley looked, but all she saw was five men and a boy of about fifteen. They were standing on the far side of the arrivals hall, staring across at the wheelchair. Four of the men were silent and blank-faced, in ill-fitting suits and heavy shoes, but the fifth was completely different. He was massive, like the side of a mountain, with shaggy hair and clothes that shouted 'money'. There were three rings on the hand that gripped the boy's shoulder.

'Here we go,' Annie murmured. Her fingers stopped tapping and she sat forward, tense and alert.

The porters pushed her straight across the concourse towards the welcoming party. The big man came to meet them, striding across the empty space with the boy in tow.

'Annie Glasgow!' His accent was so thick that it took Hayley a moment to work out what he'd said. He launched into a speech in Russian, standing four-square with one hand held out formally.

His body was huge and immovable, but his small eyes shifted continually. They flickered around the hall, keeping track of everything that was going on. When they slid across Hayley's face, she had an urge to wipe her skin, as though a slug had crawled over it.

When the Russian words stopped, Annie lifted her head to say something in reply. But the man pushed at the boy beside him, propelling him forward. Instantly, the boy began to translate.

'My father, Leonid Orlov, welcomes you to Novosibirsk and says his heart is with you in your sorrow. John was a good friend. He was happy to work with him.'

The accent was perfect, but there was no expression. The boy was simply reciting the message. And all the time his father's shaggy head was moving from side to side, scanning the concourse. Checking. Once, a couple of girls stopped to look back at him, but their boyfriends grabbed them and pulled them away hastily.

The translation stopped, and Annie raised her head. 'It's kind of you to meet us. Are you going to help us do what we came for?'

Leonid Orlov's reply was smooth and direct.

'You want to see where John died?' the boy translated.

He made it sound like a question, but Hayley didn't think his father had been asking. He knew, already, what they intended to do.

Annie obviously thought so too. 'You're friends of Frank Walsh?' she said. 'Did he tell you we were on our way?'

Her voice was slightly aggressive, but if Leonid Orlov realized that, he didn't react. When he heard what she'd said, he smiled and bowed to her.

'He is a friend of Frank,' the boy translated. 'And he is the brother of Viktor Orlov, whom you have met, I think?'

'That man who never blinks,' Annie muttered.

This man and Viktor—brothers? Hayley wouldn't have guessed that. What could dry, silent Viktor have in common with this shifty-eyed giant of a man?

The boy had heard Annie's muttered words. He caught them up and translated them and all the men laughed suddenly. Leonid Orlov bent forward and patted Annie's hand, speaking quickly and nodding as he spoke.

'My father will help you,' said the boy. 'But it is necessary to drive to Tomsk to see the place. That will take about five hours. Would you like to go now?'

Another journey? *Straight away?* Hayley groaned inside her head. She'd been promising herself a long sleep at the hotel.

Annie didn't ask for her opinion.

'Of course we want to go,' she said eagerly. 'It's what we've come for.'

She looked up and nodded, so that there would be no need for a translation. Leonid Orlov nodded back and began to give orders to the men around him, pointing to the wheelchair and the luggage. The boy stood watching, staring up at his father.

'Hey!' Annie pulled his sleeve to attract his attention. 'What's your name?'

'That is not important,' the boy said, deadpan. 'I am here only to translate.'

Annie raised her eyebrows. 'Like a machine?' she said sarcastically.

For a moment the boy didn't understand what she

meant. Then he smiled. 'No, I am not a machine. I am Yuri. But still—I am here only to translate. It is my father who can tell you the things you want to know.'

'That's good,' Annie said. She sat back and it struck Hayley, for the first time, that she was tired too. She looked very pale.

But she didn't let that interfere with her determination. The moment Leonid Orlov finished giving orders, he glanced at her, and she nodded briskly. Impatiently, even. He waved his hand and the men behind him moved into action, closing round so that he and Annie were at the centre of a tight group of people, heading for the exit. Hayley was left to follow, with Yuri and the luggage trolley.

She sneaked a look at Yuri as they went. He was no older than she was, but he was utterly intimidating. Where she was tall and solid, he was slight and elegant, with pale hair and a bony face. And he was wearing the most expensive trainers and jeans she had ever seen on a real person.

'You speak very good English,' she said. Because saying nothing was even more intimidating.

Yuri shrugged. 'My father made me learn from when I was five. It's the language everyone needs.'

'So—did you speak to John?'

'John is the man who died? Your father?'

'He was my brother. Ten years older than me. Did you meet him?'

Yuri shook his head. 'I don't think so. There are many people. My father has a lot of business.'

'Demolition?' Hayley said.

She thought he would understand straight away, but there was a long, blank pause. 'Demolition?' he said cautiously. 'I don't know this.'

'Knocking buildings down.' Hayley mimed it with her hands. 'Blowing them up. Pushing them over.'

Yuri looked baffled, but there was no more chance to explain. They were walking out of the airport building and a minibus was waiting for them, parked in solitary splendour, right outside the door.

And splendour is the right word, Hayley thought, as she climbed in. The whole vehicle had been gutted inside and refitted luxuriously. Apart from the driver and the man beside him, they were all facing each other, lounging in soft, deep leather seats with ashtrays set into the armrests. A small television stood on top of a cabinet full of glasses and bottles.

The moment the engine started, Leonid pulled an envelope out of his breast pocket. He started to speak, and Yuri went back on translation duty.

'My father says that while we travel to the place you should see the photographs that were taken before the—' he fumbled for a word and then smiled suddenly at Hayley '—before the demolition.'

Leonid was already holding out the envelope, offering it to Annie. She took it and tipped the pictures into her lap, and Hayley caught her breath when she saw the top one.

It was John. He was looking straight at them, squinting slightly against the sun and grinning into the camera. The hard hat threw a narrow shadow across the top of his face, but there was no mistaking the shape of his chin or the way his ears lay close to his head. It was John, standing in front of a tall block of flats.

The building looked ready to fall down on its own, given half a chance, but someone must have paid John to wire it, so that it could be blown up, because in every other photograph he was setting explosives into place.

As Annie leafed through them, Hayley saw him over and over again. From behind. From the side. Full face, as he looked round from drilling into the walls. Carrying a box of charges and taping wires tidily into position. There were photos of John on his own and pictures of him with other men, waving his hands around and discussing what to do. There must have been at least twenty of them, all the same.

Except for the last one. That was different.

Annie flicked past yet another smiling image—of John working near the gaping hole of the main doorway—and suddenly everything had changed. It was the same building as before, but this time it was the very moment of blowdown. The building was hovering in its place, puffing out dust. Holding in, for one split second, the forces that had already been unleashed to blow it apart.

And there, running through the doorway, blurred by the dust, but unmistakable, was John, in his hard hat.

Annie's face was grim as she stared down at the photo. Leonid Orlov spread his hands and said something in his rich, thick voice.

'It was an accident with the charges,' said Yuri. 'He went back for something he had forgotten, after the checking was done. The building fell on him.'

'That's ridiculous!' Annie said hotly. 'He was an experienced engineer. He would never have made that sort of mistake.'

Leonid Orlov picked the photos out of her lap and went through them, picking out one. And another. And another. As he held out each one, he tapped it with his ringed fingers, drawing Annie's attention to something. Hayley couldn't see what he was showing her, but she saw Annie's face grow grimmer and grimmer. Suddenly, she snatched up all the pictures, jammed them into the envelope and pushed them back at him.

Hayley was so tired that she spent most of the drive asleep. But Annie shook her arm as they came into Tomsk.

'Wake up! We're almost there.'

The site they had come to see was out on the edge of town, near the airport. As far as Hayley could tell, nothing had been done since the explosion. Great sections of wall lay tumbled across a huge swathe of ground, surrounded by other blocks of flats. The coloured inside walls were streaked and marked with rain, but they had not had time to fade and they made a strange patchwork, sprawled across the mud. Pale yellow, pale green, pale rose. In one or two places, the damp tatters of a poster clung to something that had once been part of a bedroom.

Hayley looked out of the minibus window as they pulled up. It was already beginning to get dark. Lights were flickering on in the windows of the flats around, throwing a harsh brightness on their dirty walls. By contrast, the demolition site looked dim and gloomy, scattered with a damp litter of half-burnt rubbish heaps. She thought it was the nastiest place she had ever seen.

Annie was unstrapping her seat belt. 'Help me get down there, Hayley.'

Leonid Orlov frowned when he saw what she was doing. He grunted something and Yuri muttered apologetically about stones and rough ground. Annie ignored them.

'Make them lift the chair out, Hayley. There's a perfectly good path. It's just a bit slushy, that's all.'

Hayley agreed with Yuri and his father, but she found herself sliding the door open anyway. Slipping out of the minibus, she went round to the back and opened the rear doors.

When Leonid saw that she was determined, he sent a man to help her lift out the wheelchair. Another man scooped Annie out of the minibus, ignoring her furious complaints.

'Stop lifting me about!' she hissed. 'I can *stand*, if you help me!'

59

They didn't give her the chance. One man dropped her into the chair, and the other wheeled her off, without pausing to put a blanket round her. She huddled down low, shivering and tucking her hands into her armpits.

The ground was slippery with grey slush and it was beginning to snow again. Hayley pulled on her old coat and trudged after the chair. The snowflakes caught on her eyelashes and the cold wind was raw against her face. *We'll be there in the autumn*, Annie had said. Hayley bent her head and pushed her hands into her pockets, wondering what the winter would be like. She could hear someone else following her down from the minibus, but she didn't look round to see who it was.

The site was ugly and desolate, surrounded by a broken down fence. As she got nearer, she could see that children had been rooting around in the heaps of half-burnt debris. They had wriggled through holes in the wire netting and made ramshackle dens, leaning bits of ruined plasterboard against the twisted metal that projected from the broken concrete walls.

The whole site was littered with pieces of scorched wood and charred carpet. And over on the far side was a heap of cloth sprinkled with snow. Blue denim and something grey.

Hayley stopped by the fence, holding on to the wire. This was it then. This was where it had happened. One moment John had been standing there smiling. The next— She leaned her forehead against the wire, feeling it print its hexagonal shapes on her skin. Trying not to imagine what had come next.

Away against the opposite fence, the heap of rags stirred suddenly, catching her eye. She lifted her head to look at it and saw it move. It uncoiled in the half-darkness and a pale shape glimmered, blurred by the falling snow. A face—

The next moment, without working it out, without thinking at all, Hayley was through the gap in the wire, running across the site, with her feet sliding on frozen puddles and catching on rough pieces of concrete. Behind her, she heard Annie's voice.

'Hayley! What are you *doing*?'

Closer behind, someone was scrambling after her, crashing and slipping. Muttering with annoyance. It was Yuri. He caught her when she was at the far side, grabbing her round the waist so that she staggered to a standstill.

'What are you doing?' he hissed in her ear. 'Do you want to be in a wheelchair also? This is dangerous.'

Hayley struggled against his hands. 'But he's there! Look! Can't you see?'

Yuri looked and she followed his eyes.

And it wasn't true after all. There was nothing but a bundle of denim rags, fluttering in the wind. She stopped struggling.

'What is it?' Yuri said. 'What did you see?'

'Never mind.' Wearily, Hayley shook her head. 'It was nothing. A mistake.' She slid away from him and began to work her way back across the site, clambering awkwardly over the debris.

All the way, she could see Annie watching her. She cringed at the thought of explaining herself, but when she scrambled back through the wire netting, Annie didn't say anything at all. She just reached out and touched Hayley's hand for a moment.

'Sorry,' Hayley muttered. And then, 'It's a horrible place, isn't it?'

'Horrible,' Annie said. Her face was sharp as a hatchet. She lowered her voice so that no one but Hayley could hear. 'It's horrible—but that hasn't got anything to do with John.'

'What are you talking about?' Hayley stared at her.

'It's not the right place. Oh, he was here all right—but he wasn't standing in that doorway when the charges exploded.'

'The photos—'

'I don't give a toss about the photos,' Annie said. She was trembling slightly, and Hayley suddenly realized that she was shaking with fury. 'Didn't you realize they were fixed?'

Hayley blinked, bewildered. 'But why on earth—'

'Sssh!' Annie nudged her and looked sideways. Yuri was scrambling through the wire fence. 'We can't talk about it now. But take it from me—*this isn't the place where John died.*'

8

If Vladimir's bicycle had been old, like the others, he would never have met the foreigner who came walking along the river bank.

Every kid in the village had some kind of bike. Not a good one, of course. Most of them were ancient bikes, scrounged from uncles and cousins and elder brothers. Andrei had a rusty wreck, left over from before the War, with its tyres patched and sewn a hundred times. Fyodor's bike was cobbled together from three hopeless ruins. Rika and Nadia both rode boys' bikes, repainted pink and purple to hide the scratches.

But Vladimir's was new, sent all the way from Moscow by his father. And because it was new, it was bought to last—which meant that it was four sizes too big for him. He had to stand up to ride it, straining down to reach the pedals. Tagging along behind the others until he was exhausted.

Usually, that didn't matter, because there was nowhere much to go. Just the circuit of roads round the village and up to the railway track and the school. The river bank had no proper path, and the track beside the railway was strictly forbidden.

But that morning the snow was almost too deep for cycling, and Rika decided to break all the rules. She was seventeen—the oldest of them all—and she wanted to touch the real world. She wanted to know that one day she would make it out of the village. To Petrovsk. To Novosibirsk. To Moscow. To Paris and New York and Rio de Janeiro.

'Today,' she said—and her eyes were shining—'today I'm going to take the track by the railway!'

She didn't wait for anyone, but the boys followed, because they were too old to let her beat them. Except for Vladimir, that is. And Nadia followed too. Not because she cared about Rika, but because she was born to cycle. Nothing was too steep or too far or too fast for her and her only rule was to come in ahead of everyone else. With a good bike, she could truly have cycled herself out of there and into international championships in the real world.

Vladimir was right behind them as they all swooped down towards the railway, but he knew that he would never be able to keep up. He was too small, and his bike was too big.

As soon as the others began to build up speed, he dropped out and slid off the saddle, kneeling down beside the front tyre, as if he'd had a puncture. Fyodor looked over his shoulder and Vladimir spread his hands and shrugged. *It's no good. Go on without me.*

Tough luck, said Fyodor's wave as he put his head down and cycled away. Vladimir straightened up and began to push his bike back along the stony track.

On his right was the railway embankment, as high as his head, raised out of reach of the spring floods. On his left were the trees, stretching away into the distance. Birch and pine and larch, too many to count. You could walk through the forest for a thousand miles without coming to the end of it, his father said. It was full of sables and polecats, elks and lynxes and bears.

Wolves.

In Vladimir's nightmares, the horrors always came out of the forest. Bears and wolves and crazy men with hot eyes and bony, eager hands. In the daylight, he was not afraid, but even then he walked with his face towards the trees, watching and listening.

64

That was why he didn't see the man, until he had almost bumped into him. The man was standing under the bridge, where the railway crossed the path up from the river. And he was following Vladimir with his eyes.

Vladimir stopped and looked warily at him. Strangers came by train. That was the normal way. If they were important enough, the train stopped for them on the bridge over the river. They walked up the path bringing forms to fill in, or holding papers that said they had the right to inspect the farm and the factory. If they were not important, they had to get off at Krasny Yar, sixty kilometres away, and come along the railway tracks.

This man was not important. He had no briefcase. He was wearing thick, old-fashioned trousers and a shabby, padded coat. Why would they have stopped the train for him?

But if he hadn't come from the train—he must be travelling along the river. And there was nothing that way except a little cluster of decaying cottages. Half a dozen old people clinging on to a dying village.

Vladimir scowled and climbed on to his bike.

'Please—' the man said. *Pazhalysta.*

It wasn't a Russian voice.

For a moment, Vladimir hesitated. That would be a story for the others. *While you were away, following that old railway track, you missed a foreigner—*

But the foreigner wouldn't wait while he made the story. He snatched at Vladimir's sleeve and mimed eating, scooping handfuls of air into his mouth and chewing energetically.

When Vladimir was three or four, an old man had come out of the forest, babbling about guns and torture and men with electric whips. Not a nightmare, but a real man with burning eyes, who snatched the bread from Vladimir's hand and gibbered at him out of a toothless mouth.

Vladimir's mother had sighed afterwards, and shaken her head. 'It isn't like that. Not any more. But for some people the torture is still here.' She tapped her forehead. 'And we must take them in and feed them. Share what we have. That is what life is.'

Vladimir had been terrified. His mother sat at the table with the old man, giving him milk and bread and potatoes. Listening for an hour afterwards, while he wiped the dribbled milk off his stubbly chin and mumbled about pain and starvation. When she went to fetch more milk, he pushed Vladimir away from the food, nipping at him with long, dirty nails.

When he went—looking out through a crack before he opened the door and shambled back into the forest—Vladimir's mother stood and stared after him.

'I don't know how he lives,' she said. 'A man like that.'

Remembering it, Vladimir felt the same sick terror rise inside him now. He looked at this foreigner and saw the same things. Dirt and stubble and hungry eyes. He felt the same pull of fear and shame. Tugging his arm free, he swung his bike towards the village and pedalled as hard as he could, panting up the slope.

He had almost reached the first house when he realized that he wasn't safe. All the foreigner had to do was follow him. If he knocked on the door, Vladimir's mother would take him in and feed him. He would be there in the house.

Swerving sideways, into the trees, Vladimir slid off his bike and shoved it into a bush. Then he fell to his knees on the frozen earth, scrabbling for stones. By the time the foreigner came toiling up the path, he had two in his hands and more gathered on the ground. Crouching lower, so that he was completely hidden, he waited until the two of them were almost level.

Then he threw. The first stone missed, but the second hit the foreigner on the side of his head. He staggered and put up an arm to shield his face, peering over it to see where the stone had come from.

Leaving his bike, Vladimir scuttled sideways and threw again, catching the edge of an ear. And again. And again. Each time from a slightly different position. The foreigner kept turning to try and see him, but he was always just too late.

Vladimir was almost dancing now. He had used up the first batch of stones and he grovelled for more, throwing them always from the village side, so that the foreigner backed away in the other direction. It was like herding an animal. Almost like hunting.

And suddenly it was all over. Putting both arms up, the foreigner began to run, falling awkwardly and hauling himself up again as if it were a huge effort. He didn't even stop when he had disappeared under the bridge. The sound of his feet went on, scattering the stones along the river path as he ran away.

Vladimir was triumphant. Exhilarated.

But only for an instant. Then he looked down at his hands and felt sick. They were covered in dirt and wet with melted snow. Grazed raw where he had scraped them over the frozen ground, scrabbling for ammunition.

When he was sure that the foreigner had disappeared completely, he crawled out of the trees and went back to get his bike. Slowly, he pushed it into the village and along the street to his house, leaning it against the front wall, under the eaves.

His mother screeched when she saw him, and shook his shoulder. 'What have you done? Look at your clothes! Look at your hands!'

It was almost a relief when she heated up water and made him strip for a bath.

'And you don't go out again today! You can stay in with your books and do some studying!'

He didn't argue. Once the bath was over, he spread his school books on the table by the window and tried to forget the feel of the stones in his hand. The way they flew clear of the trees and thudded against live flesh.

He was terrified that the foreigner would come up the path after all. That he would guess who had thrown the stones and totter up from the river to knock on Vladimir's door, with his bruises swelling blue and purple.

But no one came. No one came up the path until the very end of the day, when Rika swooped up from the railway, leading the others and hallooing with excitement.

When Vladimir woke up in the morning, his bicycle had gone.

He knew instantly, because there was a knothole in the shutter, right beside his bed. All year, except in the very depths of winter, he kept his bike where he had left it the day before, under the eaves of the house. He only shut it away in the shed when the snow was too thick for any cycling at all.

That morning, when he woke, the light came twinkling through the knothole, with nothing to shut it out. It fell across his eyes and he opened them, blinking. For a second he didn't realize what was strange.

When he did, he was up and out of the cottage in a few seconds, but he was too late to make any difference. The bicycle wheels had made black lines in the snow and he followed them down to the railway, expecting them to lead him under the bridge, where the foreigner had first appeared. But they didn't. They turned left and went off into the distance, along the railway track.

Slowly, Vladimir trailed back up the path. Coming that way, he saw a scrap of paper stuck on a nail in the shutters. When he pulled it down, he saw that it was an old five hundred rouble note, with writing along one edge. But he couldn't understand any of the writing, not even the script it was written in. And five hundred roubles would not buy even one wheel of a new bike.

Later on, Rika came by with the others and he showed the note to her.

'English,' she said.

She sounded out the letters, frowning at them as she straddled her bike with both feet on the ground. Behind her, the others circled on the mud, wheeling round and round and trying to catch a glimpse of the message.

But Rika's sounds didn't make any sense, even to her. She shook her head and tossed her long hair back over her shoulders, rising up suddenly on the pedals of her bike.

Then she was away, swooping and calling with the others. Racing them down to the railway track while Vladimir was left standing by the rotting fence, with half a dozen little kids clamouring round him. They twittered like birds as they tried to peep at his useless, incomprehensible letter.

He can't relax. He can't leave his feet to turn the pedals while his mind floats free, enjoying the cold air and the first crispness of the frost. The track is stony and uneven and he has to look down all the time, avoiding potholes and boulders. When he falls, he hits the bruises which the stones have left.

When he thinks, he hits bruises of a different sort—the ones left by the boy's scared, angry eyes. He had thought of himself as threatened and vulnerable before. He hadn't realized that he was dangerous too. Now the boy's eyes join those other eyes that haunt his dreams—the Wolf's eyes, and the Bear's. They follow him, accusingly.

You took my bike. You can't pretend it was a mistake. You knew what you were doing.

You knew . . .

He hopes there's someone in the village who can understand the message that he left. It is a very short message. He had no kind of paper, except a five hundred rouble note, and he had to write in big, clumsy letters, with a charred stick from a bonfire.

I will send a new bike.

He doesn't know if he can keep the promise, but he hopes he's a man whose promises can be trusted. He wants to know that about himself.

He wants it to weigh against the other knowledge, which came when he saw the boy's fear. The thing he feels inside himself, dark and silent as hidden gunpowder.

He knows that he has the power to destroy.

9

'The bastard!' Annie said. 'The filthy, lying—' She propelled herself across the hotel room, swearing and thrusting at the wheels of her chair.

All the way from the demolition site, she had been smouldering, sitting hunched into a corner of the minibus and glowering whenever anyone tried to talk to her. By the time they reached the hotel Leonid Orlov had booked, she was ready to explode. All the way up in the lift, Hayley was chanting in her head, *Please let her keep her temper until they've gone. Please . . .*

They made it—but only just. Leonid's men were with them all the way to the room, one carrying Annie and the other pushing the folded wheelchair. The chair couldn't be unfolded until it was through the bedroom door. The moment she was in it, Annie nodded curtly at the men.

'Thank you. Goodbye.'

They hadn't even got in to the lift when her control snapped and she began to rage.

'The filthy, lying—'

Hayley banged the door shut and leaned against it. 'What are you talking about? Why are you so angry?'

'Did you see those pictures Leonid had?'

'In the minibus? Of course I did.'

'I mean the ones he picked out afterwards!' Annie was frighteningly fierce. 'Did you see what he was pointing at?'

Hayley shook her head.

Annie manoeuvred the chair round so that they were facing each other. 'There was a bottle of vodka in every

71

one of those pictures. Every single one. Leonid went through them all, making sure I noticed. It wasn't the same bottle each time, but it was always half empty.'

Hayley bit her lip and thought of vodka and explosives. Together. Of John drinking and setting charges and drinking a bit more.

What had Trevor said? *She'd be better off staying in Moscow . . . Don't let her go to Siberia.* Had he met Leonid Orlov too? And seen those pictures?

'You can't blame John,' she said at last, apologetically. 'He was stuck out here for weeks, with no one he could talk to. It must have been really lonely and depressing.'

'He may have been lonely, but he wasn't suicidal.' Annie was calming down, but her voice was still tart. 'And he would never, never, *never* have drunk while he was working. He didn't like vodka anyway.'

'But the pictures—'

'Come on! It's easy enough to add in a bottle of vodka, if you've got a decent photo-editor. Just as easy as slipping John into that picture of the blowdown when he wasn't really there.'

Oh dear, Hayley thought. It all sounded too dramatic. 'John was only a demolition engineer, not a spy.'

Annie took a deep breath. 'You don't get it, do you? It's not who John was. It's who these people are and how they operate. Think of Leonid when we arrived in Novosibirsk. All those things he'd got laid on.' She ticked them off on her fingers. 'First off the plane. Porters. Wheelchair. Minibus parked slap outside the main entrance. He must have pretty impressive contacts at the airport to arrange all that. We're talking about power here. Outside the law.'

Hayley bit her lip.

'Well?' Annie said abruptly. 'You know what I mean, don't you?'

72

'Of course I know what you mean. I'm not stupid. You mean they're—'

'*Mafiya*,' Annie snapped.

Hayley sighed, and Annie glared at her.

'OK, so you don't believe me! Well, how do you explain it all?'

'Why does everything have to be *explained*?' Hayley said wearily. 'You make everything too complicated. The building doesn't fit your idea of where John died—so it's the wrong building. The photographs show that John *was* there—so they've been fixed. And Leonid Orlov has to be an evil conspirator, to make it all fit.'

Annie's eyes were steady. 'Yes. And your point is?'

'Why can't you just accept things? We know John died in that blowdown. They identified him from his teeth. So what do a few photos matter?'

'Well, if you don't care—'

Annie bit the words off short. Turning away, she wheeled herself across the room, unzipped the holdall on her bed and began to unpack. Sponge bag. Nightdress. Charger for her phone. Hairbrush and comb. Hayley watched the rhythm for a moment and then turned away and started to unpack her own case.

Annie didn't speak again until she'd zipped up the holdall and put the phone to charge beside the bed. Then she turned to face Hayley again.

'Look—it's not just the vodka. There's something else too. I should have told you before.'

She had calmed down now. Hayley shut her own case and sat down on her bed. 'What sort of something?'

'You know John rented a special phone for the trip?'

'Some kind of mobile?'

'It wasn't just a mobile. It had everything. Iridium handset. Lithium ion battery. Satellite tracking. I thought it was a waste, because the hotel phones were fine, but

John wanted to be sure we could stay in touch, even if they sent him out into the wilds. I used to phone him up every day, just for a couple of minutes.' Annie took a long breath. 'The last time he called me was the third of September. From Tomsk.'

'The day before he died,' Hayley said.

Annie's eyes flickered for an instant. Then she closed them and went on as though Hayley hadn't spoken. 'It was almost midnight. I was just going to bed, and I nearly didn't answer the phone. When I did, the signal was really bad, but I could just make out what he was saying. He said—'

She opened her eyes and frowned, getting it exactly right. Concentrating.

'He said, *Annie, look, you won't be able to get me for a while, but don't worry. I need to turn this thing off for the time being, to save the battery. I'm going out of town and there won't be much hope of charging it.* So I asked him where he was going.'

'And what did he say?'

'He didn't really answer. Just said, *I need some space, to think things through. This job's—not as straightforward as it looked. I might be home a lot earlier than you're expecting.* I said, *What's the matter?* but he just muttered something about a lorry coming, and hitching a lift. I said, *Are you crazy? Why do you need to hitch?* But the signal broke up while I was speaking. And I lost him.'

Hayley waited. She wasn't sure how she was supposed to react. Annie looked up, impatiently.

'Don't you understand? He was leaving Tomsk. Getting out.'

'So? Maybe he took a walk in the country somewhere and got things sorted. And the next day he was back on the job and—' Hayley made herself say it. '—and blew himself up.'

'That's what I thought, first of all. It took your dad two days to phone me, you know. And when he said *John was killed in an explosion. On the fourth of September*, I was too shocked to think straight. I just thought, *What a pity he didn't just keep hitching—*'

Annie stopped and bent her head, swallowing hard. Her hands were twisted together in her lap, viciously tight. Hayley looked away, embarrassed, not wanting to imagine that phone call. Not wanting to remember what it had been like when the news first came.

'Anyway,' Annie said roughly, after a moment, 'I got my brains working in the end. And then I realized—they don't fit.'

'What don't fit?' said Hayley.

'The times. John died first thing in the morning, on the fourth of September. Right? In Tomsk. And that phone call was just before midnight, on the *third* of September.'

'So?'

'So that was midnight in *England*!' Annie said triumphantly. 'But the time's seven hours ahead here.'

Hayley got it. So suddenly that it almost knocked the breath out of her. 'When you were talking to John, at midnight, it was still the third of September in England—'

'But it was already the fourth of September for him!' Annie nodded energetically. 'Almost seven in the morning. And they said the blowdown was just after eight. It doesn't work, does it? He can't have hitched that lift out of town and been back in time to get blown up.'

'We-ell—' Hayley hesitated. 'Maybe he didn't hitch a lift. Maybe he went back to the site after all. Straight after he'd phoned you.'

Annie pulled a face. 'That's what the police said. The whole case was tied up by the time I realized, and they didn't want to stir things up. *Maybe he changed his mind*, they said.'

'Well—he might have done.'

'*John?*'

That was all Annie said—but all at once he was there, as real as if he'd been standing between them. Solid, methodical John, with his calculator and his black notebook and the pen tucked behind his ear. Hayley could almost see him frowning and biting his bottom lip. He worked at thinking in the same steady way he worked at everything else. Some problems took him a long time, but he never gave up on anything. And he didn't flit around changing his mind.

'You see?' Annie swooped on the hesitation, like a swift in the sky. 'He's—he was the most consistent, reliable person I've ever known. He *could* have got back to the site by eight o'clock—but he wouldn't have gone. Would he?'

Hayley shook her head. 'Why didn't you say all this before? Mum and Dad would have believed you. They know what John was like.'

Annie just looked. And Hayley remembered the answerphone messages. *You never call me back . . . I need to talk to you . . . why don't you answer? . . .*

'Oh, leave it,' Annie said wearily. 'We can't do anything about it now, and we're both too tired to think straight. Let's get ready for bed.'

That meant Annie first, with Hayley running around to fetch things and help. By the time that was over, Hayley was so exhausted that she could hardly clean her teeth. As she slid under the covers, she saw Annie watching her from the other bed.

'Goodnight,' Annie said. 'Sleep well.'

'Goodnight.' Hayley's eyes were closing, even while she was turning out the bedside light.

She was woken up by something hitting her on the shoulder. Something hard and heavy, flying through the air.

And then a voice hissing at her. Calling across the space between the beds.

'Wake *up*, won't you! Get over here!'

Something else hit her, just as hard in just the same place. But this time she was wide awake enough to recognize it. Annie's trainer.

Hayley fumbled for the switch and turned on the light beside her. Annie was sitting up in bed with her mobile pressed to her ear, beckoning furiously.

'Quick! Come and listen!'

Still trembling from the shock of being woken like that, Hayley stumbled across the space between the two beds. Annie was obviously not going to pass the phone across, so she sat on the bed and leaned as close as she could.

'Hear it?' Annie said, in a strange, excited whisper.

All Hayley could hear was ringing. She didn't understand why Annie was holding her breath. Why Annie's free hand had clamped suddenly round her shoulders, pulling her even closer.

'Who is it?' she said. 'Who are you phoning?'

'*Sssh!*' Annie shook her and they sat in silence, listening to the sound.

Until it cut out.

'Drat!' Annie said. She put the phone down and laughed, shakily. 'That's the first time I've had a ringing tone.'

'Is that all you woke me up for?' Hayley's shoulder was sore and bruised and she was starting to be annoyed. 'I thought you were dying or something.'

'Sorry,' Annie said. 'Sorry.' She let go of Hayley and laughed again. A tight, tense laugh, on the edge of tears. 'It was just—there it was, ringing, and I suddenly

77

thought, *What if he answers? What if I suddenly hear his voice—?'*

She caught her breath and stopped, leaving the question hanging. Letting the silence gape around them.

Hayley felt uneasy questions slither through her mind. 'What if *who* answers? Who were you phoning, anyway?'

Annie turned her head away. It was the first time Hayley had ever seen her look confused. 'It was—well, actually—it was John's mobile number. The one he rented to bring here.'

'You were phoning *John*?' Hayley stared at her. 'But—'

'OK, so it's not rational,' Annie said. She sounded sad and tired. 'But you have to have something, you know. To keep you going. Some little, silly thing that will let you pretend—'

She looked down, faltering for a second. Hayley stared at her thin, frail shoulders and the bony nape of her neck and thought, *Don't tell me. I can't bear it.* But Annie had already started again.

'I went on paying the rental, just so that I could dial that number and hear the recorded message. *The phone you are ringing may be switched off. Please try later.* That was just the same as before. As if the phone was still clipped on to his belt, instead of—'

'Instead of lying under all that rubble in Tomsk,' Hayley said bluntly.

Annie looked up, grinning ruefully. 'I know. But that made the number safe to ring, didn't it? There was no chance of anyone else switching it on. Or that's what I *thought*.'

'But someone *has* switched it on.' Hayley nodded. 'Who d'you think? One of the kids playing round on the demolition site?'

'Could be,' Annie said thoughtfully. 'Or one of Leonid's men, perhaps. Or maybe your mum and dad have had it all the time.'

Hayley shook her head. 'Not them. I told you. Mum burnt *everything*. If the phone had come back to England, it would have been on that bonfire.'

'So it's still in Russia?' Annie said, in a strange voice.

'Must be,' Hayley said. 'But I don't see—'

Annie didn't wait for the end of the sentence. She sat up suddenly, transformed. Grabbing at the holdall beside her bed, she unzipped it and began to throw things out.

'What on earth are you doing?' Hayley said, catching a handful of jumpers.

'I'm looking for my blue file.' A grey skirt followed the jumpers. 'It's got the number of the phone hire company in it. What time is it in England?'

'I don't know.' Hayley looked at her watch. 'Almost five o'clock in the evening? Almost six?'

'*Which?* Oh, you're hopeless!' Annie found the blue file and heaved it on to the bed. 'Will the office be open or not?'

'You're going to ring them?' Hayley said. 'Now?'

'Of course it's got to be now!' Annie said impatiently. She found the phone number in her file and prodded Hayley in the ribs. 'Get my mobile. It's fallen on to the floor.'

She didn't explain until she had the phone in her hand. Then she spelt it out jerkily, as she punched in the number. 'If John's phone is . . . ringing, that . . . means it's . . . switched on. Right? And if it's . . . switched on . . . the phone company can . . . track it down.'

'You mean—so we can find it?' Hayley said uncertainly.

'That's right.' Annie put the mobile to her ear and grinned. 'If the satellite can pick up the signal before the thing's switched off again, they should be able to pinpoint it for us. And wherever it is—*we're going there.*'

79

10

Katya was in the museum on the day the cyclist arrived. Being bored out of her mind.

'Look, how beautiful Krasny Yar used to be!' her grandmother kept saying. 'What a lovely town!' She leaned closer to the big glass case of photographs. 'I remember those wooden houses with the carved shutters when I was a little girl. And the old church with the coloured domes.'

What a way to spend the best bit of the afternoon! Outside, the air was crisp and frosty and the low sun was catching all the windows. The bottle factory looked like something made of gold. It was the future that mattered. Who cared about the past?

Her grandmother's nose was almost pressed against the glass. 'I do believe that's—yes, look Katya! Can you see that old lady with the dog?'

But Katya's eyes were out of the window, watching the people in the street. Noticing new trainers and personal stereos and mobile phones. There still weren't many of them—but there were more than last month. *It's coming*, she thought. *Things are changing! Even in Krasny Yar.*

'You see that old lady?' Her grandmother tugged at her sleeve. 'I remember her!'

But what Katya saw, looking out of the window, was the man on the bicycle.

He came from nowhere, cycling out of the forest, on the path beside the railway line. And he was wearing—

Katya gulped with laughter, pressing her hands flat against her mouth.

'What's so funny?' Her grandmother peered round at her. 'You'd be better off paying attention.'

'Oh, but look. *Look!*' Katya nudged her. 'Look at that man. He's—oh, Babushka!'

The cyclist's clothes were the oldest she had ever seen. A thick padded jacket with the stuffing oozing out through a dozen holes. Strange, baggy trousers. A hat with moth-eaten fur flaps, and a pair of ancient felt boots, split at the sides. The cyclist's shoulders were powdered with snow and his face was red and white with cold. He looked—just *crazy!*

The wind caught him as he cleared the edge of the trees, knocking him sideways. He fell off the bike and sprawled on the ground and Katya giggled, avoiding her grandmother's eyes.

'Drunk,' said the attendant. She had come up behind, to see what all the fuss was about, and she leaned over Katya's shoulder, with her thick arms folded and her museum keeper's hat pulled forward over her bouncy red curls. 'Eleven in the morning and there's already a drunk walking down the street. That's not how it was.'

It was her catchphrase. *That's not how it was.* She'd said it three or four times since they arrived and each time Katya's grandmother had pulled herself up very stiff and straight, frowning in the other direction. There seemed to be no end to the discussion about *how it was.* For as long as Katya could remember, the old people had been at it, throwing the words backwards and forwards at each other. Better . . . worse . . . better . . . worse. *Who cared?*

Now the museum keeper's 'Drunk' sparked off a sniff and a toss of the head from Katya's grandmother. 'Poor man. It's more likely he's starving.'

The cyclist was slowly hauling himself out of the snow

81

at the edge of the road. Dusting himself down, he climbed on to the bicycle again, but the moment he began to cycle the wind caught him again, knocking him sideways.

'You see?' the museum attendant said, with bitter authority. 'Probably been drinking furniture polish.'

'Weak with hunger,' Katya's grandmother snapped.

The attendant gave her a scornful, pitying look. 'If that's what you want to think, who am I to argue? If you can't see—'

All the time, the cyclist was struggling in the snow, pulling himself on to all fours to stand up again. But the moment he managed it, he put his foot on to the patch of shiny, hard-packed snow by the entrance to the bottle factory. He sat down with a thump that made Katya wince.

'Incapable,' the attendant said triumphantly.

Yes . . . no. Drunk . . . sober. Better . . . worse. Why did old people always think you could discover things by talking? If you wanted to find out about things—well, you had to go and look, didn't you? Obvious. Katya spun round and headed for the door.

'Katenka!' her grandmother said sharply.

'I'm going to see what's really going on out there,' Katya said. And left, as fast as she could.

As she went out of the room, she heard the attendant's scandalized voice. 'Are you going to let that child talk to a drunken man? Have you no concern for her safety?'

Safety? What did they think the cyclist was going to do to her? He couldn't even stay on his feet. If he gave her any trouble, she just had to stretch out one finger and SPLAT! He'd be flat on his back.

She heard the attendant break into a lumbering trot behind her and she started to run. Down the stairs. Out into the snow. As the cold air hit her, she caught her breath, but she didn't stop. The cyclist was tottering along

82

in the gutter, pushing his bike, and she waved and called out to him.

'Hello!'

He looked round and immediately began to slither again. For a couple of seconds he stayed on his feet, scrabbling comically. Then he crashed to the ground. This time the bike was on top of him.

Katya marched across the street and began to help him up. Behind her, she could hear hands knocking on the museum windows. When the cyclist glanced across, she looked round too, and saw her grandmother banging on the glass.

'My *babushka*,' Katya said—although her grandmother was not in the least like anyone's idea of a *babushka*. She was small and wiry and very upright, with a purple hat perched on her white hair.

The cyclist looked completely blank.

He didn't understand.

With a wild leap of inspiration, Katya thought—*He's foreign. He's not Russian at all!* And that meant that—maybe—it was possible—Her heart started to pound and she scrabbled for the English words.

'You are—Amer-ee-can?'

The blankness changed to a frown.

He still didn't understand.

Oh well. Not surprising. An American wouldn't be seen dead in those weird clothes. Katya began to pull the bike free, checking the wheels to make sure they still worked properly.

Then the man worked out what she had said. His face lit up, his eyes gleamed and he let out a huge torrent of words. They were English all right, but—Katya shook her head fiercely, fending off the flood with her hands.

The cyclist tried again, with a single word. Pointing to his chest. 'English.'

'Ingleesh?' Katya was so excited that she nearly fell over the bike. 'You are Ingleesh?'

There was another tidal wave of language. She rapped him on the arm.

'You must to speak slowly.'

'Sorry,' the man said, in slow motion. 'I'm sorry.'

Katya looked him up and down. This might be the most exciting thing that had ever happened to her. On the other hand, he might just be a lying Estonian drunk. She looked severely at him.

'It is true? You are English? Where is your passport?'

The man shrugged wearily and pulled his pockets inside out, to show they were empty.

Estonian, Katya thought. Resigned and disappointed.

But she had no intention of sharing her suspicions. The museum attendant was bustling across the street, ranting in Russian.

' . . . and there's your grandmother thinking you're going to get your throat slit. And all for what? What can you do for a drunk like that? You have to be careful in these days . . . '

'He's not a drunk,' Katya said, with dignity. 'He's an Englishman.'

'Same thing,' said the attendant scathingly. She rolled her eyes up to the sky, took her cap off, ran her hands through her hair and put the cap back on again. 'You think I don't know decadence when I see it?'

'You don't know anything.' Katya was suddenly full of confidence. What did old people understand about the world? 'You think it's a drink he wants?' She turned to the cyclist and switched back to English, groping for the words. 'You want—vodka?'

She mimed it as well, for the attendant's benefit, tossing back an invisible glassful. The man looked horrified.

'Bread,' he said in English. 'Please.' And then in Russian as well, pointing at his mouth. *'Khleb, pazhalysta.'*

Katya shot a smug glance at the attendant. 'You see? He's an Englishman, and I'm going to take him home. My father knows very good English. We shall feed the poor, hungry man.'

She couldn't manage to explain that to the cyclist, so she simply nodded, pointed at her mouth and beckoned. Then she turned for home, pushing the bike to make sure that he followed her.

'Your grandmother will go mad!' the attendant called after them. 'You could be killed by this man.'

'In the street?' Katya said, over her shoulder.

She began to walk off, but she realized quickly that the cyclist could not keep up with her. She had to slow down to his pace.

As they went, she examined him. He was filthy and unshaven, but—not the ugliest man she had ever seen. Quite young. And maybe English after all. Katya tossed back her long hair and smiled at him. But he didn't react. All his energy was going into walking.

They were going so slowly that Katya's grandmother caught them up before they reached the end of the street. Katya braced herself for a tirade, but the museum keeper had obviously been lying about that. The grandmother looked sharply at the cyclist, patted his hand, and pointed to the bike.

'Katya. I will walk with him. You ride to warn your father. Tell him to heat water for a bath. And soup.'

'Ride? This bike?' Katya said loftily, looking at the crossbar.

'I can't see another one.' Her grandmother stared her out.

Katya compromised. Putting one foot on a pedal, she pushed off with the other and scooted down the road. As she swung round the corner, she glanced back. The cyclist was picking his way up the road, grabbing for her grandmother's arm every time he slipped.

Katya wove her way round the corner and through the network of streets to her own house, avoiding the shiny patches where the new snow was already trodden down hard. She swerved abruptly whenever she met a car, but there weren't many of those. Just the occasional battered black Zhiguli.

When she reached the flats, she pulled the bike into the lift with her, hauling it up on to its back wheel so that it would fit. It dripped a pool of melted snow on one corner and left a trail from the lift to the front door of the flat.

Her father was sitting at the table, writing long, thoughtful comments in the margins of his students' essays.

'Papa!'

He put down the pen and raised his eyebrows at the bicycle. 'Something's happened?'

'I've found an Englishman!' Katya said dramatically. 'Babushka is bringing him home.'

Her father looked astonished. 'A tourist? Here?'

'Not a tourist. A cyclist!' Katya gave a little, gasping laugh, out of breath.

Her father stood up and took the bike away from her. Carefully he slid it behind the couch where she slept. Then he put his hands on her shoulders. 'Now. From the beginning, please. Slowly. Who is this Englishman of Babushka's?'

'*I* was the one who spoke to him,' Katya said, nettled. 'I spoke to him in *English*. Babushka and the museum woman were just arguing about him. If it hadn't been for me—'

'Yes, yes, I understand. He is your Englishman. But why is he coming here?'

Katya remembered the message. 'Soup, Babushka said. And a bath. He came out of the forest on a bicycle. He—'

Her father pushed her ahead of him, into the kitchen. 'Heat up the soup while I start the bath.'

There was hardly room for them both in the kitchen. Katya wedged herself at the far end, beside the stove.

'All the soup?'

Her father shrugged. 'All the soup, I suppose. And, I'll have to put on the rest of the pans. There's no hot water this morning.'

The water was just coming to the boil when they heard the whine of the lift. And then the sound of footsteps. Babushka's were unmistakable, slow and precise. But the cyclist sounded dreadful, dragging his boots like an old man. Katya ran to the front door and threw it open, to check that it was really him.

Her father came out of the kitchen looking distant and polite. What Katya thought of as his teacher's face. But the moment he saw the cyclist, his expression changed. The cyclist looked even paler than when Katya had spoken to him, and he was wheezing badly.

Katya's father pushed past her and slipped his arm round the man's shoulders. 'Come in, dear friend,' he said in English. 'There is food and a bath and then you can go to bed. We will look after you.'

As long as she lived, Katya never forgot how the cyclist looked when he heard his own language, spoken so that he could understand it.

He is not ready for all this. Not prepared for the kindness of people who speak to him in his own language. He knows, without asking—without even thinking—that he can trust them. They do not want anything from him. They are distressed by the sight of his bruises and his filthy, unshaven face.

Don't trust me! he wants to say. *Be on your guard! I'm not a poor, harmless stranger. I'm dangerous—like a landmine in the middle of the forest. Suddenly, at any moment, I might blast you into pieces.*

But he doesn't know how or why. He can't remember what it is that he's done, or why the Wolf and the Bear are hunting him. All he knows is that he is weak from hunger and from cycling. He must have food, so that he can keep moving on.

So all he says is, *Thank you. Thank you, you are very good.*

And he lets them take him in.

11

On the map, it looked like nowhere. Annie's finger ran north from Tomsk, up the river to Petrovsk. About two hundred miles. And then north-west, and into a blank, empty space.

'It *can't* be there,' Hayley said. 'That's not a place. There's not even a road.'

'It is there,' Annie said bitterly. 'I've checked the figures three times.'

'So what's it doing? Just lying around in the middle of the forest?' Hayley felt like crying with disappointment. *After all the hassle we went through to get it . . .*

It had been a real struggle. The mobile rental company was perfectly happy to do the tracking, but not to pass over the results. Annie had spent an hour on the phone, arguing with the manager.

'It's a matter of security,' said his frosty voice, from an office in Surrey. 'Our clients have to be able to trust us.'

'They can't trust you if they're *dead*!' Annie yelled down the phone. 'And I'm the person who's been paying the rental.'

'Our contract is with Mr Cox. If you're able to produce his death certificate, maybe we could reconsider . . .'

'How can I produce his death certificate when I'm in the middle of Siberia?'

'I don't think that alters the principle . . .'

She was definitely losing the argument until Hayley had a sudden inspiration.

'What about the newspaper reports?' she hissed. 'About the explosion. They'll be on the Net, won't they?'

Annie grinned and gave her a thumbs up as she passed on the idea.

There was a grudging hesitation at the other end. 'Well, I suppose that might be acceptable—'

'Well get a move on, then!' Annie snapped. 'But for heaven's sake track the phone *first*. Otherwise you'll lose the signal.'

By the time she'd convinced them, her own phone's battery was almost flat. She had to give them the hotel number so that they could call her back.

The return call didn't come through until four in the morning. Hayley had dropped off to sleep and she woke up to a cascade of noise. The phone was ringing. The people in the next room were thumping on the wall. And Annie was yelling at the top of her voice.

'Get it! Get that phone and bring it over here!'

The room was dark except for Annie's bedside lamp. Hayley carried the phone across and sat on the end of the bed. Annie was wide awake, as though she hadn't slept at all.

'Yes . . . yes, that's right . . . Beethoven's the password . . . thank you.' She put a hand over the phone and hissed at Hayley. 'Get my notebook and a pen. Quick.'

She scribbled down the map reference, read the numbers back down the phone, and signed off in a calm, businesslike voice.

'Thank you, that's great . . . yes, of course I will. Thank you. Goodbye.' But when she put the receiver down and pointed across the room, her hand was shaking. 'Get the map book, Hayley. Quick! It's in that blue file.'

She was almost shouting. The people next door thumped again, but she ignored them and grabbed the file from Hayley. Pulling out the book, she found the right page with shaking hands.

'It's . . . it's . . . oh, hold the book while I look!'

They bent over the map together. And there it was, in the middle of nowhere.

Annie frowned at it. 'What would John have been doing in a place like that?'

It was on the edge of a sea of nothing. Forest and bog and endless winding rivers. *If you got lost there*, Hayley thought, *you could be lost for ever*. At home, *lost* didn't mean much more than *mislaid*. But here— If you dropped into that emptiness, how would you ever find yourself again?

'We've got to go there,' Annie said, somewhere around seven o'clock in the morning. She sounded crisp and determined.

Hayley struggled up in bed, rubbing her eyes. 'You're not serious?'

'Of course I am. It's what we came for, isn't it?'

'But look at the *map*. How can we get to a place like that? Ask a taxi to drive us into the forest? Hire a floating wheelchair to sail down the river?'

'So what d'you think I'm going to do? Give up and trot meekly back to England, just because it's difficult?' Annie's face was like stone. 'Don't kid yourself. I'm going—there.' She jammed her finger down on the map. 'And if it's humanly possible, I'm going tomorrow.'

Hayley propped herself on one elbow and stared across the space between the two beds. 'So how are you going to do it?'

'Like this.' Annie reached into the blue file and pulled out a small white rectangle covered in incomprehensible Cyrillic letters. When Hayley frowned, she flipped it over to show the English on the other side.

91

It was Leonid Orlov's card.

'I'm going to phone him,' Annie said. 'And ask him to take us there.'

'You're crazy,' Hayley said. 'I thought you had him down as some kind of mega *mafiya* boss. You think he's going to organize an expedition into the forest—just because you ask him to? To find a *mobile phone*?'

'No harm in asking,' Annie said. 'And if he agrees—' Her eyes glittered suddenly. '—well, won't that be interesting . . . ?'

She phoned as soon as it was nine o'clock.

Within twenty minutes, Yuri was knocking on the door of their room, smiling nervously. The moment Annie opened the door, he launched into a little speech. It sounded as though he had been practising it all the way up in the lift.

'My father understands how you feel about the mobile phone. He understands that you want to have it back. He will send someone into the forest to find it for you. All you need to do is write where it is.'

He had the pen and a notebook ready in his hand.

'That's so *kind*,' Annie said effusively. But she wheeled herself backwards, away from Yuri and the notebook. 'Only . . . it's not just the phone we want. We want to see the place where it is. For ourselves.'

Yuri's hand wavered. 'But there is nothing there. Only trees. And mud.'

'And the mobile,' Annie said sweetly. 'That's the interesting thing, isn't it? Please go back and say to your father that we need to visit this Nowhere-in-the-Middle-of-the-Forest. We can't go back to Moscow until we've been there.'

Yuri looked at the notebook in his hand. For the first

time, Hayley felt sorry for him. He looked very cool, but he was only the same age as she was, and he'd obviously been given precise orders about what to do. He had one last try. 'It is very hard to travel in the forest. Especially for you. Why do you want to make a difficult journey for such a little thing? All you have to do is tell my father—'

'Ah, but it's not a little thing to me.' Annie's voice was like syrup now. 'If anyone's fetching the phone, I just have to go too.'

Yuri shrugged, glanced at Hayley and gave in. As the door closed behind him, Annie's sugary smile vanished.

'Well?' she said sharply.

Hayley frowned. 'You really think Leonid's going to agree?'

'Depends how much he wants to find that mobile.' Annie fished in her sleeve and pulled out the piece of paper where she'd written what the phone company told them. 'Quickly! Go and flush this down the toilet.'

'What?' Hayley stared at her. 'After all the trouble it took to get it?'

'Of course. Hurry up! The only place I'm keeping that information is inside my head.'

'But suppose you forget it?'

Annie looked scornful. 'Do you think it's not burnt into my brain?'

Hayley gave in and went into the bathroom, ripping up the paper as she went. It took three flushes to get rid of it all, and the cistern was still refilling for the last time when Yuri knocked on the door again.

This time, his father was right behind him. Hayley let them in and Leonid came striding into the room, with both hands held out. There was a great cascade of Russian, accompanied by a lot of hand-waving.

Then Yuri said, 'He will take you.'

'Is that *all* he said?' Annie looked suspicious.

Yuri shrugged. 'You don't have to know the rest. But he thinks you are very stubborn and stupid and he is angry about being—' He searched for a word.

'Blackmailed,' Hayley said boldly.

Yuri's smile was sudden and unnerving. 'I think so.' He gave Hayley an appreciative look.

Leonid launched into another tirade, seizing the map book and flapping it in Annie's face. There was something threatening in the way he loomed over her chair, but she kept perfectly still, staring him straight in the eye. When he had finished, she spoke to Yuri, without turning her head.

'What was all that about, then?'

'He says that you should tell him where you want to go.' Yuri's voice was expressionless. 'If you give him the reference, he can work out a route.'

'I'll show him on the map,' Annie said. 'Roughly. We can be more precise when we're almost there.'

Yuri translated that into Russian, in exactly the same deadpan way.

It's like a dance, Hayley thought. *A kind of ritual they have to go through.* What Leonid wanted was the exact map reference. That was obvious. He could see that Annie wasn't going to tell him, but he spread the map on the arm of her chair and made her show him the beginning part of the journey. Pushing all the time for a little bit more than she was prepared to give. Hayley could feel an electric tension all round them.

When he decided that he had as much as he was going to get, the atmosphere changed suddenly. He straightened up and began to talk briskly, moving on to practical arrangements. Hayley understood that, even before Yuri translated.

'We shall need special cars. To Petrovsk it is not so bad. But after that the roads are very difficult. And to get

94

into the forest, a boat is better. That will take time to arrange, even for my father. So we shall set out tomorrow. Yes?'

Annie nodded. 'At nine o'clock in the morning?'

Yuri consulted his father. Then he said, 'Earlier. We shall be here at half past seven.'

'We'll be ready.'

'And we shall have to stay a night in the forest. It will not be possible to go and come back in one day.'

Annie hesitated for a moment, looking over Yuri's shoulder, at Leonid. Then she nodded. 'OK. If that's what it takes.'

And that was it. Leonid shook Annie's hand, patted Hayley on the head and went. Yuri lingered for a second, looking at Hayley as though he might say something, but his father called him from the corridor and he went at once.

'Well!' Annie said, when the door closed. 'That was pretty interesting, wasn't it?'

Hayley nodded. 'Why did Yuri say the boat would take time to arrange "even for my father"?'

'Because his father can arrange *anything*, of course. Bit of protection, bit of drugs, bit of black market dealing. Anything. I bet he's got the police in the palm of his hand.' Annie looked at Hayley's doubtful face and grinned. 'You still don't believe he's *mafiya*, do you?'

Hayley frowned. 'I thought the Mafia was an Italian thing.'

'Not here it's not. Home-grown Russian crime and corruption. In the bad old Soviet days, it was the Communist Party bosses who had everything sewn up in towns like this. Those networks never got swept away. Just privatized. People like Leonid are coining it in. Haven't you noticed his watch? And Yuri's trainers? And the cars? He's probably a millionaire.'

Hayley still wasn't convinced. 'If he's a millionaire—why is he interested in a little thing like John's mobile phone?'

'I don't know.' Annie drew in a long, slow breath. 'But I'm not going to let him get anywhere near it unless we're there too.'

There was an edge to her voice that made Hayley shiver.

12

What was the point in bringing home an English cyclist if he didn't *talk*? Katya had a million questions to ask him. Maybe he needed to eat his soup first—her grandmother glared at her, forbidding her to interrupt that—but why was he taking so *long*?

She sat at his elbow, fretting impatiently, and as he swallowed the last spoonful, she gave him her best, most charming smile.

The cyclist put his spoon down. 'Thank you,' he said in English. His voice was almost too weak to hear.

Katya opened her mouth—and met another glare from her grandmother. The grandmother didn't speak anything except Russian, but she knew how to look after people.

'No talking now,' she muttered. 'Help him into the bath, while the soup is still warm in him. And then bed. He needs to sleep.'

Katya's father leaned across the table and repeated the instructions in English. The cyclist nodded and said them over again. 'A bath. Bed.' They could see him struggling to get to his feet.

The grandmother prodded Katya. 'Help him. Take off his boots.'

'His boots?' Katya squealed. They were disgusting. Old and splitting and thick with mud.

'You want *me* to get down on the floor?' her grandmother said.

Katya pulled a face and slid off her chair. As she tugged at the first boot, she saw the cyclist looking down at her,

97

distant and vague with exhaustion. Inside the boot, his socks were worn into huge holes. His feet were white and numb with cold and his skin was wrinkled from being wet. The boots had blistered the skin on top of his toes.

Her grandmother stood up and went into the kitchen to get out the salt. Katya heard her pouring it into one of the pans of boiling water.

'Sergei!' she called. 'Katya! Fill the bath.'

It was an awkward manoeuvre, because the kitchen and the bathroom were side by side and both tiny, but Katya and her father were used to it. They worked the big pans round the tight corner between the doors and emptied them into the bath. Then they went back to heave the cyclist on to his feet.

The grandmother followed, with a chair to put by the bath. When the cyclist was safely sitting down, she chivvied the others out of the bathroom and closed the door.

'Enough!' she said. 'Let him have his bath in peace, and then he can sleep.'

'But we don't know who he is!' Katya hissed. 'Or where—'

'Patience.' The grandmother tapped her lips with a bony finger. 'Until the right time.'

The right time came very slowly. When he was dry after his bath, and dressed in the warmest clothes they could find, the cyclist fell into the grandmother's bed in the flat's only bedroom. He was instantly asleep, without moving or making a sound.

And he was still asleep at eleven o'clock at night.

'Like a dead person,' the grandmother said, settling herself in the big armchair beside the unfolding couch. 'I will spend the night here, next to your father. Katya, please prop the bedroom door open.'

Katya sighed and looked impatient. So what if the cyclist did wake up? Did Babushka really think she couldn't handle him? All the same, she wedged the bedroom door well open, with a heap of books. And two or three times in the night she opened her eyes and watched the other bed.

But the cyclist didn't stir, all night. And when Katya left for school in the morning, he was still sleeping.

'Better not to talk about him,' the grandmother murmured as she held out Katya's coat. 'Silence is best. Until we discover who he is and why he's here.'

Katya didn't say a word at school. But when she walked back down the road at lunchtime there was a car parked outside their block. She looked at it, thoughtfully.

As she reached the lift, she met two policemen coming out. They had almost passed her when one of them stopped and turned.

'Have you seen an Englishman around here?' he said. Almost casually. 'Tall and fair. Very dirty.'

'Why—yes.'

The moment Katya said it, she knew there was something wrong. The second policeman turned as well. Too eagerly.

'You've seen him today?' He must have heard the urgency in his own voice, because he checked himself. 'It's nothing, you understand. We just need to check his papers.'

But he has no papers, said a cold little voice in Katya's brain. He had turned his pockets inside out and they were empty. Suddenly, she was very wide awake. Cautious and alert.

'I saw him yesterday,' she said. 'Not today.' It was true. He had been hidden under the bedclothes when she left

99

for school. 'My grandmother and I met him outside the museum and brought him home for a meal.'

'He was a stranger?'

'He was *hungry*!' Katya said. 'What would you have done? Would you have left him there, in the street?'

The second policeman—the younger one—looked away quickly. Katya saw the corner of a smile. But the other was persistent.

'So—he had a meal. And then what?'

'Then—' Katya frowned, like someone trying to remember. Both policemen were looking at her now. She felt wary and uneasy, without knowing why.

'Then I went to bed,' she said vaguely.

'You don't know what time the Englishman left?'

She shook her head, wide-eyed and dumb, and the older policeman pushed by impatiently, heading for the car outside. The younger one glanced at her and she gave him a bright, interested smile that made him turn away too and hurry after his colleague.

When she reached the flat, her grandmother opened the door before she could knock.

'Did you see the police? Did they speak to you?'

Katya nodded. 'They asked me what time the Englishman left last night.'

'And you said?'

'I said I was in bed and I didn't know.'

The grandmother let out a long slow breath. 'Thank God for his mercies. I was afraid—' She broke off short.

'Why did they come?' Katya said.

'It was Galina from the museum.' The grandmother pursed her lips. 'I ought to have guessed that she would report the Englishman. She was born to be an informer, that one. She told the police he had gone off with us, and they came round to find him. We told them he had gone last night.'

'And they believed you?' Katya said.

The grandmother shrugged. 'How can we tell? I hope so.'

The cyclist came out of the bedroom looking at Katya warily.

'It's all right,' Katya's father said in English. 'She is a clever girl. The police still think you left last night.'

The cyclist let out a long breath and Katya's father stood up.

'Let's talk while we have lunch.' He often marked all the way through the meal, but today he dumped the pile of essays on his chair. 'There is a lot to understand.'

Katya would have talked about the police straight away, but her father was different. He was slow and methodical and he started at the beginning, talking in English, but translating for his mother.

'You came through the forest? On a bicycle?'

The cyclist nodded. 'There was a track to begin with. Later on I walked along the railway track.'

The grandmother clicked her tongue when that was interpreted, and Katya imagined the effort of lifting the bike over the sleepers. Again and again and again.

'How many days?' her father said.

The cyclist hesitated, counting on his fingers. 'Three— no, four. With the bicycle.'

'And no food?'

'No food. But I melted the snow in my hands to drink.'

'And why are you travelling?'

The cyclist's eyes flicked left and right. He shrugged and spread his hands, not answering.

Katya's father tried again. 'Where are you going?'

There was a long silence. The cyclist stared hard at each of them in turn. Then he leaned forward suddenly, putting his arms on the table.

'I don't know where I'm going,' he said abruptly. 'I don't know my name or what I do or where I live. All I know is that I was ill in the forest, and some people took me in. But I couldn't stay there. I can't stay anywhere for long, in case—'

He stopped.

'In case?' Katya's father said.

There was another silence. The grandmother was watching them all with sharp eyes, looking from one face to another. Suddenly, she lifted her ruined right hand— the hand she always kept hidden. She laid it on the table in front of the cyclist and Katya saw him take it in. The long, pale scars. The distorted fingers.

'I also have suffered in the forest,' the grandmother said quietly. 'When I was young, I also hid from the police and trembled when there was a knock at the door. How did you think I understood you so quickly, when the police came?'

The cyclist stared at the scars. Katya couldn't tell whether he heard what her father was saying as he interpreted.

'Usually it is better not to speak of suffering, even to oneself,' the grandmother said. 'I have learnt this as well. But if you never speak—if you never trust anyone—then you die.'

'How do we know who can be trusted?' the cyclist said, when he had the words in English. He didn't lift his head to look at them.

Katya's father didn't speak. He simply reached out and touched his mother's hand, running a finger lightly over the twisted thumb. The cyclist followed with his eyes. Softly, as the finger moved, he began to talk.

'I don't know how I got into the forest. All I know is that I have to keep hidden and keep moving, because I'm in danger. There are people looking for me. Only—I can't remember who they are.'

102

'And so the enemies are all around,' Katya's father said. Suddenly he sounded old and weary. 'In every dark corner, in every new face, you see one. Yes? I am right?'

'Exactly right,' the cyclist said.

'And these enemies—why are they looking for you? What do they want?'

The cyclist shrank back suddenly, with his face changing, loosening, giving way. The grandmother reached out with her good hand and took hold of his wrist.

'You are safe here,' she said in Russian. 'Don't be afraid!'

But he *was* afraid. His face was dark with fear and his hands were shaking.

'You mustn't keep me here,' he said. 'It's dangerous. *I'm* dangerous.'

The girl doesn't understand. He can see it in her face. She is still living in a clean world, where good and bad are in two different camps. Either—or. When he says, *I'm dangerous*, she thinks that all he means is, *My enemies will attack you as well*.

But the grandmother and the father, they know. They know how the darkness winds through everything. When the knock came on the door, the grandmother looked through the spyhole and made a sign, and the father said softly, in English, *The police are here*. And both of them watched his face, to see how he reacted.

Afterwards, when the police had asked their questions and gone, he said, *Why did you hide me? You don't know anything about me. If the police are looking for me, I'm probably a criminal*.

The father translated for the grandmother, and she said something in Russian, and laughed.

That proves you're English. If you think the police are always on the side of the law.

They are sheltering him—but they don't assume that he's innocent. Because they know that no one is entirely innocent. He wishes he could stay here and remember what it is he's done and why he feels guilty and afraid. He would trust these two to judge him fairly.

But he can't stay, because he brings danger wherever he goes. Even though he means no harm, the Bear pads after him, and the Wolf looks for his trail with cold and deadly eyes.

He has to move on.

13

It took Leonid exactly twenty-four hours to arrange a boat. The next morning, at half past six, the telephone rang and Yuri was on the other end of the line.

'It is all settled. We shall come to fetch you in an hour. You are ready?'

Groan, thought Hayley. *Double, treble groan.* But she said 'That's fine. We'll be ready.' She put the phone down and rolled over to switch on the light.

Annie was awake, propped up on one elbow. 'How long have we got?'

'An hour.'

'He's punctual.' Annie pulled a face. 'Help me get into the bathroom and then have a go at phoning Trevor and Chris.'

'Mum and Dad? But it'll be the middle of the night there.'

'Don't care. We ought to tell them where we're going and who's taking us. Now get on with it.'

It was a rigmarole. Fold up the chair to get it through the bathroom door. Unfold it again. Go back to help Annie up. She could stagger a couple of steps on crutches if she had to, but she was liable to fall at any moment. Hayley hovered until she was safely installed in the chair. Then she took the mobile and went back into the bedroom to dial home.

She expected the phone to ring for a long time. And then her father's sleepy voice, irritated until he found out it was her. *Don't you know what time it is?*

But the answerphone was on. It was an old recording and it was a shock to hear her mother's voice, brisk and cheerful, the way it used to be. *No one in the Cox family can take your call at the moment. But if you like to leave a message . . .*

Hayley rang off and worked out what she needed to say, to make sure she got all the vital details in. Then she rang back again.

'Dad? It's Hayley. We're travelling into the forest with a man called Leonid Orlov. John's mobile phone company—World Telecoms—knows exactly where we're going. We ought to be back tomorrow.'

She turned off the phone, wishing Trevor had been there. Wishing she had heard his voice.

They didn't have even an hour to get ready. After forty minutes, Yuri was knocking on the door, while Hayley was still throwing things into her suitcase. There were two large men standing behind him.

'We have come to carry your luggage. The cars are outside.'

'But we haven't had any breakfast.' Hayley threw in her old coat, slammed the lid down and locked the case. 'We must have something to eat.'

Annie brushed that aside. 'Don't fuss, Hayley! We can easily get something to eat on the way. Isn't that right, Yuri?'

'I think—excuse me, please.'

Yuri disappeared abruptly into the lift, leaving them alone with the two men. It was obvious that neither of them spoke English. They didn't attempt to talk. One of them scooped Annie out of the wheelchair and headed through the door, ignoring her protests. The other one folded the chair, picked it up and reached for the suitcases.

'Please,' said Hayley. 'I can—'

If he understood her, he didn't take any notice. Before she could blink, he was heading out of the room, with both cases, one tucked under his arm and the other in his free hand.

Oh well, Hayley thought. She grabbed Annie's crutches, locked the bedroom door and raced for the lift. It was tiny and cramped, and Annie was protesting loudly.

'Why don't you put me *down*? I can stand if you hold me up.'

It had no effect. She stayed suspended in mid-air. The man with the wheelchair and the cases had bypassed the lift completely. All the way down, they could hear his feet thundering on the wooden stairs, and the wheelchair bumping as he dragged it down behind him.

Annie was furious. Her lips were clamped tight shut and she was staring into space, not looking at either Hayley or the man who was holding her. If Hayley had dared, she would have giggled.

The lift was slow, as well as small. It stopped three times on the way down and two more people crammed themselves in. The third person recognized impossibility when he saw it and let them go. By the time they reached the ground floor, the wheelchair was standing ready and Annie was dumped into it, without ceremony.

'Thank goodness,' she muttered. 'Now let me push it myself.'

There was no hope of that. The men had obviously been told to take care of her and they weren't going to let anyone interfere. Not even Annie herself. They swept her off across the hotel foyer and presented her to Leonid Orlov, who was sitting in state in a large armchair, surrounded by three or four other men. He nodded pleasantly and said something in Russian. Then he looked round.

'Yuri!'

Immediately, all the other men began searching and calling, but Yuri didn't appear. It was Hayley who saw him first. He came hurrying out of the dining room with a waiter behind him, carrying a big cardboard carton. When he saw Leonid, the waiter began to talk very fast, gesturing at the carton and shaking his head apologetically.

Yuri grinned and came across to Hayley and Annie. 'He is upset because he cannot bring a better breakfast. And there is only this old cardboard box to put the food in. He does not want my father to be angry.'

'What's all the fuss about?' Annie said impatiently. 'All we need is a piece of bread.'

Yuri looked shocked. 'There is bread, of course—but that is not enough. He has put in eggs as well. And butter and jam. And some meatballs.'

Meatballs for breakfast? Hayley pulled a face behind his back. But Annie looked impressed.

'You got them to produce that lot? With no warning? You're a fast operator.'

Yuri shrugged modestly. 'It is normal. They like to help my father and his friends. Shall we go to the cars now, and then you can eat.' He moved behind Annie's chair.

'It's all *right*,' she said irritably.

She reached for the wheels and spun it forward faster, away from him. He was only just in time to skip round her and open the doors.

Outside, three vehicles were parked, one behind the other. Their drivers were walking up and down beside them, stamping their feet and blowing on their fingers.

'This is the expedition fleet, is it?' Annie said.

Hayley hadn't realized that they were all going. The front car was obviously Leonid Orlov's own, a big green Range Rover with smoked glass windows and smart bags in the boot. The two behind it were more humble things, a couple of Nivas, one black and one grey. They were the kind of car a child might have drawn. Square boxes on wheels with flat, hard seats.

'This is yours,' Yuri said, opening the front passenger door of the first Niva. 'Misha will drive you. He is a good driver—but he does not speak any English.'

'Aren't you coming in our car?' Hayley said. That seemed the obvious arrangement.

Yuri avoided her eyes. 'My father prefers me to ride with him. But there is no problem. We shall all meet at the river.' He held out his arms to Annie. 'Can I help you? Or should Misha lift you into the car?'

'Have you got any idea how difficult it is to lift someone into a car?' Annie said tartly. She nodded to Hayley. 'Let's show him again how we do it.'

Hayley stepped into position and Annie issued the instructions, staying firmly in charge.

'Let me put my arms round your neck. Right, now hold on to my waist. Good, now up . . . Are you watching, Yuri?'

Once she was in her seat, she took the cardboard carton on to her lap and began to share out the breakfast. Hayley found herself sitting in the back, reaching forward for bread and hardboiled eggs.

'Maybe we'll give the jam a miss,' Annie said. 'At least till we get to the boat. Fancy some meatballs?'

'Cold?'

'Oh, don't be so picky. We don't want to upset Leonid, do we? Take them now. It's not going to be easy once we've started.'

It wasn't easy anyway. Annie couldn't twist round to hand them over. Hayley had to hold on to the eggs and the bread with one hand, to stop them rolling off her lap, while she leaned forward for the meatballs. As she stretched over Annie's shoulder, she was sharply aware of

Misha in the driver's seat. He was staring ahead, not reacting at all.

There was something not quite right about that.

But Hayley wouldn't have thought anything of it— except for one thing. As her hand closed round the meatballs, Annie grinned.

'Do you think Leonid Orlov eats cold meatballs for breakfast? Out of his hand?'

Misha's mouth twitched.

Hayley was half turned away, but she saw it out of the corner of her eye. And she knew, for certain, that he was trying not to smile at the idea of his boss with a handful of cold, greasy meatballs. He'd understood what Annie said.

Yuri had been lying when he said that Misha didn't speak English.

Slowly, Hayley sat back, thinking about it. It was only when she was in her place again, with the car pulling away, that she realized what the danger was.

Annie obviously hadn't seen that tell-tale twitch. The first thing she said was, 'So what do you think the old devil is up to? Why has he laid all this on?'

'Maybe he's just being nice,' Hayley said carefully.

'Nice? Oh, come on! No one gets to be a *mafiya* boss by being nice. He changed completely when I told him about the phone. Didn't you see?'

'He's very cunning,' Hayley said, trying frantically to think of a way of giving a coded warning. 'Why do you think he's put us in this car and not in his own?'

Oh come on, Annie, come on! Surely that's enough of a hint.

But it wasn't. Annie said scathingly, 'It's just the old front seat thing. He knows I need a front seat, and men like him can't bear to sit in the back. And he's probably making some plot to get the map reference out of us.'

'Well, maybe we shouldn't talk about it then.' *Or we'll hand it to him on a plate.*

110

'But this is our only chance to talk.' Annie sounded impatient. 'Once we reach the river, we'll all be together, on the boat. And Leonid will be leaning on us for more information. We've got to decide how to feed it to him so he never gets enough to guess—'

But we won't get the chance, if you blab it out now.

At that moment, the car went round a corner and Hayley moved, almost without thinking. It seemed like a chance to whisper in Annie's ear without being too obvious. She lurched forward.

But she had forgotten about the food on her lap. It showered down, rolling through the space between the two front seats. An egg hit Misha's shoe and another jammed itself under one of the pedals. Meatballs rolled down his trouserleg and Annie's skirt.

'Oh *dear!*' Hayley said elaborately, diving forward to try and reach them. She was still aiming to mutter a warning.

But Annie foiled her, by pulling away and turning in her seat. Frowning down at the eggs and the meatballs. Hayley was so frustrated that she could have screamed. She was on the verge of saying the warning crudely, out loud.

Misha speaks English. He's spying on us.

But before she could get the words out, Misha's massive shoulders began to heave up and down. He threw his head back and bellowed with laughter and then turned round—terrifyingly, taking his eyes off the road altogether—and ruffled Hayley's hair, grinning at her in an unmistakable way. *Nice try, English girl.*

'Glad he thinks it's funny,' said Annie.

'He's enjoyed the whole conversation,' Hayley muttered, scrabbling for the eggs and meatballs.

Annie finally got the message. She raised her eyebrows and glanced sideways at Misha, but he was solemn again, staring straight ahead at the road. Annie watched him for a second and then leaned back in her seat.

'I hope they've brought something else for lunch,' was all she said. 'It's hours before we reach Petrovsk.'

14

'What is this danger?' Katya said. She was squashed into the kitchen, watching her grandmother kneading dough. Wondering how she could be so calm. 'Why would anyone chase a man like that?'

The grandmother glanced over her shoulder, into the other room. The cyclist was playing chess with Katya's father. Before he moved a piece, he hesitated, with his hand in mid-air, thinking.

'Imagine,' the grandmother said slowly. 'You wake in the forest—and you have lost yourself. You try to remember your family, your home, your friends—there is nothing. How do you feel?'

'Afraid.' Katya frowned, trying to imagine it better. 'Yes, very afraid. And exposed. As if there are eyes all round me, watching.' She saw the cyclist's hand move again, reaching for a pawn. 'Do you think that's all it is? That he is afraid just because he can't remember?'

Her grandmother patted the dough into a circle and reached for the rolling pin. 'You want it to be more?'

Katya looked down, to avoid her eyes. The grandmother nodded across at the window.

'Take a look out there. Tell me what you see in the street.'

Katya leaned across the table. There was a car in the road, parked opposite. The man in the driving seat was reading a newspaper.

'Him?' she said. 'You think he's watching this building?'

The grandmother shrugged. 'Maybe. Maybe not. In the old days, they would have pushed their way in and taken him. Now—who knows? But there are still people in the town who like to know what's happening.'

'So there are real enemies looking for him? He's right?'

'Who knows?' The grandmother's fingers moved neatly and swiftly, cutting little circles of dough. 'Maybe it's really him they're watching for. Maybe they just want to know what's going on.' She straightened and put a hand against her back. 'And maybe you could help me, instead of sitting there like a queen. My fingers are getting old and stiff. Fetch the filling for these.'

Even old and stiff the grandmother's fingers were twice as fast as Katya's. Katya had to concentrate as they spooned little piles of filling on to the dough and sealed the circles and she had no time to think about the cyclist and the man outside. Not until her father appeared in the kitchen doorway.

'I have decided,' he said, as though they had been discussing it. 'We must send our visitor to Petrovsk. Whoever he is, he must be English. He should find a British Consul there to look after him.'

'But—' Katya's eyes strayed towards the window.

The grandmother kicked her foot to make her stop, nodding through the door at the stranger's back. Katya's father pushed past them and looked out into the street.

'I see,' he said slowly. He sighed and looked at his mother. 'It could be nothing, of course. Just snooping.'

The grandmother shrugged. 'Do we need to take a risk?'

'Perhaps we can be careful.' Katya's father considered for a moment, pulling at his moustache. 'If he goes to the station in a car . . . and if his ticket is bought already . . . '

114

'He has money?' the grandmother said acidly.

'Very little.' Katya's father sighed again. 'But there is . . . the bicycle. If that could be sold, discreetly . . . '

He let his voice trail away. Katya saw her grandmother's lips purse.

'What else can we do?' her father said defensively. 'Can you think of another way to get the money?'

Katya manoeuvred the bike back into the lift and her grandmother squeezed into the opposite corner, as far away as possible. When they reached the ground floor, she looked across at Katya.

'You understand what to do? What we have worked out?'

'I suppose so. But I'm going to look stupid.'

'You think that will kill you?'

The grandmother slid out of the lift and marched towards the main doorway. As she stepped into the open air, she changed completely. Her face lit up and she called back over her shoulder.

'Come on, now. I'll show you.'

Katya hadn't been expecting that. Before she could say anything, the grandmother took the bike from her and straddled it. Pushing off with one foot, she began to cycle up the middle of the road.

Eighty years old and cycling in the snow! Katya put a hand to her mouth. Suppose the bike slipped over?

It didn't slip. Her grandmother pedalled to the corner, very upright, with her hair sticking out from under her fur hat. Then she put one foot down to turn and cycled back, with a broad smile on her face.

The man in the black car put his paper down and applauded, winding the window down to call out to her.

'Bravo, Babushka!'

Solemnly, Katya's grandmother bowed, first to the car and then—elaborately—to the apartment window. The cyclist was standing there, making sure he was visible.

'Now you.' The grandmother pushed the bike at Katya.

'What if I fall?' Katya sounded as pathetic as she could.

'Of course you'll fall,' her grandmother said briskly. 'Keep near the soft snow.'

Unsteadily, Katya pushed off. She slid the length of the block, wobbled, skidded and fell over.

'Faster!' her grandmother said. 'And look towards the end of the road, not down at the ground.'

Katya did it again and fell off again.

And again.

And again.

It was half an hour before she felt it was convincing to wobble up to the corner without falling off.

'Very good,' the grandmother said under her breath, when she brought the bike back. 'Next time, you can go all the way. Don't forget to wave at the window, to make sure he notices our visitor again.'

Katya beamed up at the window, giving the cyclist a flamboyant wave. Then she pushed off, heading for the corner of the street. *At least I haven't got to fall this time.* Her ribs were sore enough already and there was a long graze on her shin, under her trousers.

The moment she was out of sight, she slid off the bike and waited. Her grandmother came strolling round the corner to join her.

'The man's not following?' Katya said anxiously.

'With our guest at the window?' The grandmother shook her head. 'He dare not leave. Now give me the bicycle. I'll see you at the market.'

She took the handlebars, climbed on and pedalled off, swooping round the next corner like a bird. Katya stumped after her, glancing nervously over her shoulder.

When she reached the market, she had trouble finding her grandmother. In the end, it was the bike she spotted. It was over on the far side of the market, beyond the stalls. There was a row of old women sitting against the wall, where the ground was free of snow. Each of them had a pathetic little heap of things for sale. Old saucepans. Jars of pickled cucumber. A winter coat or two.

Slumped against the wall, with her fur hat off and a scarf tied round her head, Katya's grandmother merged into the line. She might have been any old, poor woman. Katya or her father would have stood out disastrously, but the grandmother was unremarkable. Just another *babushka*. Katya began to stroll round the stalls, keeping an eye on what was happening.

For the first half hour, only a few people drifted by. They picked over the coats and bought the odd jar of pickled cucumber. One or two of them bent to examine the bike, but when they muttered a price Katya's grandmother laughed raucously. Sometimes, all the old women laughed.

'It's no use,' Katya hissed, pretending to look at the bike herself. 'No one wants it.'

The grandmother folded her hands. 'Don't take any notice of these people. They aren't important. The right people won't come straight away. They will wait for me to lose heart and drop the price. Then they can offer me even less.'

'So how will you know they are the right people?'

'I shall know.'

It was a long wait. At last, when the light was starting to go and the stalls were beginning to close, two men came dawdling along the row, picking at the coats and fingering the saucepans. When they reached the bike, they began to look it over, talking to each other with sour faces.

'Pity about the tyres.'

'They're like that on that model. The newer one is much better.'

'The colour's pleasant.'

'Yes, but you can't match it. To get rid of those scratches, you'd have to repaint the whole thing.'

They spun the wheel, tried the brakes, knelt down to look along the front forks. All the time, Katya's grandmother sat very still, waiting. These were the right people. Even Katya could see that.

All the same, when they named a price, the grandmother spluttered scornfully and pulled the bike away from them, suggesting ten times as much. They shook their heads and jeered at her.

Then the haggling started in earnest. Halfway through, the grandmother hauled herself stiffly to her feet and began to wheel the bike away. Twice, the men shrugged and started to walk off. But in the end they agreed on a price and the men started to count out the notes.

Katya's grandmother watched them ferociously. 'Not that one—it's ripped to bits. And don't you try that dirty paper on me, either. I want good notes.'

It was almost dark before she was satisfied. She examined the notes one last time, rolled them together and zipped them carefully into the inside pocket of her coat. The moment the men disappeared, Katya ran up to her.

'You're brilliant. You're an *actress*!'

'Just old enough to have done it before.' The grandmother hauled herself painfully to her feet. 'Let's go to the station.'

As soon as they were away from the market, she pulled off her scarf and stopped by a shop window, to pat her hair tidy. Then she put on the purple hat, settling it firmly on her head.

118

The queue at the ticket window was halfway across the station hall and everyone in it was muttering. Behind the window, the ticket clerks were changing over, chatting to each other and drinking tea. Katya shuffled her feet restlessly.

'We have to do this today?'

'Tomorrow, the queue will be twice as long,' her grandmother said patiently.

'But I'm hungry.'

'When this is over, we can eat *pelmeni*. Look. Now there are only fifteen people ahead of us.'

She had dropped the headscarf into a bin before they joined the queue. Now she was herself again, the woman who had run a kindergarten and brought up Katya's father to be a professor, in the days when that was a good career. When they finally reached the ticket window, she was crisp and efficient. They came away with a ticket for the last train that night. And there was an hour to get the cyclist on it.

'He won't be ready.' Katya said, panicking. 'It's impossible.'

'Of course he will be ready.' Her grandmother steered her towards the payphone. 'You know what we arranged.' She dialled their number, but all she said when Katya's father answered was, 'Twenty minutes.'

Then she and Katya began to walk back to the apartment, heads down against the snow. The flakes drove at them out of a dark sky, swirling suddenly bright in the patches of yellow light around the street lamps. They settled for a second and then the wind stirred them up, so that they eddied like smoke round Katya's boots.

As they walked, the grandmother kept her eye on the cars going past. Most people had shut themselves in for the evening already, but every now and again a car nosed along the road, slowing down as the snow piled up on its windscreen.

They were almost at the last corner when the grandmother put up her hand to flag one down. The first two cars sailed past, but the third pulled in beside them and a young man stuck his head out.

'I can't go far.'

'To pick up a friend round the corner,' the grandmother said, 'and take him to the station. How much?'

Katya didn't catch what the young man said, but it was obviously satisfactory. Her grandmother bundled her into the back of the car and then walked round to the front passenger seat. Katya heard her giving instructions to the driver.

' . . . and you pull up at the front door, right outside. He will be ready.'

The driver looked wary. 'If I have to wait, it will be more.'

'There will be no waiting. Pull up outside the door and then go straight on, round the block.'

The driver muttered a bit, looking doubtfully at her, but the grandmother sat calm and dignified, ignoring his eyes. In the end, he did what she said. They pulled up outside the flats, right by the front door. The car was still parked opposite, but it was facing the other way, and they were blocking its view. The grandmother turned and spoke over her shoulder.

'Hold your door open, Katya. And lean out, so that Papa can see it's you.'

Katya's father and the cyclist must have been standing ready in the entrance hall. The moment Katya showed herself, the front door of the flats flew open. Katya had a quick glimpse of her father's face and then the cyclist came hurtling across the pavement and into the car. He pulled the door shut behind him and crouched low on the seat beside her. She saw that he was wearing her father's old trousers and his thick overcoat.

'Quickly to the station, please,' Katya's grandmother said. 'Our friend has to catch a train.'

The driver looked sideways at her, suspiciously, and she gave him a charming, unruffled smile as he pulled away from the kerb. They had disappeared round the corner before the watcher had time to start his engine.

As they drove, Katya tried to see the cyclist's face, but it was too dark now, and the patches of light flitted by too fast. It was only when they reached the station and got out of the car that she saw how pale and tense he was. He was biting his bottom lip.

Katya pulled at his sleeve as the grandmother hustled them into the station. 'You know how to do?' she said in English.

He smiled suddenly, surprising her. 'Your father wrote it down,' he said, miming to make sure she understood. Copying not just her father's quick scribbling, but his little frown and the way he chewed his moustache as he wrote on and on. And on.

'Much words!' Katya said.

'Very much!' the cyclist smiled again.

They were at the platform now. The train was crowded and people were pushing each other, jostling for the best spaces. Katya's grandmother took out the ticket and pressed it into the cyclist's hand, curling his fingers round it. She held up four fingers, to show him it was a fourth class ticket, and pointed at the carriage with a flood of Russian that he obviously didn't understand.

'She says sorry.' Katya struggled with the English. 'Is only four—fourth. We have no more money—'

The cyclist interrupted her before she could work out how to say it.

'It's fine. Don't worry. You're very good.' And then, to the grandmother, pointing first at her and then at his own heart. 'You have a very good heart. *Khorosho*. Thank you. *Spassiba.'*

His eyes were grey and very clear. Full of things to say, but without words. Gently the grandmother patted him on the arm. Then she pushed him on to the platform, peering after him to be sure that he got into the right carriage.

She didn't move from where she was standing until the train pulled away. As it disappeared out of the station, she turned to Katya.

'Now he is gone for ever. We don't tell anyone where he went. We never speak about him at all. Do you understand?'

Katya met her grandmother's eyes and somewhere between the two of them the cyclist dissolved, growing thin and insubstantial, until he blew away, like the snow in the wind.

He ignores everyone else in the carriage. It is the only way to stay sane. If he looks at them, he will watch their eyes, noticing those that glance away, shifting from one thing to another. And those steady, cold eyes that never blink.

He pulls the curtain back and looks out of the window instead. The train slides out of the station in the gathering darkness, leaving the town behind. The trees close round on both sides, glimmering ghostly white as the lights flicker over the snow on their branches. Behind that shell of light, the forest stretches, black and impenetrable.

Suddenly, in his mind, he sees himself climbing out of a lorry, on the edge of a shabby town. It's the end of the road, with nothing beyond but forest. Like the forest around him now, but warmer and without snow.

He sees himself wait, watching the lorry disappear. When it has gone, he walks deliberately off the road and into the forest. Towards the setting sun.

The whole thing is so clear and real that he knows it has happened to him, some time in the past. But he can't get into the mind of that past self, to know why he behaved like that. Where is he aiming? Does he think he can cross the forest?

Leaning his face against the glass of the window, he stares out into the night.

15

*T*o Petrovsk *it is not so bad*, Yuri had said. But before they were halfway there, the road surface began to deteriorate. Bumping around in the back seat of the Niva, Hayley wondered how much worse it could possibly get.

It got a lot worse.

Once they were past Petrovsk, the tarmac was patchy. Sometimes it ballooned into a great swathe, wide enough for all three cars to drive abreast. Sometimes it was so narrow that they had to go at walking pace to keep out of the boggy mud on either side.

And sometimes it just stopped.

The first time that happened, Hayley thought they were at the end of the road. There was nothing visible ahead except a short slope with a muddy wallow at the bottom.

'What happens now?' she said. 'Do we have to walk from here?'

'Of course not!' Annie was fierce. She tore her map open and stabbed at the lines. 'There's a road all the way down to the river. It says so. We've just got to get through the mud and we'll find it again.'

She pushed the map at Misha, pointing. He shook his head doubtfully, flicking his fingers to show what he thought of the map. But before Annie could lose her temper, someone jumped out of the car in front and came squelching back towards them.

Misha wound down his window and there was a heated conversation. Finally, he pulled a face and wound the window up again. Then he started the engine and pointed ahead, to show which way they were going.

One by one, the cars lumbered down the slope. As they hit the bottom, mud splattered roof-high, smacking against the windows and sliding down in long streaks that obscured the view. The Niva laboured through the slough and up the slope on the other side. As they topped the rise, the tarmac started again, winding away into the distance.

'See?' Annie said. 'Easy! This car's *made* for roads that keep vanishing. I love it!' She laughed triumphantly, as if they were out on a picnic.

Crazy, Hayley thought. But then the whole expedition was crazy. They were driving along an unknown road that broke up underneath them, in a car that juddered at every pothole, with petrol cans rattling around in the back. The light was already going and it had started to snow. Big flakes danced ahead of them and streamed away behind, touched with red from their tail lights.

They were heading into nowhere, fast. If the car broke down, Annie would be completely stuck and nothing short of a helicopter would get her out.

So what did she do?

Laugh.

Misha caught the mood and he laughed too, grinning sideways at Annie. In the darkness of the back seat, Hayley shuddered, feeling completely isolated.

'Is it much further?' she said, in a disapproving voice.

Annie glanced back at her. 'What's the matter? Getting saddle sore?'

Hayley didn't pretend to think that was funny. 'I'd just like to get there,' she said stiffly.

'It's hard to tell how far we've been.' Annie shrugged. 'I think we still have two villages to go through. But it was only about a hundred miles from Petrovsk to the river in the first place. It can't take *much* longer.'

125

It took another two hours. They drove through the tiny villages—clusters of half a dozen houses in the middle of the forest—and somewhere beyond the second one they came to a stop, in the dark. Misha turned off the engine and got out to talk to the others. They could see the snow settling on his shoulders as he walked away from them.

Annie peered through the windscreen. 'I can't see a thing out there, but I think we're at the river. Go and see what's up, Hayley.'

Hayley pushed the door open. Snowflakes caught in her eyelashes and cold air hit her in the face, taking her breath away.

'Don't hang about!' Annie said fretfully. 'If I get cold it takes me ages to warm up again.'

'Put your coat on top of your fleece.' Hayley passed it over. 'And there's another blanket here as well.'

She got out and tucked it round Annie's knees. Then she pulled on her own coat and went to see what was going on.

The men were together in a group, in front of the Range Rover. As she approached them she realized that they were standing on a small jetty, looking along the black river. Yuri was on the edge of the group and she inched up to him.

'Are we waiting for a boat?'

He nodded. 'My father is angry. They promised to be here when we arrived. He is trying to telephone the captain, but it is not possible to get an answer.'

'Will the snow stop them?'

Yuri shook his head. 'The boat will come. Do not worry.' He sounded completely tranquil. 'When my father says that something should happen, it is certain.'

The way he said *my father* was beginning to jar on Hayley. She walked past him, to the end of the jetty, and looked down at the water. There was no light for it to reflect. If it hadn't been for the small sounds it made round the jetty, she might have been looking into an utter void.

After a second Yuri followed her, his feet ringing hollow on the wooden boards. 'Annie Glasgow—' he said, tentatively.

Hayley didn't look round. 'What about her?'

'When we come off the boat, there will be no road. Only a track. Maybe.'

'So?' Hayley knew exactly what he meant, but she made him spell it out.

'Maybe it will not be possible to drive. If we have to walk, she cannot come. The wheelchair is no good in the forest. Perhaps you two should stay in the car and go back to Tomsk?'

Hayley heard her father's voice in her mind. *Annie's a very determined person. But she may just have to give up.* He hadn't realized what a lot it would take to make that happen.

'Annie won't go back,' she said, still looking down at the water. 'She'll get there somehow.'

'Maybe if we knew . . . exactly how far we have to go from the river?' Yuri said delicately.

So that was what he was after. Hayley shook her head and wished she didn't like him. 'No good asking me. If you want to find that out, you'll have to discuss it with Annie.'

She tried to make herself meet his eyes and challenge him. *Why do you always play your father's games?* But she wasn't brave enough. After a moment or two, Yuri walked back down the jetty, to join the group round Leonid.

After they had waited for half an hour, the boat came chugging down the river. They saw its single light, like a star, even before they heard the noise. By the time it reached them, they were all lined up on the jetty. Annie was still in the Niva, which had been driven forward to the very edge, and Hayley realized why as soon as she saw the boat.

It was a little, dilapidated ferry, with room for three vehicles at most. Hayley watched the men as they sized it up. The boat was sitting high in the water, so that the cars couldn't drive straight on. There would have to be some kind of ramp.

Leonid was not helping them. He stood slightly apart, with his hands in his pockets and his eyebrows raised. The boat's crew produced a rough arrangement of planks lashed together and looked up at him for approval, but he shook his head and pointed at one of the lashings. They had to retie it three times before he let them put it into place and waved to Misha to drive on to the ferry.

Annie put her head out of the window as they passed, and grinned at Hayley. 'He's not going to risk his precious Range Rover by sending it first, is he? Come and pull me out if we land up in the river.'

There was no problem. The Niva bumped over the planks and on to the ferry and the men rushed forward to adjust the ramp as the boat settled. The other Niva was loaded and, finally, Leonid permitted them to drive his Range Rover aboard. He followed on foot, with Hayley and Yuri.

'Now we can sleep,' Yuri said cheerfully. 'We have five hours on the boat, or maybe six.'

Hayley couldn't believe it was going to be so long. She went over to see Annie. 'Do you want to come out of the car? It's going to be ages before we land again.'

'Looks a darn sight more comfortable in here than it does in that cabin. It's all narrow wooden benches in there, isn't it? Leave me here and I'll have a nap.' Annie was cosy now, wrapped in a cocoon of coats and blankets,

128

and her face was warm and pink. 'Wouldn't mind some tea, though, if there's any going. Even Russian tea.'

There was a samovar in the main cabin and the men were already clustered round it. Hayley wriggled through and fetched Annie a glass of tea. She waited until Annie had finished it and settled to sleep and then she walked down to the front of the boat. Pushing her hands into her pockets, she peered through the snow, into the darkness ahead.

It was the middle of the night, and she was just thinking of finding somewhere to doze, when she saw a line of lights ahead of them, up in the air. What on earth—?

The lights jerked to the right, all together, and stopped again. Suddenly she realized what she was looking at. There was a low railway bridge across the river—barely high enough to let their boat pass—and a train had paused on top of it. Lights shone out from its windows, strung over the river like a line of stars.

The train began to move again, slowly crossing the bridge, and Hayley watched it idly, staring at the windows as they slid past. Some of the curtains were pulled shut, but at some windows there were faces pressed to the glass. Once, a couple of little boys waved wildly at the lights of the boat, bouncing up and down and slapping at each other. Once, a woman with long dark hair flourished a bottle of vodka, tilting her head back to drink.

And then, as the train started to gather speed, there was another face. A pale, familiar face, staring out at the falling snow—

Hayley caught her breath, flinging herself forward to the front rail of the boat, watching the face slide across the bridge and away into the trees on the bank. For a moment after it disappeared, she was struggling for air. Holding on to the rail so hard that it almost froze her fingers.

'What is the matter?' said a voice from behind her. 'What were you watching?'

She turned and found Yuri closer than she expected. Near enough to touch. 'It's nothing,' she said. 'A mistake.'

'Another mistake?' He raised an eyebrow. 'Like the mistake on the building site? What do you see, Hayley, that makes you breathe so fast?'

In the dark, he didn't seem so cool and intimidating. Hayley noticed how gentle his voice was and she wondered what it would be like to tell him the truth. *I see John. Suddenly, for no reason, I think I see him. He's not there, but every time there's a moment when I'm taken in. When he looks so real that I can't believe—*'

She turned her head away. 'It's nothing. Really. I've just been a bit unsettled. Ever since John died.'

Yuri was silent for a moment. Then he said, 'I don't think that—if I were dead—my sister would travel so far to see the place. It's good to have a brother that you love.'

His hand came out towards Hayley, as if he might be going to touch her, but he didn't. After a while, he went away and left her standing alone by the rail.

16

Ivan wasn't really expecting anyone off the overnight train from Krasny Yar. Not a passenger. There might be half a dozen fat old *babushkas*, with their hair tied up into headscarves and their luggage bundled into shopping bags, but they were no use to him. They would waddle off down the road or jump on to an early bus, chatting away to each other and cackling with laughter. But as for *customers*—pah! The Krasny Yar train was a dead loss.

He tilted his hat forward over his eyes and put his feet up on the dashboard, next to the smart new notice he had had made.

Ivan Danilovich Suva—Taxis

That was an exaggeration at the moment. So far, he had only one taxi, and that was old and battered. But he had plans. You had to think big in this world—and he knew how to do it. Plaster the town with posters that said *Ivan Suva—Taxis* and that was the first name that would spring into people's heads. Soon he would have two taxis. A fleet. Branches in other towns. All he had to do was arrange for the posters.

He wasn't quite there yet, but he'd made a start. His cousin had printed him off a thousand computer labels and he kept them ready in his pocket. Every now and then, he slapped one on to a wall, a door, a notice board. *Ivan D. Suva—Taxis.* Every time he walked past one of his stickers, he felt the future opening out in front of him.

131

He leaned back and closed his eyes, dreaming of his gleaming fleet of cars. Dozens of smart, professional drivers signing on every morning, ready to receive orders.

Right, men, it's another great day for I.D.Suva—Taxis. *Remember, this is no ordinary taxi operation. You are the spearhead of a transport revolution. We are aiming at Complete Customer Satisfaction.* Dramatic pause. Hundreds of eyes fixed on his face. *What are we aiming at?*

And the answer, from a thousand throats, as the drivers roared their loyalty. *Complete Customer Satisfaction!*

Someone tapped on the window suddenly, right next to his ear. He jumped, so hard that his heart thudded in his chest. Opening his eyes, he saw a pale face pressed to the window, so close to his own that he could see himself, tiny and perfect, in the stranger's eyes. Even the badge on his jacket was clear in the reflection. *I. Danilovich Suva—Taxis.*

The man was flapping a piece of paper at him. Ivan wound down his window and greeted him, in his firm, professional voice. Welcoming and efficient.

'Do you want to take this taxi?'

He could have saved his breath. The stranger simply flapped the piece of paper harder, until Ivan took it and read the message.

Please will you take me to the British Consul, it said in Russian.

British Consul! The words danced on the paper, letting off fireworks and doing crazy dances in front of Ivan's eyes. This was it! This was the moment he'd waited for and planned for. The reason he had spent hours huddled over his radio, tuned to English language programmes. Now the opportunity had come—and he was prepared.

Tourist Trade!

'Hi,' he said, in his best American accent. 'Great to meet you, guy! You English are wonderful people!'

The tourist frowned at him, looking tense and anxious. Ivan's confidence wavered slightly.

'You speak English?'

The tourist nodded. Rather uncertainly.

'Then jump into my cab, mate!' Ivan reached across and opened the passenger door. 'Best cab in town!'

'Do you know where to find the British Consul?' The tourist was still hesitating.

'I find out. Faster than all these others.' Ivan swept a hand scornfully towards all the other cars. 'You can trust I.D.S. Taxis. We are better than—better than cricket!'

'I hate cricket,' the tourist said absently.

And then he stopped and said it again, as though the words had somehow startled him.

'I. Hate. Cricket.'

Ivan was struggling. What was this? Typical English humour? 'I hate the circus!' he said, experimentally.

The tourist just looked bewildered. 'The circus?'

'It is the same. You are English and you hate cricket. I am Russian and I hate the circus. This is a joke. Yes?'

'No,' the tourist said. 'I'm sorry—'

For a second, Ivan thought he was going to back away and find another taxi. The other drivers were looking at them already, wondering why Ivan was taking so long to agree with him. The tourist would go to one of their cars and they would get the fare, even though they had not struggled to learn English for tourists. Ivan was incensed by the unfairness of it.

'Oh, very good! So now you won't take my taxi! Just because I didn't understand this *I hate cricket*.'

'No, no, it's not that,' the tourist said hastily. 'Forgive me. I was—' He held back for an instant and then began to speak quickly, leaning in through the car window. 'I was in the forest. I had a fever. Before that, everything's a blank—my whole life. But when you talked about cricket, I suddenly remembered the *boredom*—'

'You have lost your mind?' Ivan said politely.

'I thought it had all gone, for ever. But if I can remember about cricket—' The tourist touched his forehead. 'Maybe it's all in there. Waiting.'

Unexpectedly he laughed and slid into the seat next to Ivan. Catching his mood, Ivan started the engine.

'Very good! I will find the British Consul! Yes? We shall discover who you are. Come!'

They raced away from the station and round three corners, into the main boulevard. Ivan leaned sideways, chatting as he drove.

'First, we shall go to the police.'

The tourist stiffened suddenly.

'Do not be afraid,' Ivan said, to encourage him. 'We will just ask them where is a British Consul. Then we shall go to the Consul. Do not be afraid! I will not desert you!'

He patted the tourist's hand, visualizing what would happen next. The British Consul at the telephone, calling Moscow. Moscow calling international. Computers buzzing. Faxes. E-mails. Internet searches. And at last— brought at high speed, by modern telecommunications— The Name! And the tourist throwing his arms wide.

Ivan! My friend! Without you, I would be nothing. I would not even know that I hate cricket. I owe everything to you!

And then—oh yes!—

Please come to visit me in England. You are like my brother.

He drove faster, squealing round corners, and looking away from the road to grin encouragingly. The tourist was sitting on the edge of his seat. Ivan understood. He was willing the taxi forward. He wanted more speed!

When they reached the police station, Ivan didn't even turn off the engine. 'Wait here. I shall run.'

He burst into the building so fast that the man behind the desk looked up in amazement from his newspaper.

'Please tell me!' Ivan said urgently. 'Where is the British Consul?'

He should have known that nothing in Russia happened fast enough to leave the engine running. Half an hour later, the car was still parked and he was still in the police station, with the tourist beside him.

The policeman behind the counter was insisting that the tourist had to fill out a report form.

'That's what the regulations say. For every enquiry, I must make a report. I must see this man's papers.'

Ivan could feel the tourist listening nervously. He translated what the policeman had said. 'You must fill in this form and he is asking for your papers.'

'I haven't got any,' the tourist said. 'If I had papers, I would know who I am.'

That was true. Ivan looked at the policeman, out of the corner of his eye. How much had he understood? Nothing, by the look of it. He was glowering impatiently and tapping his fingers. Ivan spoke a bit faster, trying to look as though he was explaining.

'It won't be good to tell him that you have lost your mind. He will keep you here, I think. You must try to fill in his form.'

'How can I fill in a form?' the tourist said. 'I don't know anything.'

Ivan changed to Russian and spoke to the policeman. 'This man cannot give you his papers, because he has lost them. That is why he wants to see the Consul.'

The policeman looked at the tourist and then back at Ivan. 'Where did he lose his papers?'

'In the forest. He was walking in the forest.' Ivan

remembered a programme he had heard on the radio. 'This is a thing the English do very often in England. They go walking.'

'Still he must fill in the form,' the policeman said stubbornly. 'What is his name?' When Ivan hesitated, he turned to the tourist and barked out a single word. In English. 'Name?'

'I don't know,' the tourist said.

For a split second, Ivan felt his whole dream collapsing. It was all ruined. He would never be the wonderful man who solved the problem. He would never be invited to England and shown the West. They would take away the tourist and send him to hospital until his mind was right. It was all over—

The policeman picked up a pen. 'How do you write that?' he said to Ivan, in Russian.

Hardly believing that he was doing it, Ivan wrote down what the tourist had said, on the margin of the policeman's newspaper. *I. Dontknow.*

'And the first name?' the policeman said.

Ivan didn't risk another question. He said the first English name he could think of that began with the right letter. 'Ian. His name is Ian.'

He wrote that on the newspaper too, and the policeman copied the name into the first space on the form. *Ian Dontknow.* Then he looked up. 'Address? Date of birth?'

Ivan pretended to ask. Made them up. Felt himself beginning to panic.

'Address in Russia?'

Not wise to make that one up. Ivan gave his own address, because it was the only one he could think of.

The policeman nodded and began to scribble busily, writing a report of the incident. When he had finished, he passed it across to Ivan. 'Please read this to him. Then he must sign it. There. At the bottom.'

Ivan took the form and the pen and turned to the tourist. 'This says that you have lost your passport and papers in the forest and you are going to the British Consul to get new ones. Now you must sign at the bottom.'

'But—' the tourist started.

'It's all right. You just have to write "I don't know". That is enough.'

The tourist wrote it, solemnly, in the box at the bottom, and Ivan handed the paper back.

'That is good.' The policeman slid it into a file. 'Wait here.'

He disappeared into a back room, and there was another half hour's wait. Ivan had a hundred questions to ask about England and how things were there, but he was afraid the tourist would give himself away. They sat in silence until the policeman reappeared.

Ivan bounded up, eagerly. 'Yes? You have the British Consul's address?'

The policeman shuffled his papers together. 'Tomorrow. Come back tomorrow and I will give you the address of the British Consul in Novosibirsk.'

'Novosibirsk?' Ivan was appalled. 'There's no one here?'

'I am instructed to send all British persons to Novosibirsk. Come back tomorrow and I will give you the address. Goodbye.' He closed the file and turned away.

The tourist looked questioningly at Ivan. 'So what is happening?'

'Tomorrow we shall have the address. For today—' Suddenly, Ivan realized that there was no choice about today. If the police decided to check up, the tourist had to be at the address on the form. 'Today you will come home with me.'

Svetlana was furious.

She stood in the kitchen, with a twin on each hip, and hissed at Ivan under her breath.

'So where do we put him? Where will he sleep? You're going to give him our bed? And what makes you think we have food for a guest? Why do you always do things before you think?'

Her mouth trembled, ready to collapse into sobs. She did a lot of sobbing at the moment. Ivan patted her hand.

'This is good luck. You will see. He is English, and he will be grateful to us.'

'Grateful!' Svetlana snorted. She thrust the twins at him and turned away to rummage in the vegetable basket.

Ivan went back into the other room and sat down on the couch. Olga had climbed up on to the tourist's knee and she was chatting away to him, with her head bobbing. The frilly net bow on top of her hair was tickling his chin as she waggled her head, but he wasn't complaining. He was just listening to her babble, with a rather dazed look on his face.

'My darling,' Ivan said, 'our guest is English. He doesn't understand Russian words.'

Olga looked round. When she saw Ivan with the twins, she wriggled off the tourist's lap and ran across the room to her father. Ivan had to juggle both the babies into one arm so that she could sit on his knees as well.

'Tell me some English words!' she ordered.

Ivan nodded. 'Very well. To begin with, you must say *Hello*.'

Olga repeated the word carefully, frowning with concentration and making a fat Russian *l* at the back of her throat. 'Helllllo.'

'Very good,' Ivan said.

She beamed and jumped off his lap. Running across to the tourist, she looked up solemnly at him. 'Helllllo.'

138

He smiled at her. 'Hello.'

She was ecstatic. Spreading her arms, she began to dance round the room, chanting the word. 'Helllllo, helllllo, helllllo!'

Svetlana stuck her head round the kitchen door, looking sour. Before she could say a word, Ivan jumped in.

'Olga is learning English. You see how good it is for the children to have visitors?'

Olga did another twirl. 'I'm learning English!'

'Hello,' the tourist said in English, looking hopefully at Svetlana.

She disappeared, banging the door. Olga ran back to Ivan, still chanting, and tried to scramble on to his lap, and the twins started to wriggle fretfully.

'Please,' the tourist said tentatively. 'Can I—?'

With relief, Ivan went and dumped both the twins on to his lap. Then he scooped Olga into his arms and sat down again.

'Now then, my little chicken, my dove. Do you want to see where England is? Shall we look in the map book?'

It was a good idea. Olga adored the map book. She stopped chanting, gave a little squeal and ran across to the bookcase. With both hands, she pulled at the atlas.

Ivan took it out for her and put it on the floor. Opening it, Olga flipped through the pages and stabbed joyfully with her finger.

'Here!'

She always picked on the map of the United States, because she loved the patchwork of colours. Ivan laughed and shook his head.

'Let me show you.'

He knelt down beside her—and suddenly he had a Grand Inspiration. It was no use asking the tourist

139

questions, because he couldn't remember the answers. But maybe something else could be surprised out of him.

He patted Olga's hand. 'I'll teach you the names of the towns. Yes? You can say them after me.' He looked at the kitchen door. 'But *softly*, because of Mama.'

Olga nodded seriously and Ivan began to say the names, almost whispering, pointing to each one on the map as he said it.

'London, Bristol, Birmingham.'

Olga repeated them, even more softly, trying to match the sound of what he'd said. 'Lyonndonn, Breestle, Bermeengum.'

All the time, secretly, Ivan was watching the tourist. But there was no sign that he was even listening. He was joggling the twins on his lap, pulling funny faces to keep them quiet.

'York, Newcastle, Liverpool.'

'Yok, Newkahstl, Lyeevairpull.'

No hint of recognition from the tourist.

'Glasgow—'

Ivan's finger was moving on to Edinburgh when the tourist looked up, suddenly.

'Glasgow,' he said. And again, lingering on the word. *'Glasgow.'*

Ivan rose up on his knees. Eagerly. 'This is where you live?'

The tourist didn't answer. Instead, he said, 'Annie Glasgow.' And stopped in surprise, looking at the air in front of him as though the words were hanging there.

'This is a name?' Ivan said eagerly. 'Your name, perhaps?'

'Not mine,' the tourist said slowly. Bewildered. 'But—'

He faltered and then said the words again in a voice that made Ivan catch his breath. A voice that stopped

140

Svetlana dead, as she opened the kitchen door, ready to yell again.

'Annie Glasgow.'

He feels a wave that almost engulfs him. A sense of—of himself, certainly, but of someone else too. A sharpness, like lemons, like cold air coming in off the sea. Something that needs all his own sharpness to meet it. And, at the same time, he's holding his breath because it's so . . . fragile. Like an eggshell, like a spider's web. Hold it too roughly, and it would be broken for ever.

The feeling is so strong that he can't speak. The little taxi driver is gazing at him, trying to understand. Turning away from him, he meets the eyes of the wife who was so angry before.

She is standing in the kitchen doorway, staring at him with a kind of gentleness. As though she can see what it is he sees. As though she has heard it in his voice.

That sharp, fragile, precarious sweetness. Worth anything you could do to protect it, to keep it . . .

17

The ferry moved even more slowly than the Niva, nosing its way up a sprawling, shallow river with evil spluttering noises coming from its engine.

Hayley thought they would stay aboard at least until it was light. She settled herself in the deck cabin and dozed with her boots off, as close to the stove as she could get.

But the sky was still a dark grey when Yuri shook her shoulder.

'Hayley! We've stopped.'

Annie and Leonid Orlov were sitting side by side in the front of the Niva with the light on. They were bending over Annie's map and Leonid was obviously annoyed.

He beckoned impatiently and Yuri scrambled over to join him. Hayley followed, pushing her feet into her boots. By the time she caught up, Yuri was at the car window, translating.

'Where do we go now?'

Annie indicated a direction on the map. 'This way. Three kilometres and then—'

Leonid looked up quickly, catching the sense of what she was saying.

'—and then I'll tell you the next bit,' Annie finished.

For a moment Hayley thought there was going to be an argument. But instead, Leonid sent two of his men on to the river bank with torches, to reconnoitre. They came back in a few moments, talking quickly and pointing.

'They have found a track,' Yuri said. 'Maybe it goes in the right direction. We shall try.'

142

One by one, the cars lumbered down the planks on to the decaying jetty. It had almost stopped snowing, but there was a thick layer of snow on the jetty and along the river bank. Under the trees, the ground was clearer and Hayley could see the track leading into the forest.

As they set off along it, Annie looked back at the boat. 'Poor devils,' she said. 'They're just going to sit there, I think. Waiting for us to get back.'

'More comfortable than driving down here,' Hayley muttered.

The track was nothing like a real road. It was made of rough earth, pitted with potholes. The Niva swerved and lurched as Misha tried to avoid them, but it was hard to spot them in the dark. And often there was no choice anyway. Hayley was exhausted from bracing herself against the jolts.

At least she could do that. Annie couldn't. Whenever the Niva hit a bump, she bounced right out of her seat and back again. Hayley could almost feel the bruises. But Annie never complained. Just occasionally, when a particularly vicious bump caught her by surprise, she winced and put a hand to her mouth.

The bouncing had another effect as well. Annie suddenly touched Misha's arm and said, 'I need to get out.'

He didn't pretend not to understand. Just pulled up and let Hayley scramble out of the back. She slid down into the darkness, wondering what was underneath the thin coat of snow on the ground. Solid earth or squelchy mud? Whichever it was, she had to open the passenger door and wait for Annie's crisp instructions.

'Right. Swing my legs round. Wait while I put my arms round your neck. Now hold on to my waist . . . '

As if I didn't know, Hayley thought furiously. *I've done it often enough, haven't I?* But she'd learnt one thing on the journey. Annie liked to be in charge. So she bit her tongue and obeyed orders, while Misha examined the ground under the trees, prodding the snow with his foot to find somewhere firm.

He carried Annie across there, and then left Hayley to support her. Both the others cars had stopped immediately, to wait for them, and Hayley had to shield Annie with her body while she manoeuvred her legs apart and held her skirt out of the way.

'And if you put your feet there, you'll get them peed on,' Annie said tartly.

Hayley had a brief, delicious dream of loosening her hands a little. *Whoops! Oh, I'm sorry, Annie!* Maybe if she fell into the snow, she would realize—

But then again, maybe she wouldn't. Hayley had a dismal feeling that Annie was tougher than that. So she held on tight and waited for the next order.

'OK.'

That meant, *I've finished.* Very brisk. Drop the skirt and wave to Misha, so that he could carry her back into the car. And then they were off once more, bumping their way into the forest. In spite of the jolting, Hayley fell asleep again, slumping against the uncomfortable metal side of the Niva.

She woke when they stopped and Annie said, 'Hayley? Time to get out.'

OK. Give me a chance. I'm not your slave, said a moaning voice in Hayley's head. Then she woke up properly and realized that Annie meant something different this time.

It was early morning and the vehicles had stopped on the edge of a clearing. Once there had obviously been a small village there. A dozen wooden cottages stood round the edge of the clearing and flakes of old paint showed how bright the clearing must have been, when they were all inhabited and cared for.

144

Now scrubby trees and tangled undergrowth silted up the garden patches and sprouted through collapsing roofs. Most of the cottages were ruined and decaying and only two or three showed any signs of life. Their shutters were closed—nailed down—but their stovepipe chimneys were smoking vigorously. Beside one was a goat, chewing at a sickly bush. Beyond it was a patch of ground that seemed to be cultivated, although the plants were shrivelled and crisp with frost.

The men were climbing out of the cars in front, and one of them pointed ahead, at the nearest cottage. Hayley looked and saw the door open.

A dumpy middle-aged woman came out, pulling on a thick overcoat. Her hair was tangled and unbrushed and she was wearing old felt boots. She stumped towards them through the snow, peering at the cars and watching the men warily.

Annie saw her too. 'I must get out!' she said. 'I must be there when they talk to her.'

Hayley groaned. 'You won't understand.'

'I must be there!'

With a sigh, Hayley tapped Misha on the shoulder, pointing behind her, at the wheelchair. The dumpy woman had stopped at a distance. She showed no sign of coming any closer to the cars.

Misha looked at Annie and pulled a face, waggling his hand to show that the ground was rough.

'Please!' Hayley said. 'I can take the chair up there if you carry her.'

She was signalling frantically, so that Misha had to understand, even if he was still pretending not to speak English. Reluctantly he climbed out of the car and opened the back, to get the wheelchair out.

Even empty, it was hard to haul along the track. Hayley pulled it after her and parked it on the flattest piece of

145

ground she could find. Then she ran back to fetch some blankets while Misha carried Annie over.

Yuri followed her to the car. 'Hayley—it would be better if you two stayed here. You will not be able to understand.'

'Then you can translate!' Hayley said. Now that she had struggled with the chair, she felt as fierce as Annie. 'You don't think we've come all this way to miss what happens, do you?' She pushed a blanket into his arms. 'Help me with these.'

She wondered whether Leonid would interfere, but he was concentrating on the woman ahead of them. When it was obvious that she wasn't going to come any nearer, he took a step forward and called to her, in a loud, commanding voice.

Instead of answering, she shrank back, glancing over her shoulder. He called again and suddenly the woman gave a high-pitched shriek and cried out, like a child. Not words at all. Just a throaty, frightened noise, something between a shout and a moan.

For a moment they were all still, like figures in a tableau: the baggy, grey-haired woman with the child's voice; the three muddy vehicles; the crowd of men in heavy overcoats; and Annie in the chair, with Hayley and Yuri beside her. It was still snowing slightly and the flakes drifted down, lodging in Annie's bright brown hair, settling on Yuri's shoulders, clinging to Hayley's eyelashes.

Slowly, the door of the furthest cottage opened. A hunched old woman shuffled out, leaning on a stick. Immediately, Hayley realized that the first woman was relatively young, even though she had wrinkles and grey hair. She was forty, maybe, or fifty. This second woman belonged to a different generation altogether. She was much smaller—shrivelled and bent—and she moved very slowly, every step a separate effort. Her hands were knotted with the effort of supporting her weight on the stick.

But her eyes were alert. All the way across the clearing, she watched the visitors, glancing from one to another and back at the cars. Hayley saw her take in the wheelchair and the way the group divided into two parts, one grouped round Leonid Orlov and one round Annie.

When she reached the first woman, the older one stopped and said something inaudible to her, stroking her arm and patting her heavy, rounded shoulder. The child-woman unfroze and began to babble, pointing at the strangers and waggling her head about.

'What's she saying?' Annie hissed.

Yuri frowned and shook his head. 'It's nothing, I think. Nonsense. I can't understand.'

It was snowing harder now. The little old woman was wearing a thick, heavy coat, but she shivered as she walked painfully towards them. When she was close enough to be heard, she began to speak in a precise, formal voice. Annie looked at Yuri. He listened for a moment and then started to interpret.

'She says welcome. She is called Irina Petrovna Goncharova and the—the other one—is called Frosya. They are inviting us into the cottage.'

'Thank goodness for that,' Annie muttered. 'Let's get going before we're all frozen solid.'

Hayley took hold of the chair handles, but before she could attempt to push it, Leonid Orlov signalled to the men round him. Four of them came across and picked up the chair. Carrying it between them, they headed for the door of the nearest cottage.

Hayley stumbled along behind. As she reached the doorway, the child-woman—Frosya—began to pull at Annie's coat. Annie jerked out of her hands.

147

'Please—' Yuri said quickly. 'We should take off our coats and our boots. It is polite.'

Not only polite, but necessary, Hayley realized as she stepped inside. The wooden walls were thick, the shutters were permanently closed and the wood stove in the corner was going flat out. It was stiflingly hot in the cottage.

It was also cramped. There was only one room and most of the space was taken up by two beds. There was a large one beside the stove—high and old-fashioned, with a heavy wooden frame—and a smaller one by the window. Once the wheelchair was brought in and the coats were heaped up by the door, there was only just room for them all to squeeze in.

Hayley found herself sitting on the big bed, not looking too closely at the heap of dirty rags that covered it. The whole place smelt strongly of wood smoke and, under the wood smoke, of other, more basic things.

Annie began to speak while Leonid Orlov and his men were still crowding in.

'Yuri, please will you tell these people that we are looking for a mobile phone. We know it's here somewhere, because there is a signal coming from this place.'

Yuri looked over his shoulder first, at his father, but Leonid waved him on and he began to speak. Hayley caught the word *telefon* and saw Irina Petrovna raise her eyebrows, mockingly.

When he translated her reply, Yuri was grinning. 'She asks how there can be a telephone here. You can see that there are no wires, she says.'

'Well, you could have explained properly.' Annie looked impatient. 'Hayley, pass my coat across.'

Hayley dug it out of the heap and Annie found her mobile in the pocket and waved it dramatically.

'Telephone. OK? Understand?'

Irina Petrovna shrugged and shook her head. It was obvious that she had never seen anything like that before.

'Damn,' Annie muttered. 'I was so sure . . .'

Hayley nudged her. 'Don't take any notice of that,' she whispered. 'Look at the other one.'

Frosya had turned her back on the phone and her face was set stubbornly.

'She knows something!' Annie said quickly. 'Ask her, Yuri!'

She sounded unmistakably sharp and angry. Even before Yuri began to speak, Frosya was shaking her head, hiding her face with her fists. Irina Petrovna frowned and said something to Annie.

'She is telling you that they have done nothing wrong,' Yuri muttered. 'And it is not good to be angry with Frosya.'

'For heaven's sake!' Annie lowered her voice, but she couldn't keep the irritation out of it. 'I don't want to upset anyone, but I *have* to know if they've got John's telephone.' She waved hers in the air and said the word again, trying to make it sound Russian. '*Telefon.*'

Suddenly, the bed Hayley was sitting on began to creak and shake. There was a wheezing sound behind her. She looked round and saw a tiny, shrivelled old man heaving himself up out of the heap of rags.

'*Telefon,*' he said, pointing at Annie. '*Telefon!*' He laughed rustily and then launched into a long sentence, pointing at Frosya and Annie and at the ceiling.

Frosya responded pettishly, hiding her face in her hands, and Irina Petrovna put an arm round her shoulders and began to whisper in her ear.

'What's going on?' Annie fretted. 'Yuri—?'

But there was no need for a translation. Irina Petrovna whispered again and Frosya stood up sulkily and clambered on to the bed where the two of them were sitting. They all froze, watching her.

Slowly, she slid her hand up the side of the shutter. Hayley's heart jolted as she saw what the hand was heading for. There was an ancient, filthy gun balanced on the top edge, draped in cobwebs.

But Frosya didn't disturb it. Her hand stopped just below the gun and she slid her fingers deftly round the edge of the wood, fumbling in the space behind. When she pulled her hand out again, she was holding something small. Something black and silver.

'That's it!' Annie said, breathless and excited. 'Quick, Hayley!'

Hayley stood up, but Leonid Orlov was quicker. His hand shot out and he wrenched the phone away from Frosya. She started to wail and Irina Petrovna asked a sharp, angry question.

'She asks us what right we have,' Yuri said apologetically. 'It was a visitor who left that phone as a present for Frosya. She found him in the forest and brought him here. He was very ill and he needed everything done for him. He was helpless. She saved his life.'

'A visitor?' There was something odd in Annie's voice. She fished in her pocket again and pulled out a photograph. 'Show them this, Hayley.'

It was a picture of John.

Frosya took one look and gave a little cry. Her hand shot out and she snatched the picture, cradling it to her and smiling at it. Chattering in her peculiar voice.

John? Hayley remembered him hoisting her above his head and laughing. Tall and strong and cheerful. Roaring up the road in his old sports car. Frosya was stroking the photograph tenderly with one broad red finger, like a mother stroking the face of a baby.

150

'Yuri,' Annie said, 'ask her—'

But Annie wasn't in charge any more. Leonid elbowed Yuri out of the way and began to bark questions at Irina Petrovna, thrusting his face forward so that it was only inches from hers. The old woman sat in silence, staring coldly at him and giving very short answers to what he said.

'What's going on?' Annie said desperately. 'What's he saying?'

'It is better to wait,' Yuri said stiffly. 'I will tell you when my father has finishing asking.'

It seemed like hours. Annie was gripping the arms of her chair, rippling her fingers with impatience. Hayley was hardly breathing. She kept looking from Irina Petrovna to Leonid Orlov, trying to work out what was going on, but the language was impenetrable.

'What did Irina Petrovna say?' Hayley muttered. 'You've got to tell us that, Yuri.'

'Of course.' The translation was very hurried. 'She says you look tired. She is offering you the bed in her house so that you can rest properly.'

'That's not what I meant,' Annie said irritably. 'What did she say about the photograph?'

'That is—' Yuri looked quickly at his father and then back at Annie. 'It is nothing. He was not here. It was someone else.'

'But the *photograph*—'

Yuri looked unhappy. 'The fat woman, she is—you can see what she is like. This picture is like a toy to her. Like a doll. That's all.'

'That *can't* be it!' Annie was almost crying with disappointment and frustration and exhaustion. 'Your father's got to tell us what's going on!'

She spun her chair round to glare at Leonid, but his eyes slithered away, not meeting hers.

151

'So what do we do?' Hayley said. 'I mean—we've come all this way. Are we just going to take the phone and go back again?'

'Of course we're not,' Annie hissed. 'No one's moving me until I've talked to every single person in this place.'

Hayley glanced nervously at Yuri. 'What does your father say?'

'He says—'

Yuri paused for a second. Hayley wondered whether he was hunting for a word or simply deciding how much to tell them. Either way, he made his mind up very quickly.

'My father says the same as you. We will make these old people tell us everything they know. We will squeeze it out of them.'

He smiled, obviously glad to be agreeing with Hayley and Annie again.

18

'What is going to become of the poor man?' Svetlana leaned across Olga, whispering it into Ivan's ear. 'What will you do tomorrow?'

They had taken Olga into bed with them so that the tourist could have her little folding couch. She was fast asleep, snuggled into Svetlana's arm. On the other side of the thin wall, the tourist was snoring gently and the twins stirred in their cot, unsettled by the sound.

'Tomorrow we are going back to the police,' Ivan said patiently. 'To find out the address of the British Consul.'

'And then?' Svetlana hissed. 'Ivan—he has no money. He speaks no Russian. How can he travel to Novosibirsk on his own? What will he do when he is there?'

She was getting more and more agitated, hissing the words. Ivan was bewildered.

'I thought you wanted to get rid of him?'

Svetlana tossed her head. 'We took him in and he's ours to worry about. He needs to get home if there's someone waiting for him.'

'Someone?' Ivan said. 'Are you thinking of Annie Glasgow?'

He was teasing, but Annie Glasgow had been in his mind too. For some reason he imagined her standing on the map, right on the black dot that said *Glasgow*. She was looking out, across the coloured shapes of Norway and Sweden and Estonia, towards Russia . . .

Just a simple Scottish girl, walking through the heather in her tartan dress. Singing to her sheep as she thinks of the missing tourist. Will ye no come back again? *While English lords and Japanese businessmen march over the hills shooting all the birds and the deer.*

'He's missing her,' Svetlana said gruffly. 'And once he's in England, he'll surely be able to find her. It's such a small country.'

'Scotland,' Ivan said dreamily. 'Maybe she's in Scotland.'

Svetlana pulled his hair. 'Don't go to sleep! Keep thinking about Novosibirsk and the British Consul. How will he get there.'

'The train? The bus?' Those were the obvious answers, but Ivan had a feeling they weren't going to be good enough for Svetlana.

He was right. 'The train! You would just push him on to a train? With no money and no Russian and no memory? How will he avoid being robbed? How will he find his way when he gets to the city?'

'What else can he do? There is no British Consul here.'

'You must *drive* him to Novosibirsk.'

'Drive him?' Ivan hadn't expected that. Suddenly he was wide awake again. 'But—the petrol. To Novosibirsk and back is seven hundred miles.'

'You can find petrol when you want to.' Svetlana's voice was scathing. She didn't need to mention the hunting trip Ivan had made at the beginning of last winter, just after the twins were born. He knew very well what she meant. 'You have to take him.'

Olga stirred and turned over, flinging both arms out and mumbling softly. Ivan and Svetlana both froze, waiting for her to settle down again. She muttered and mumbled, wriggled a few times and then fell back into a deep sleep.

By that time, somehow the argument was over. Next

time Svetlana spoke, she was talking about the food Ivan would need to take for the journey.

'You must set out early. You can drive there in ten hours. Yes?'

Ivan visualized the distance on the map and tried to recall what he had heard about the road. 'Maybe. If it doesn't snow too much. But I'll need to arrange things first. I have to take enough petrol for the whole journey, to make sure I can get back. That means borrowing some cans from Dimitri.'

'No problem. He will lend them.' Svetlana nodded briskly, winding up the discussion. 'If you are there when the police office opens, you can maybe set out by ten o'clock. So you will be there before dark. Almost.' She closed one eye, calculating. 'And the next day, all you have to do is find the British Consul. That will leave plenty of time to drive back I think?'

Ivan gave in. 'I'll be home before midnight.'

'So why are you awake now?' Svetlana said, accusingly. 'With all that driving, you need to sleep, or you'll be too tired.'

She settled under the covers and fell asleep almost instantly, but Ivan wasn't so lucky. She had made him think about time and distances and where he was going to buy petrol and he couldn't settle until he had it all sorted in his mind. He tossed and turned for hours, working it out, and it was almost light before he slept.

When Svetlana shook him awake, at seven o'clock the next morning, it was all clear in his head. He told her the whole thing, with all the timings and every detail in place. But they both knew it was only a plan. The nice, neat scheme you start with, before the muddle of real life messes it up.

In real life, the police office opened late. And when it did open, there was a different policeman on duty. He took his time finding the right file and reading it. And as he read, he watched them both over the top of the papers.

The tourist sat fretting on the narrow bench beside the counter, with his strong shoulders hunched over and his head bent. He was picking nervously at his fingers.

That's not how he ought to be, Ivan thought. *A big man like that*. But he didn't say anything. He kept as still as he could, waiting for the policeman to reach the end of the papers. He didn't like the silence or the way those bulging, bloodshot eyes moved over the words. Towards that signature, at the end of the form.

The file thumped down suddenly on to the counter. 'The Consul's address is not here,' the policeman said roughly.

Ivan's heart jerked. He stood up and went forward. 'Is it possible to find it?' he said. Sounding as mild and polite as he could.

The policeman gave him an odd look, glanced at the tourist and then flicked through the papers again. 'Well— maybe. Wait here.'

He went into the back room and Ivan heard him make a telephone call. His voice rose and fell, but it was impossible to make out any of the words.

Distractedly, the tourist stood up. He began to move around, examining the room where they sat. Tilting his head to peer up at the ceiling and turning round to run his hand over the window frames. Once, he even knocked on the wall beside the counter, putting his head on one side to hear how it sounded.

Keep still! Ivan wanted to say. *It's better to be careful*. But he didn't dare to raise his voice in case it drew attention to them. He was afraid that someone who understood English would come in and see the form.

He pulled at the tourist's sleeve. 'We should sit still. If we annoy the policeman, it will take longer. What were you doing?'

'Just looking,' the tourist said. 'At the building.'

'This is an old city,' said Ivan. 'With lots of interesting buildings. You know about buildings?'

'Oh yes.' The tourist was confident, not even pausing to think.

'So—you are a builder!' Ivan pounced on the clue. 'An English builder. Yes?'

The tourist frowned and shook his head. 'No, I don't think so. That's . . . not quite it.'

'An electric man? The one who does the water? The— on the walls?'

The tourist shook his head again, looking puzzled.

'Perhaps you are—'

But before Ivan could think of anything else, the policeman came marching through from the back room. He slapped a piece of card down on to the counter and pulled the form towards him.

'You!' he said to Ivan. 'Come here.'

Ivan stood up and went to the counter. The policeman's hand was resting lightly on the form, just below the signature.

I don't know.

'There is a problem here,' he said.

Ivan felt his hands begin to tremble. He looked down, to hide his nervousness. 'A problem?'

The policeman's fingers tapped the paper, lightly, lightly. 'What should we do about it?'

'I don't know,' Ivan said—and then heard his own words. Even though they were in Russian, the English words on the paper leaped up to match them. *I don't know.* He looked up involuntarily, to see whether the policeman had noticed.

157

He had. The bloodshot eyes met Ivan's in a steady stare.

'What should we do about it?' the policeman repeated.

It felt like a dead end. Words hovered on the end of Ivan's tongue. He was on the brink of explaining everything, of trying to get the man to understand.

Then the fat fingers tapped the paper again—and he suddenly realized what was going on. He almost laughed with the relief of it.

'Well?' the policeman said, impatiently.

Ivan slipped a hand into his pocket, took out a hundred rouble note and laid it on the counter. The bloodshot eyes looked down at it, without any expression.

Reluctantly, Ivan added another note. Still no expression.

The third note was more than he could afford to lose. Only the policeman's fingers, tapping again, brought it out of his pocket.

But it did the trick. Ignoring the money, the policeman peered at the form, ran his finger along the signature and shrugged. Then he picked up the piece of card he had brought through from the back room.

'This is the address you want?'

'Thank you,' Ivan said, looking down to check. 'That's what we need.' He turned away quickly, nodding to the tourist to follow him.

As they went through the door, he glanced back at the counter. The policeman was slipping the papers into the file. There was no sign of the money.

Now he was three hundred roubles down, there was an extra problem with the petrol. It meant borrowing money as well as petrol cans from Dimitri. They had to chase all round Petrovsk to find him, and when they had tracked him down he had to be told the whole story.

And all the time, the day was ticking away. They didn't start the hunt for petrol until well into the afternoon. According to the plan, they should have been halfway to Novosibirsk by then.

'Maybe we should set out tomorrow?' Ivan said, when they finally got back to the flat.

'Are you mad?' said Svetlana. 'That way, you would lose three days' work instead of two. What's wrong with setting out now?'

'But it will be dark soon. It's after five o'clock.'

'So?' Svetlana rolled her eyes. 'What have you done all day? Nothing except sit about. If you leave now, and drive all night, you can reach Novosibirsk by morning. Ready to look for the Consul, just as we planned.'

The tourist was watching her face, trying to work out what she was saying, but Ivan didn't translate. He bent down gloomily and picked up the bag of food she had put together. 'Let's go,' he said. 'Yes?'

'Yes,' said the tourist. He turned to Svetlana, spreading his empty hands apologetically. His meaning was clear. He wished he had something to give her, but there was nothing. 'Thank you,' he said. 'Goodbye.' He looked down. 'Goodbye, Olga.'

Olga threw herself forward to hug his knees. She had picked the word up already. Almost. 'Goodbarry! Goodbarry!'

Ivan waited for Svetlana to stick out her arm for the polite handshake she would have given anyone else. But instead, she reached up and patted the tourist's cheek.

'God churney,' she said awkwardly, reddening at the sound of her own voice.

Ivan was astounded. He had long ago given up hope of teaching her any English, and he thought she had forgotten it all. Her accent was so thick that the words were barely comprehensible, but the tourist understood.

'Thank you, my friend,' he said. Very slowly, to make sure she caught the words. Then he bent forward and kissed her cheek.

Svetlana would have yelled at anyone else. But all she did was step back quickly, blinking. Scooping up Olga, to hide her face.

I see, Ivan thought. *An English not-exactly-builder that women like very much.*

It unsettled him, seeing Svetlana behave so unlike herself. As a kind of reassurance, he took the long way out to the Novosibirsk road, looping round by the station. That meant that he could drive past the other taxis, standing hopefully in line. He hooted at them and waved his hand, pointing out of town to show that he had a good job. A long drive. There was no need for them to know that he wasn't getting paid.

The other drivers yelled and waved back enviously, peering at the car to see who the passenger was. *I. D. Suva—Long distance commissions undertaken*, Ivan thought, back to his usual buoyancy. *Foreign customers a speciality. English spoken.*

Then they were rattling westwards towards the last shreds of light, with the wind coming straight down the road, into the windscreen. Snow whirled in the headlights and the battered roof-rack sang like a ship's rigging over their heads.

For half an hour or so, they struggled to talk, but neither of them could make out the words well enough. Gradually the conversation died away. Ivan saved his attention for driving and the tourist stared out at the darkness.

The road unravelled between walls of trees. Trunk after trunk was caught in the beams of light, the birches ghosting past like skeletons and the pines clumped and dark in the shadows. Sometimes there were fields.

Sometimes there was a village. Once they saw the big chimneys of a chemical works. But mostly it was trees. And there was no other traffic, except a lorry or two, thundering past in the other direction.

On and on and on.

After three hours, Ivan began to fall asleep. Twice he jerked himself awake, with the tourist shaking his arm. The third time he shrugged and pulled into the side of the road.

'I must take a break,' he said. 'Not long. Just—'

Before the end of the sentence, he was asleep, leaning against the steering wheel with his folded arms as a pillow.

The next time he woke—maybe it was after a few minutes, maybe it was hours—the tourist was outside. He had come round the car and he was tapping at the window next to Ivan's ear. Gesturing, to show that he would take a turn at the driving.

'But you have no papers,' Ivan said sleepily, opening the door so that he could be heard. 'No—'

The tourist ignored that. He pushed until Ivan slid across into the passenger seat. Then he climbed in and started the engine. Ivan kept awake for a moment or two longer. Just long enough to think, *He's driven one of these cars before. He knows just how to handle it.*

Then he floated away into a dream of bricks and bagpipes and bonnie Scottish lassies.

Is anyone following? He can't be certain. When there is a long, straight stretch of road, he sees another set of headlights behind, a long way in the distance. He jams his foot on the accelerator as hard as he can, but at the next straight stretch the headlights are closer.

They gleam in the darkness, like cruel eyes. Sometimes they seem to shift and flicker, sometimes they are steady and unblinking. But never both at once. The two never mix. The two men in his dreams won't be in the same car.

161

When he sees the headlights for the fifth time, he decides. On the next stretch of winding road, he starts to hunt for a track into the forest. When he finds one, he slows down abruptly, switches off his headlights and turns off the road.

As the wheels bump on to the uneven track, he sees the taxi driver stir for a moment and then settle back to sleep. A nice man. Kind to his children. He thinks what a simple life it is, being a taxi driver. Easier than—

Than what? He still can't remember. But just for a second, back in the police station, the feeling of it had gone shuddering through him.

Something to do with buildings. Something to do with the way they're made and how they hold together. He understands how the police station works, how its weights and forces balance each other, sturdy against collapse. He knows just where the weak points are.

And, inching down the track, in the dark, he remembers another building, put together in just the same way. Not a police station. A hotel.

He's not an electrician, but he sees himself walking through the hotel with a box of electrician's tools in his hand. He's following a surly Russian. Up and down stairs, into basements and through long corridors. It is always the Russian who examines the wires and tests the sockets. His job is different. His job . . .

But he can't remember that. All he can remember is the name of the hotel. It sounds suddenly in his mind, not in his own voice, but in the Bear's voice. Harsh and discordant.

Hotel Iksa.

Slowly he drives on down the track between the trees. When he is sure the car is completely hidden, he switches off the engine and turns round in his seat, looking back over his shoulder.

His hands are shaking and he is sweating. But it's not because of the headlights going past on the main road.

19

Hayley never wanted to hear another word of Russian in her life. They'd spent the whole day going from one dilapidated cottage to another, asking the same questions and getting the same useless answers. All the cottages smelt. And everyone in the village was ancient, except for Frosya.

There was a crazy old woman with a goat in her garden and hens all over her house. A miserable wreck of a man on crutches. Another one, without crutches, who coughed and spat all the time. And Frosya's withered, cackling father.

They all rambled on and on, saying the same things about the man who had come out of the forest. *Frosya found him . . . he had the tick fever . . . they looked after him in the Komendant's house . . . he went away . . .* There was never anything new, but Annie insisted on having every boring word translated.

By the evening, Hayley was exhausted and disappointed and bad-tempered. Miserably she dragged the wheelchair through the snow to Irina Petrovna's cottage, with Misha behind her, carrying Annie. Irina Petrovna bobbed in ahead of them and chattered at her husband, who was sitting up in the big double bed. He looked very frail, but when he saw Annie, he pushed back the covers and started to swing his legs out of bed.

'Oh no!' Annie said. 'You mustn't—Yuri, tell them. We don't want to take that away from them. We can sleep in chairs.'

Irina Petrovna took a lot of persuading, but in the end Yuri convinced her to keep the bed and produce some padded quilts for Annie and Hayley. When that was done, he backed away to the door.

'I must go now. We shall stay in the cars tonight. I hope you sleep well.'

'We'd sleep better if we knew what was going on,' Annie said sourly.

Yuri went slightly pink. 'There is nothing,' he muttered. 'If my father knew something—why would he stay here?'

Then he bolted, as though he was afraid he had said too much. Annie glowered as he closed the door behind him, but she looked resigned.

'Makes sense, I suppose. Perhaps we'll get some more information out of them in the morning.'

They tried to settle down for the night, but it wasn't easy. Annie stayed in her wheelchair by the stove, packed round with padded quilts, but Hayley had to manage with an ordinary wooden chair. The quilts she had kept sliding off her knees and her head was full of confused and complicated thoughts. It took her hours to go to sleep.

And when she did doze off, she wasn't asleep for long. With four of them sleeping there, the cottage grew very stuffy. Irina Petrovna's husband snored, the shutters creaked, and the stove spat and crackled. By five o'clock, Hayley knew that she wasn't going to sleep any more, and she was beginning to get cold.

She pulled on her boots and her old coat, crept across to the door and turned the catch. It was still dark outside, but the moon was almost full and new snow glimmered all the way across the clearing. She slipped out of the cottage and padded down the side of it, towards the forest behind. She went very slowly, feeling her feet sink into the snow and watching her breath billow ahead of her in the cold air.

Under the trees, it was darker still. The ground was soggy, covered over with a crust of ice that crunched under her feet as she walked. The moonlight caught the bare branches of the birch trees and threw strange cold shadows down the trunks.

Hayley walked into the trees until the cottages were just hidden, picking her way carefully. When she was completely surrounded by trees, she stopped and leaned back against the trunk of a pine, closing her eyes and listening to the silence.

Whatever happened here, she thought, *John is dead*. The words had been running round in her head all night. *John is dead*.

But in the dark forest, there were no impossibilities. Only birch and pine. Black and white. And the thick, cold silence.

When she heard the footsteps, she didn't open her eyes. She let herself pretend that it was John walking towards her, ducking between the trees and stepping carefully over the frozen water. Avoiding the jagged edges where she had broken the ice. She saw the moonlight catch the side of his face and the long line of his jaw. She imagined it glancing off the pale gold of his hair.

The footsteps came right up to her and stopped. She held her breath, cradling the impossibility. Not just seeing him, but feeling that unmistakable, physical sense of his presence.

Then a voice said, 'Hayley?'

And of course it wasn't John at all. It was Yuri. She opened her eyes and laughed, foolishly.

'It's strange, isn't it? Being in the forest when it's dark.'

'You couldn't sleep in the house?'

She shrugged. 'It was better than being in the cars, I expect.'

'Maybe you were thinking?' Yuri said it very delicately, watching her face. 'Wondering about your brother?'

'Of course I was.' But she couldn't tell him what she had been thinking as he walked towards her. She asked a question instead. 'The man who was here—the one Frosya brought out of the forest—where is he now?'

'I don't know,' Yuri said. 'Irina Petrovna says that he went back into the forest. I think she is telling the truth.' He looked down, chipping at a patch of ice with his foot. Then he said, tentatively, 'Is it very terrible? When a brother dies?'

He sounded uncertain. Almost afraid of his own question.

'Of course,' Hayley said. She was hesitant too, because she didn't understand why he needed to ask.

'Even if you have argued?' Yuri still wasn't meeting her eyes. 'Is it still terrible to realize that you will never see him again?'

His lowered face was sombre in the moonlight.

'I do see him sometimes,' Hayley said.

She didn't know why it was so easy to tell him, when she had never told anyone else. Only that she wanted to console him. To turn his mind away from whatever was driving his questions.

He looked up, startled. And then laughed nervously. 'You mean that you imagine him?'

'I . . . suppose so.' What else could it be. 'But it seems real at the time. You remember when we were on the building site? In Tomsk?'

Yuri nodded. 'You saw something—like his face?'

'It's always like his face,' Hayley said slowly. 'But there was nothing there. You saw it yourself. Nothing except a bundle of rags.'

'And on the train?' Yuri said. 'When we were in the boat?' His voice was very tense. Breathless.

In her mind, Hayley watched the train go by. She saw the long string of lighted windows and the pale face looking out of the last one. The thought of it made her giddy.

'Yes, I saw him on the train too. Looking out of the window.' She leaned back against the tree trunk and closed her eyes for a moment.

When she opened them again, Yuri was staring at her. He looked unhappy and the moonlight threw long, pale shadows down his cheeks.

'I wish you had not told me,' he said softly.

Then he turned and began to run back towards the cars, weaving between the trees. As he reached the edge of the clearing Hayley saw his father coming to meet him. She heard the faint sound of their voices talking for a moment.

And then Leonid Orlov started shouting.

Hayley heard a car door slam. The rough, coughing noise of engines starting up. Suddenly, her brain began to work properly, and she started to run back towards the clearing. But it was too late.

As she came out of the trees, she saw all three cars pulling away from the cottages. Bumping on to the track that led out of the village and down to the river. Their headlights glared in the darkness, destroying the delicate balance of moonlight and shadow.

'You can't do that!' Hayley yelled. 'Stop!'

She tripped and fell, landing in a dirty mixture of mud and trampled snow. Hauling herself on to her knees, she saw the cars swing right and away. For a brief moment, the back of the Range Rover was lit up by the Niva's headlamps and she saw Yuri's face pressed to the rear window, grim and staring.

Then the cars disappeared into the forest and all Hayley could do was gaze after the headlamps, watching the faint patches of light that came and went, came and went between the endless trees.

'The bastards!' Annie said. 'The complete, utter—'

She swore for five minutes, without faltering, in sheer powerless rage. Spitting and hissing, with her weasel-face dead white. Hayley stood speechless and wretched, knowing that it was all her fault. Irina Petrovna and her husband were sitting up in bed, but they obviously didn't understand what had happened.

Finally the swearing collapsed into a dreadful coughing fit that shook Annie's whole body. Irina Petrovna let herself down carefully from the bed and walked across the room. There was a jug of milk standing on the table and she poured a cup and stood over Annie while she drank it. When the coughing had stopped, she looked at Hayley with her head on one side. Enquiring.

'They've gone,' Hayley said helplessly. 'The cars—the men—'

She pulled the door open and pointed at the space where they had been parked, shrugging and spreading her hands to show that she didn't know where they had gone or what was going to happen next.

The old woman shook her head sadly. It was clear that she understood. She patted Hayley's arm and then she turned to Annie. Slowly and clearly, she began to make signals. First a shrug that was quite different from Hayley's. Patient and resigned. *Well, that's how it is . . .*

She pointed at Annie and Hayley and then at the floor in front of her. *You're here . . .*

Then she swept her arms wide, embracing everyone, and tapped her head. *We'll think.*

Hayley smiled, but Annie gave a sour, wretched laugh.

168

'What's the point of thinking? It's too late for that. Leonid's got what he came for, hasn't he?'

'What do you mean?' Hayley said.

Annie's face twisted scornfully. 'Don't be thick. Why do you think he brought us all the way here? Not just because of a mobile phone. He's desperate to find John. And now he knows where to look.'

'You think—' Hayley hardly dared to say it. 'You think that really *was* John on the train? Alive?'

'Don't you?'

'But—that body. They checked the dentist's records—'

'You think Leonid couldn't fix those?' Annie said impatiently. 'With *his* contacts?' Her voice was bitter now. 'Of course John's alive—until Leonid catches up with him.'

'So it's my fault—'

'Why didn't you tell *me* you'd seen him? Instead of blabbing it out to Yuri.'

Annie had managed not to say it until then. But she couldn't keep the words out any longer. Hayley looked away, biting her lip.

'What will they do when they find him?'

Annie didn't reply in words. Instead, she pulled the little photograph out of her pocket and held it up so that Irina Petrovna and her husband were watching too. She pointed first at where the cars had been parked and then at John's face. Then she drew her finger savagely across her throat, with an ugly grimace. The meaning was unmistakable.

They've gone to kill him!

20

I t was the bumps that woke Ivan.

He dreamed that they were driving over a great plain covered with giant pumpkins. The car bounced over one orange hillock after another until the bumps forced their way out of his dream and into his waking, conscious mind. He woke and saw not pumpkins but something worse. They seemed to be off the road altogether, following a dreadful potholed track through the forest.

'What is this?'

Wherever they were, it wasn't the road to Novosibirsk. He sat bolt upright and grabbed at the steering wheel before he was properly awake. The tourist pushed his hand away, without hostility.

'Do that and we'll crash,' he said.

Ivan rubbed a hand over his short, spiky hair and straightened his collar. 'This is the wrong road.'

'The road to Novosibirsk is too dangerous,' the tourist said. 'Anyone could find us on that. All those taxi drivers by the station know which way we went.'

Anyone could find us . . .

'People are chasing you?' Ivan was outraged. This was the man who had taken Olga on his knee. He had got round Svetlana, the most suspicious woman in the world. He had been welcomed into the bosom of the Suva family. And all the time— 'This about losing your memory is a lie! Yes? You're a criminal! You're running from the police!'

'No! It's not that!' The tourist hesitated. 'At least—I don't think it's the police who are chasing me.'

'Not the police?' Ivan went cold all over. 'Is it the *mafiya*?'

The tourist looked cautious. 'Maybe. When you say *mafiya*—what do you mean?'

'Are you kidding?' Ivan rolled his eyes up at the roof. 'Everyone knows the *mafiya*. They have contacts everywhere. Criminals, the government, the police—everyone. You see a man in an American car with big schemes and lots of dollars? *Mafiya!*'

The tourist swung the wheel to avoid a spectacular pothole. 'Could be,' he said. 'That could be what I'm running away from.'

Ivan felt sweat trickle down his back. A good deed. That was all he had done. A simple good deed. If he'd had the choice, he would have put the tourist on a train and been back outside the station with the other drivers. But, no, he'd let Svetlana talk him round—and what was his reward?

OK, Suva, we're hauling you off to see the Boss. You mess with the mafiya *and you get what you deserve, brother. No sweat. What made you think you could step into the big time, you pathetic little taxi driver?*

All he'd ever wanted was an ordinary family and an ordinary life, and now here he was, stuck out in the *taiga* with the *mafiya* after him and his precious taxi bumping over potholes that would destroy its suspension.

He gripped the edges of his seat. 'This is madness! If the car breaks—if we run out of petrol—what then? We shall freeze to death. We shall starve. Wolves will eat us. You don't understand the danger. We must go back.'

'I can't go back,' the tourist said stubbornly. 'There might be a trap.'

He swung the wheel just too late to avoid a giant

puddle. Ice cracked and water sprayed up round them. Ivan looked sideways, wondering which of them was stronger. What would happen if it came to a fight?

He didn't think his chances were good. The tourist was six inches taller than he was.

OK, Suva, so you use your wits. Quick thinking, that's your strong point.

'Maybe you drive *into* trouble,' Ivan said cunningly. 'Maybe there is a trap waiting at the end of this track.' He mimed it, driving an innocent left hand taxi into the cruel jaws of his right hand. He squeezed the left hand murderously and shuddered. 'You think it's so easy to avoid the *mafiya*?'

For the first time, the tourist looked uncertain. The car slowed almost to a halt. 'Where does this track go?'

Ivan blew a raspberry. 'You think I know? You think I know all the tracks in Siberia? This is not like your little England, chum. This is a big country. With oil and gas and gold. And wolves and bears. Everything. You think we have only one road?'

The car stopped. The tourist turned off the engine, took his hands off the steering wheel and looked down at his fingers. They were shaking.

'Imagine what it is,' he said, 'to know nothing about yourself. Except that someone wants to kill you. How do you make a plan, if you don't know your enemies? Or yourself? All I know is that I don't want to die. Help me, Ivan.'

Anything else, Ivan could have resisted. Threats. Bribes. Lies. Flattery. But this *Help me* cut him to pieces. It was what Olga said when she wanted him to pick her up, so that she could see further. *Help me, Papa!* The tourist said it in exactly the same pleading voice.

Ivan could almost hear Svetlana scolding him. *Will you believe any story he tells you? Are you so soft? Such a fool?* But it

172

was no use. He did believe it. He put a hand on the tourist's arm.

'What can I do? No one can help you until you remember who you are. Where you come from and why the *mafiya* are chasing you.'

'Do you think I haven't tried?' the tourist said desperately. 'How can you hunt for your memory if you've lost it?'

Ivan thought how his father had yelled at him when he lost things.

Remember, boy! Are you an idiot? Where did you put it? Remember! REMEMBER!!

His father was a huge man, a Georgian, with shoulders like a bear's and a temper fuelled by vodka. When he began to shout, Ivan was so terrified that he couldn't remember anything at all.

It was always his mother who rescued him. She wasn't afraid of standing up to his father, even though he was three times her size.

'Don't be a fool, Daniil! You think his brain will work if you shout? People don't remember when they're trembling!'

Then she would put an arm round Ivan and lead him into the kitchen, where it was quiet. Where his father wouldn't come, because it was her place. After a while in that small, safe room, he would calm down and she would talk to him gently, helping him to remember.

The feelings came back to him. The way his brain fluttered round in his head, refusing to settle to anything, like a bird trapped in a house. The calm slowness of his mother's voice, stilling the panic so that the bird flew down into her hands, folding its wings and settling its ruffled feathers.

Quiet.

Calm.

Safety.

Ivan looked at the tourist and recognized that frantic terror in the whiteness of his face and the way his hands fretted in his lap.

'Let us change seats, old chum,' he said gently. 'I know a safe place for you. Quiet and safe. When you are there, it will be easier to remember.'

He thought there might be an argument, but the tourist was too tired for that. He opened his door and clambered out of the car as if it were an enormous effort. Ivan jumped out as well, and patted him on the back as they crossed over.

'Don't worry. It is a good place I am taking you to.'

The tourist nodded and slipped into the passenger seat. Even before Ivan had started the engine, he was asleep with his head tucked against the door and his fluttering hands lying still in his lap.

It was a long time since Ivan had been to Petrovsk 9, but the road came back to him as he turned north-west again. It unravelled like an ancient story. Although its yellow surface was cracked now, the verges were almost as bare as the day the road was made. The wind had scoured them free of snow and they were black and barren in the light from the headlamps. Beyond them, the forest was full of starved and stunted trees that poked bare, stag's-horn branches into the dirty air.

When the factories were busy, there had been a kind of energy to the pollution all round the city. Now it was a desolation, a seeping despair that mirrored the soul of the place. The empty factory buildings lined the road, giving way to blocks of pale, decaying flats.

Most of them had been built in one great burst in the nineteen fifties, when the town was a secret and the government was pouring money into its factories and research laboratories. Half the flats were empty now, boarded up and covered with graffiti.

Turning off the main road, Ivan wove his way along the smaller streets, driving smoothly and carefully, so that the tourist did not wake. Even when they pulled up, he only stirred a little and turned over, pillowing his face against the back of the seat.

Very quietly, Ivan got out of the car, locking the door behind him. He could see Grigory already, high above his head. It was almost midnight and freezing cold, but he was sitting on the front windowsill of his flat, peacefully cleaning the windows. Moving the cloth over the glass in a slow, methodical manner.

The lift was broken as usual. Ivan climbed the stairs without hurrying, but he was breathless by the time he reached the sixth floor. He rested for a moment, leaning on the doorframe, before he pushed at Grigory's door.

It was still unlocked. Every time Ivan expected that would be different, that Grigory would have decided to protect himself, but it was always the same. Anyone could walk in, unannounced. Ivan let himself in and shut the door behind him.

The flat was even barer than last time he visited. Two chairs and a table under the naked electric bulb. A mattress on the floor and a cooker against the opposite wall. Four icons propped up on top of the cupboard and a broom leaning in one corner.

Stillness.

'Grigory,' he said quietly.

'Ivan.' Grigory smiled at him through the glass. Then he swung himself into the room and closed the window. 'All day I have been waiting for you.'

Ivan shrugged awkwardly, not accepting what Grigory implied, but not rejecting it completely. There were things they never talked about.

175

'I have brought someone who needs quiet and safety,' he said. 'Will you take him in?'

'Of course.' Grigory dropped his window-cleaning cloth into the sink. 'He is in your car?'

'Asleep,' Ivan said.

'Shall we go down to see him?'

As they went down the stairs, Ivan kept looking sideways at his brother, trying to see some change in him, but Grigory was the same as he had always been. Short and stocky, with blunt features and dry, reddened skin. His fair hair was cropped close to his head and he moved easily, without looking at Ivan. Smiling.

'You're doing well,' he said. 'You have a bigger car.'

'Three years ago,' Ivan said.

'And Svetlana and the baby? They are well?'

'Very well. But Olga is six years old now. We have twin boys as well. Vadim and Fyodor.'

'Six years old? So long since we met?' Grigory did look round then, a steady look, without judgement.

Ivan tried to think of questions that he could ask in return, but it was difficult. Grigory's life never changed. In the end, he said, 'Your beard is grey.'

'Yes.' Grigory looked at him and a corner of his mouth twitched. 'For two years now.'

The tourist was still asleep in the car. They stood looking at him through the window.

'He does not speak Russian,' Ivan said. 'He is English.'

Grigory shrugged. 'If we need to talk, we shall find a way.' He peered through the window with a kind of open, frank interest, like a child.

'He has forgotten who he is,' Ivan said.

He opened the door and shook the tourist's shoulder. The eyelids flickered and the tourist's blue eyes moved vaguely for a moment and then focused on Grigory's face.

'My brother,' Ivan said, in English. 'In his flat it is quiet, mate. And no one will find you.'

The tourist frowned for a moment, but before he could speak, Grigory reached into the car and took hold of his hand. Slowly he drew him out and began to walk towards the flats. Ivan locked the car door and went after them.

Grigory signed to them both to sit down at the table and put bread and salt in front of them, and a bowl of apples. Although the window was closed the flat was very cold.

'I can't stay,' Ivan said restlessly. That was how Grigory affected him. Always. He touched the tourist on the shoulder. 'Good friend, you are safe here. I will come back to see you in a week, or maybe two.'

The tourist hesitated. 'They won't find me?'

'Never,' Ivan said. 'Who would come to this place?'

'You won't tell anyone that I'm here?'

'Never,' Ivan said again. He reached out and gripped the tourist's hand, sealing the promise. 'I will never tell to anyone. And soon I will come back to see you.'

Slowly the tourist nodded. Ivan let go of his hand and patted it.

'My brother is called Grigory. He does not speak English, but he is a good man. You can trust him. He will help you.'

'Yes,' said the tourist. He did not even look at Grigory, as if there was no need. Ivan felt a curious stab of envy.

'Goodbye.' He stood up to leave, and Grigory stood too.

'Wait,' he said. He took one of the little icons from the cupboard and held it out, cupped in both hands. Ivan saw the Mother of God staring up at him with eyes like dark pits and a stiff child sitting regally on her knee.

'For Olga,' Grigory said. 'From her uncle.'

It was all Ivan could do to take it in his hand. But he

knew his brother well enough to understand the deal. Grigory was quiet and slow, but he was not without resistance.

'Thank you,' he said. He dropped the icon into the pocket of his overcoat. 'Now I must go home.'

He drove away from Petrovsk 9 twice as fast as he had come. The car bounced and jolted on the broken road and he pushed a cassette into the new tape player and drowned out his thoughts with a strong beat and a pair of voices singing American lyrics.

By the time he reached Petrovsk, he was in another world. Civilized and dynamic. He snapped the tape off and began to weave his way through the back streets to his own apartment block.

There was a green car filling the space where he usually parked. He looked at it enviously for a moment, but he didn't stop to wonder whose car it was or where the owner had gone. He was suddenly very hungry and he remembered how long it was since he had eaten. He ran towards the lift, full of careless thoughts about food. Glad to be living his own life and not his brother's.

He sits across the table from the man called Grigory, eating bread and apples. While they are eating, there is no need to do anything else. If their eyes meet, Grigory smiles, but the smile is without pressure, and he understands that it is not necessary even to smile back.

When the food is finished, they wash the plates in the sink and dry them. Then Grigory kneels down in front of the cupboard where the icons stand. Slowly and methodically, he begins to take the packets and saucepans and tools out of the cupboard, lining them up neatly on the floor.

When the cupboard is empty, he lifts out the shelf and stands it against the sink. Then he picks a screwdriver off the floor.

There are four screws holding the base of the cupboard in place. Without hurry, Grigory unscrews them all and takes out the wooden base. Underneath, beside the floor joist, there is a long, narrow space. He moves back so that his visitor can see.

Then he puts everything back into position again. Exactly as it was before, except that he leaves the screws untightened, sitting in their holes.

You are safe, his eyes say when he straightens and stands up. *They will not find you.*

He remembers the electrician lifting the floorboards like that. In the Hotel Iksa. He remembers how the electrician stepped back, letting him peer into the space underneath.

Most of those Russian buildings are easy to suss out. Walk round the outside once, and you can tell exactly how they're made. Exactly where to lay the charges so that they'll come straight down, like a house of cards.

But the Hotel Iksa is an old building. Solid and stubborn. He has to crawl all over it, making sketches in his notebook while the electrician pretends to check the wiring.

It's not really illegal, after all. Just a few undercover enquiries. And he's not going to do the demolition himself. He's only the consultant. The man who gives advice about where the charges ought to go.

What harm can you do, just making a plan?

21

*T*hey've gone to kill him—and you're the one who did it. You've killed your brother. Annie wasn't saying that. But the words burned in the air.

Irina Petrovna had gone out, signalling that she would talk to the other people in the village. Her husband had put his head back on the pillow and fallen asleep again. Annie and Hayley were on their own, with the unspoken words scorching the silence. They seeped out of the cottage walls like the smell of wood smoke. They echoed in Hayley's head like the hissing of the stove.

You blabbed to Yuri. You've killed John.

'There must be something we can do!' she said desperately. 'Can't we get out of here and find John before they do?'

Annie's voice was scathing. 'And how are we going to do that?'

'I thought—maybe—can't you phone?'

'Go on then, genius! *You* phone!' Annie snatched the mobile off her arm rest and almost threw it at Hayley. '*If* you can think of anyone to phone.'

The battery was virtually flat. Hayley saw that as soon as she switched it on. And anyway, who was there to phone? The hotel in Tomsk? Frank Walsh, in Moscow? Her parents?

None of them would be any use. She found the hotel number in Annie's notebook and tried that, but all she got was incomprehensible crackling. And the odd words she did catch sounded totally Russian.

'You see?' Annie said bitterly. 'The batteries are useless. John's mobile is even worse. Completely dead. We can't charge it, because there's no electricity here. There isn't a hope of getting out.'

'Can't I . . . walk?' Hayley didn't fancy the idea, but it must be possible.

'Across the river? I don't think so. Even if it freezes hard, you'd take days to reach the nearest village. Assuming you didn't die of hypothermia the first time you fell asleep. And I'm stuck here like an idiot anyway, until someone appears with a car. Like—never.'

Hayley's mind ran round in circles, trying to think of another way out, but she couldn't. It was true. The snow outside was too deep for the wheelchair, and the nights were numbingly cold.

'We could die here,' Annie said gloomily.

Another bonfire at home? Hayley didn't want to think that.

'We can't give up yet,' she said defiantly. 'I'm going to find Irina Petrovna. I'll try and ask her who else comes here. After all, they've got tea. They must get that from somewhere.'

She picked up the phrasebook and opened the door.

Outside, she could see Irina Petrovna's footprints on the new snow, heading down the slope. She followed them to Frosya's cottage and knocked on the door.

Inside, someone said something in Russian. Hoping that it meant *Come in*, Hayley opened the door and stepped inside. There were no lights lit, and the shutters were closed, so that she couldn't make out who had spoken. She took another step forward, pulling the door shut behind her, to keep out the cold air.

Instantly, the old man in the bed reared up and fell forward, grabbing at her arm. She reached out both hands to catch him, and he snatched them and held on tightly. He was peering at her face and jabbering excitedly.

Hayley tried to pull away, muttering apologetically and ridiculously in English. 'I'm sorry, I didn't know . . . I thought . . . I won't disturb you . . . '

But he wouldn't let her go. He dragged her closer to the bed, shouting insistently.

'Look, I don't know,' Hayley said. 'I can't understand—'

That just made matters worse. He shook her arm and shouted louder, pulling at her sleeve and pointing towards the gun balanced on top of the shutters. Then he gave her a push that sent her staggering across the room towards Frosya's bed. The effort brought on a fit of coughing that doubled him up.

Hayley was terrified that he would have a heart attack if she argued. She scrambled on to the bed and was rewarded with a toothless, coughing grin. He pointed up yet again, obviously encouraging her, and she slid her hand up the side of the shutters, just as Frosya had done.

She was aiming for the gun, but, just before she reached it, something made her feel round the side of the shutter. She wriggled her hand into Frosya's hiding place, running her fingers along the ledge.

At first, she thought there was nothing there. Then she reached further along, standing on tiptoe, and her fingers met two things. Something soft, and something hard and flat, standing on its edge. She glanced down at the old man, wondering whether she dared to pull them out.

He was obviously delighted to see her rifling Frosya's treasures. He chuckled maliciously and then lapsed into another fit of coughing.

Manoeuvring her fingers round so that she could get a better grip, Hayley pulled out the two things. The first was a little cloth bag, full of odd beads and buttons. It was

182

obviously Frosya's and she pushed it back quickly. The second thing—

When she saw what it was, she almost dropped it.

She was holding one of John's notebooks.

Even without opening it, she knew that it had to belong to him. He always used the same kind of book. Small and black, with hard covers. She flipped through the pages, trying to read the writing, but it was too dark to make anything out. Holding it tightly, she jumped off the bed.

The old man had started to giggle to himself. A malicious, toothless snigger that made her feel sick. She couldn't wait to get out of the cottage.

'This is my brother's,' she muttered. 'I need to look at it properly.'

The old man nodded and mumbled, sniggering crazily under his breath. He seemed to have forgotten about the gun. Hayley shuddered and scrambled out of the cottage as fast as she could.

Annie went very quiet when she saw the book. Her hand hovered over it, without touching it, as though she couldn't bear to begin. 'It won't be any use,' she muttered. 'It'll just be full of sums. Lists and costings and things like that. John never wrote—never *writes* anything interesting in his notebooks.'

'There might be something,' Hayley said.

She knelt on the floor beside Annie and opened the book at the first page. As usual, John had written nothing on that except the date when he began to use the book. With a space left below it for the date of finishing.

'The second date's blank,' Hayley said. 'Look. This is the one he was using when he—it's the last one.'

Annie peered at it. 'That's the date he left home. Must be just the Russian job in there.'

Hayley began to leaf through the pages. The first few looked incomprehensible but familiar. Sketches of a ten floor building. A schedule for soft-stripping. Dates and numbers and a rough wiring plan.

'Looks like that block in Tomsk,' Annie said. 'Nothing special there. Is that all?'

Hayley flipped on further and found some more sketches. A three storey building this time, not large but obviously fairly complicated. The sketches were covered with measurements and notes and after them came more elaborate drawings, marked carefully with small crosses.

Annie pulled a face. 'What's *that*? Why would they bother to blow something that size?'

Hayley turned over to the next page. There was a list of dates like a rough schedule. A page headed *Soft-stripping*, with lists of numbers and weights and some hieroglyphs she couldn't understand. And a few notes in jargon. *4 skins. Furnace demic. Two days to burn wood and clat.*

'What on earth was he doing?' Annie frowned. 'It can't have anything to do with the flats in Tomsk.'

'Maybe he had other things going.' Hayley tapped the crosses with her finger. 'He was supposed to be a consultant, wasn't he? Perhaps they were consulting him about this building too.'

Annie shook her head. 'He would have told me. He always told me about what he was doing. And this is really detailed. He must have spent ages going round the building. I don't understand why he didn't say anything.'

Hayley shrugged and turned to the next page.

They were both expecting more sketches of the same building, but what they saw was completely different.

It was a church.

A square church, with a massive doorway and long, narrow windows, set high in the walls. In the centre was a round, squat tower, topped by a single onion dome.

'What was he up to?' Annie stared at it. 'Why would he draw a building like that?'

'Maybe he just liked it,' Hayley said.

Annie shook her head. 'He never used his notebooks for anything except work. If he drew it here, he must have had a reason. It's got to mean something.'

They both leaned closer, trying to make out the details. Even in Irina Petrovna's cottage, the light was bad and they had to concentrate to see properly. They were so busy that they didn't know that the door had opened until the cold air hit them.

By then, it was too late to hide the notebook. They turned and saw Frosya staring at them with her round face turning pink and her jaw clenched.

Hayley was too embarrassed to speak. Until then, she hadn't thought much about what she'd done. Finding the notebook had knocked it all out of her mind. But now she saw herself through Frosya's eyes, trampling on the bed and robbing the secret hiding place. She cringed.

Annie didn't cringe. She went straight into a fierce verbal attack, pointing her finger at Frosya and shaking the book.

'What do you mean by hiding this? Hey? It's my fiancé's notebook! You stole it, and you didn't show us even though you knew we were looking for him! What did you think you were playing at?'

Frosya might not understand any of the words, but she couldn't help picking up what Annie meant. Her mouth began to tremble and she looked across at Irina Petrovna's husband for support.

He had woken up when Annie began to shout. Now he propped himself up on one elbow, slowly and creakily, and began to talk to Frosya. Whatever he said to her sent her off into a long, energetic babble.

Hayley couldn't tell whether or not the old man

understood anything of what Frosya was saying. He kept trying to interrupt her, but that only made her worse. They were both talking and their voices rose in competition.

'Oh blast it!' Annie muttered under her breath.

'Give me the book,' Hayley said. She interrupted the old man, holding the book out and pointing at the church. 'Where is this? Is it a real place?'

He leaned forward, peering at it. But before he could say anything, Frosya came running across. The moment she saw the picture, a beam spread over her face and she started to chatter again, nodding and pointing past Annie. Waving her arm in a way that suggested a long distance.

'It's real,' Hayley said. 'Annie, do you see that? Frosya knows where it is!'

'Great,' Annie said sarcastically. 'So it's west of here. Big deal. That's really precise, isn't it? Somewhere between here and Moscow.'

Frosya looked anxiously at her, dithering into silence.

'Why don't you smile?' Hayley muttered. 'Can't you see she's petrified of you?'

'It's not exactly a smile situation, is it?' snapped Annie. 'This church could be really important—some kind of clue. But we can't find out where it is, because we can't understand a word anyone says.'

'What about the map book? We could show them—'

'Left it in the car, didn't I?' Annie scowled.

Hayley felt like shaking her. She was going to mess everything up by being so bad-tempered. Couldn't she see Frosya shrinking away?

Turning her back on the wheelchair, Hayley tried to make contact with Frosya herself, by pointing.

'Can you' (point) 'and I' (point) 'go to see this church?'

She held the book flat and walked her fingers across the paper to the great doorway in the drawing, tilting her head questioningly. Frosya looked puzzled and unhappy.

Doggedly, Hayley made the signs again, even more slowly. And again.

Suddenly Frosya began to grin. Seizing Hayley's hand, she started trying to drag her towards the door, chattering excitedly.

'Hang on,' Annie said. She sat up in her chair and took charge. 'If she's going to take you there, you'll have to plan it, Hayley. You'll need warm clothes. And what about the time? Can you get there and back in the light?'

The old man was obviously saying the same kind of thing to Frosya, pointing at the boots and coats by the door, and tapping his watch. But it didn't look as though she agreed. She kept on tugging at Hayley's arm.

It was Irina Petrovna who sorted it out. She came in when everyone was talking at once and she didn't attempt to break in. She simply stood by the stove, with her hands folded, until the voices died away. When there was complete silence, she asked a single question and listened first to what her husband said, and then to Frosya's hectic, disjointed mumbles.

When she had it all straight in her mind, she drew, taking two empty pages of John's notebook.

Five little stick figures, one in a wheelchair. A sunset. And there they all were again, in bed this time. Then, on the next page, a sunrise, with an arrow to show that the sun was coming up and not going down. And a clock showing eight o'clock.

The building she sketched at the bottom of the page was not as tidy as the church John had drawn, but it was obviously the same place. And there were two of the little figures walking off together towards it.

She looked up, to check that they all understood.

'So how far is it?' Annie said, still impatient. She ran her finger between the walkers and the church and then tapped the clock, questioningly.

Irina Petrovna laughed, shaking her head. *Patience.* Then she talked to Frosya for a long time, obviously trying to get her to work something out. When she had it, she drew again—arrows and clocks beside the little walking figures—Hayley almost wished she hadn't.

'Looks like three hours there and three hours back.' Six hours walking. With no one except Frosya. And it was snowing again. 'Do you think it's really worth going?'

'You won't know, will you?' Annie said quickly. 'Unless you go.' She was gripping Hayley's hand and her face was frighteningly alive. Burning with determination. 'You've *got* to go.'

Hayley met her eyes. She meant to say, *It's ridiculous. Going all that way in the snow, just to look at a church.* But she didn't say it. Because she understood, suddenly, that Annie would go crazy unless something was happening. Unless she was *making* something happen. She couldn't endure being passive.

'All right,' Hayley said. 'We'll go first thing in the morning.'

She tapped the sunrise and the two little figures walking to the church, and nodded at Frosya. And Frosya grabbed her hand, laughing and patting it.

22

The moment he walked into the flat, Ivan realized what the green car was doing in the street. He understood why everything had been so still as he turned his key in the lock. But, by then, it was too late to alter what was going to happen.

He came through the door and saw Svetlana sitting on the sofa bed, with her hands clenched into fists. Her eyes were swollen from crying, and there was a raw, red bruise on her cheek. When he came in, she looked up wildly and her mouth twisted.

Ivan took one quick step towards her—and someone came from behind and grabbed him, clamping both arms to his sides. A man like a gorilla pulled him off his feet, swinging him towards the window.

In front of the window, two chairs had been pulled round to face the sofa. The men who sprawled on them were young and hard-faced. They wore new suits, with the sleeves pulled back to show ringed fingers and white shirt cuffs, and one of them had a gun lying casually across his lap.

The other one was holding Olga.

His big hand clamped her mouth shut, squashing her cheeks out of shape. His fingers were shiny with tears and snot, but she wasn't crying now. Her wide, frightened eyes were fixed on Ivan's face.

'It's all right, baby,' Ivan said soothingly. Stupidly.

Svetlana made a small, angry noise and the two young men laughed.

'That's right,' said one of them sarcastically. 'Papa's home and everything's fine.' He had a fair, square Russian face and he wrenched Olga's head round so that he could grin at her.

'Leave her alone,' Ivan said. 'What do you want?'

The man with the gun was darker and smaller. A Khant maybe. 'There is no need to be agitated, Ivan Danilovich,' he said. 'This will not take long.'

The gorilla twisted Ivan's arm up sharply, behind his back, and the two young men laughed again.

'What . . . won't take long?' Ivan said, gasping for breath. 'We have . . . nothing to give you. Why have you come?'

'We have come to help you,' said the Khant smoothly. 'You have been badly treated. Misused and exploited.' He shook his head, parodying sympathy.

Round his feet was a litter of toys, scattered where Olga had left them. In the room behind, Ivan could see the twins asleep in their cot. He hardly felt it when the gorilla pushed at his arm again. The pain was nothing compared with the fear that gripped his whole body.

'You have been ill-used,' the Russian said. 'Exploited by a stranger with a bad luck story. Isn't that right?'

'I don't know what you mean,' Ivan panted. Trying to find a way to think.

The Khant clicked his fingers. 'Show him the photograph, Gennady.'

The gorilla clamped one arm tightly round Ivan's body. With the other hand, he pulled a picture out of his inside pocket and held it under Ivan's nose.

It was the tourist, of course. And yet—it was not the tourist, even though the face was the same. It was someone laughing and confident, shielding his eyes against the sun. Someone who knew exactly who he was.

'Don't bother to lie,' the Russian said wearily, giving

Olga's face a squeeze. 'We know you picked up this man at the station. The other drivers told us. Your wife has identified the photograph and we know that you set off towards Novosibirsk together. So you see, there is no problem. All we need is an address in Novosibirsk.'

For a moment, Ivan thought it was going to be easy. He thought he could save the tourist and his family as well. 'If I can reach into my pocket—' he muttered.

The gorilla loosened his grip and Ivan felt for the piece of card with the Consul's address written on it.

But before he could find it, the Khant smiled lazily. Insultingly. 'We shall phone our contacts in Novosibirsk, of course, to check what you say. When they've found the man—then we'll leave you in peace.'

Ivan pulled out the useless piece of card and looked down at it. He could see the tourist sitting in Grigory's flat with the bread and salt in front of him. And he could hear his own voice speaking, meaning every word. *Never! I will never tell to anyone.*

His throat was dry.

'Ivan?' Svetlana said. Anxious and urgent.

The Russian laughed suddenly. 'Don't be a fool, Ivan Danilovich. This man is, of course, a criminal. Good at deceiving people and gaining sympathy. It is not your fault that you were taken in. And any promises made to such a man are, naturally, of no importance.'

It wasn't true, of course. The Russian didn't even try to make it sound true. He was offering the words as an escape. An excuse for Ivan's conscience.

Ivan could hear his own breathing. The only sound in the room, or so it seemed. In. Out. In. Out. Olga had begun to whimper, snivelling through the Russian's fingers.

'How can you hesitate?' Svetlana hissed. 'What are you?'

Ivan didn't know what he was. There was no voice in his head to tell him. He had dreamed of being a hero and he couldn't keep a simple promise.

Never! I will never tell to anyone.

The Russian barked, suddenly, 'Search him! Go through his pockets!'

The gorilla grabbed both Ivan's hands and pulled them behind his back while the Khant jumped up to search his pockets. He started with the jacket, pulling out Ivan's wallet and driving licence and spreading his papers on the table. Then he moved on to the overcoat.

It happened very quickly. The Khant's hand went deep into the right hand pocket of the overcoat and dragged out Grigory's icon. In the light from the window, the gold background glinted suddenly.

'Well!' said the Russian, pleased with himself. He leaned over Olga's head and snatched the icon out of the Khant's hands. 'What's this? A gift from Novosibirsk?'

Ivan clamped his mouth shut, until the lips bruised, but it was too late. The moment Svetlana saw the icon, she began to shout.

'I know where he's been! I know! He hasn't been to Novosibirsk at all! Don't hurt Olga! Let her go! I'll tell you!'

'Svetlana, they'll kill him—!'

But she didn't even hear. She was on her feet, reaching out for Olga, and she was speaking as fast as she could. Telling them where the tourist was.

'It's my husband's brother—Grigory Danilovich Suva! That's where the icon came from! He's a religious maniac! He lives in Petrovsk 9! I'll give you the address—'

The gorilla let Ivan go and he slumped on to the sofa, hiding his face in his hands. There was a voice in his head now, but it was not heroic or comforting.

Big man. Big talk. Making promises you can't keep. Why

did you open your mouth in the first place? You had no right to promise—

The Russian pushed Olga off his lap and she ran straight past Svetlana to Ivan, throwing herself at his legs. Hugging them with both arms.

'Papa! Papa!'

Ivan picked her up and held her tightly, burying his face in her hair.

The Khant had whipped a mobile phone out of his pocket and he was talking quickly, passing on Grigory's address to someone in Petrovsk 9. *It's over,* Ivan thought wretchedly. *It's over. They'll get him now.*

His brain was still protesting, still trying to think of a way to warn the tourist. But there was no way. Even if the men left them alone to try, it was impossible to phone, because Grigory—of course—had no telephone. And as for driving there—even if he jumped into the car straight away, and drove like a demon, he would never make it in time. It was all fixed. It was already happening.

Ivan raised his head and saw the icon, flung down carelessly on the table. The dark eyes gaped like black pits, shafts that spiralled down and down and down into nothing. *Failure,* said the stern face against the gold background. *Failure, traitor.*

Olga was patting his cheek and Svetlana came across and put a hand on his arm, but he could not meet their eyes.

Traitor to your family, said the voice in his head. *Traitor to your guest. Traitor to yourself. Traitor, traitor . . .*

He felt his life fall to pieces.

In Petrovsk 9, in Grigory's flat, there is no sound. One man is asleep, curled easily on the mattress. The other is just waking, because he always wakes early.

193

He stretches and opens his eyes, seeing the pale beginnings of light at the uncurtained window. He stares at it tranquilly, ready for whatever is going to happen.

The sleeping man is dreaming of the one they call the Bear. Of his heavy face, bent over the black notebook, his small, shifting eyes scanning it greedily. Sliding impatiently past all the notes on costing and soft-stripping. He doesn't want those explained, even though Misha is standing there, ready to interpret.

What the Bear wants to know about is the explosives. How many charges. Where to put them. How to wire them up. He has it explained to him three times, growling technical questions that Misha can barely translate.

The sleeping man shifts uneasily, hearing the Bear's thick voice overlaid by Misha's expressionless English.

You must keep silent about the hotel. If they know there is a buyer with plans, they will make the price bigger. If the plans are secret—the price will be small. So you must not speak. Or you will pay a price as well.

It's a pack of lies. All except the threat. Does he know that then, while he's listening? Or only later? Does the knowledge seep in slowly, like something you see in the dark, out of the corner of your eye? Something you try to ignore?

He doesn't want to get mixed up with knowing anything. He's only the consultant, after all. The man who makes the plans.

It's better not to know too much . . .

23

Hayley thought she had enough warm clothes for the walk to the church, but Irina Petrovna didn't agree. Before it was light, she got up and began rummaging in the battered old painted box in the corner of the room. She pulled out a collection of thick, ancient garments and brought them across to press them on Hayley. Not instead of Hayley's own coat and trousers, but as extras.

There was a pair of men's trousers that had to be held up with a piece of cord. A baggy fur coat, old and smelly but still with an amazing thickness of coarse, springy hair. A long scarf knitted in purple wool. Mittens. A hat with ear flaps.

When Hayley had had some bread and some warm milk, she started to wrap herself up. By the time everything was on, she could hardly put her arms down by her sides.

'I feel like an onion,' she muttered to Annie. 'All layers.'

'She's just making sure you don't freeze to death,' Annie said sharply. 'Smile, or she'll be insulted.'

But Irina Petrovna wasn't insulted. She looked at Hayley and laughed. Then she pointed across the room at a pair of old felt boots, with two pairs of socks looped over the top.

'Oh please!' Hayley said. '*Please!* I've got my own boots.'

She would have put them on, but Irina Petrovna knocked them out of the way and pointed at the felt boots again.

In the end, it was simplest to give in. Hayley tugged

on the extra socks and then began to work her feet into the boots. 'I can't believe I really need all this stuff.'

'Just stop moaning and get on with it!' Annie said shortly.

That was how she'd been all day. From the moment she opened her eyes, she'd been snapping like a mousetrap. One careless remark and FZAP!

The idea of being left behind was driving her crazy.

'Are you sure you'll be all right on your own?' Hayley said.

Annie looked round the room and shrugged. 'Have to be, won't I?'

'But how—?'

'I'll manage. All right?' It was obviously not a subject for discussion. Annie wheeled over to her bag and unzipped a pocket. 'Take the camera. If I can't get to see this place myself I want some photos.'

Hayley stowed the camera in a safe pocket, about three layers down. And then it was time to go.

Frosya was outside already, equally bundled up, with a scarf tied over her head. Her shabby brown coat was bulging softly. Hayley couldn't begin to guess how many jumpers she was wearing underneath. She looked like the middle-aged women Hayley had glimpsed doing their shopping in Tomsk—except that Frosya was skipping around like a five year old, excited by the thought of the trip.

'OK then,' Hayley said awkwardly. 'I suppose we're off. See you tonight. Bye.'

'Goodbye,' Annie said curtly. 'Have fun.'

She wheeled up to the door, with her face set, so that she could watch them go. Irina Petrovna came outside, pushing a bundle of food into Frosya's pocket and talking seriously to her. Giving instructions of some kind.

Then she smiled at Hayley and touched her lightly on the cheek. Her hand was warm.

'Goodbye,' Hayley said. 'See you later.'

It was barely light, and very cold. Hayley could feel the air moving through her nose and down into her lungs and the sensation brought her to a standstill for a moment. But Frosya had already set off enthusiastically. She was ploughing through the snow, head down, taking the path that led towards the river.

When Hayley had arrived, coming up that track, in the dark, in the Niva, the forest had been a dark wall on either side, solid and threatening. Now as the sun came up, the trees round them took on an airy, luminous brightness. The slanting sunlight danced in the network of branches, dissolving the space into an intricate tracery of snow.

The track was easy all the way down to the water's edge, and they covered the distance steadily. But then they turned right, into the trees. And immediately they were into untrodden snow.

Frosya was carrying a long stick and she prodded as she walked. Some of the ground was boggy under the snow. In other places the river had frozen over and there was snow lying on the ice, so that the edge of the bank was hard to see. Frosya kept testing, nodding when it was all right to take the next step. Prod—feel—nod—step. Prod—feel—nod—step.

It was an unvarying ritual. Hayley imagined her learning it when she began to go into the forest on her own. When her parents realized that she was never going to grow up like other children. *This is what you must do in the snow, Frosya. You must never forget* . . .

It didn't stop her talking. All the time they were moving, she was babbling excitedly. After a while, when it was obvious that Hayley couldn't understand anything, she pointed at Hayley's pocket, motioning to her to pull something out.

'The camera?' Hayley produced it hopefully.

But that was the wrong thing. What Frosya wanted, it turned out, was John's notebook. The moment it appeared, she leapt on it, almost wrenching it out of Hayley's hand. Flicking to the picture of the church, she started chattering again, tapping the drawing first in one place and then in another. Hayley didn't understand any more than she had before, but her heart started to beat faster. Whatever Frosya was saying was important enough to turn her cheeks pink and make her eyes shine.

It began to snow, lazily, a few fat flakes drifting down out of a flat grey sky. Frosya closed the book and dropped it into Hayley's pocket to keep it dry, patting the pocket affectionately.

After that, it was steady walking, following the river. It was unbelievably slow. When they had been going for an hour and a half, Hayley looked back and saw the smoke from the cottages they had left behind, hanging over the trees behind them. They had come almost no distance, even though her legs ached and she was warm and sweating under all her layers. Only her nose was burning cold.

Once or twice, Frosya glanced at the smooth, easy surface of the ice that was beginning to form at the edges of the river. Once she even climbed down the bank and tested it with her foot. But, to Hayley's relief, the ice groaned and cracked, and Frosya scrambled up the bank, shaking her head.

There was no way out of plodding through the snow. It was tiring and monotonous and the sun had disappeared under a layer of leaden cloud. But gradually Hayley's walking fell into a rhythm and the time ticked past. Two hours. Two and a half hours.

They took longer than Irina Petrovna had predicted, and Hayley knew it was her fault. Frosya was slow and methodical, but she kept up a steady pace. She looked as though she could walk for ever. After two hours, Hayley began to wilt, and by the time they had been going for three hours she had to keep stopping to gather her strength.

Frosya didn't complain. She simply stood with her hands folded, beaming patiently. Waiting until Hayley had recovered enough to go on. Plod, plod, plod.

They came on the church quite suddenly. Hayley was expecting to find it in a village and ever since she noticed the smoke behind them, she had been peering over the tops of the trees, looking for something similar ahead of them. Watching for more smoke to show up, pale against the sky.

But there was no village. Nothing at all. Just a sudden flat clearing on the river bank and the church coming up out of the snow.

It was a white church, with black shingles on the roof. The walls were as intricate as the forest behind them, decorated with pillars and blind arches, but there was not a trace of colour on them. There were hardly any windows either. The building was a block of shadowed white, a shade darker than the snow, rising up to the black onion dome. It was big and solid, but it looked light as air, insubstantial as an ice sculpture.

When Frosya saw it, she caught hold of Hayley's hand, nodding and babbling her strange, clumsy words. What she meant was perfectly clear.

Come on! Come and see!

'Wait!' Hayley said, pulling out the camera. 'I have to take a picture.'

Frosya fretted impatiently while she did it. The moment the camera was packed away again, she grabbed Hayley's arm and began to lumber across the open space, dragging Hayley after her.

The snow was deeper there, with no trees to shelter the ground, and they had to take giant strides, hauling their feet out after every step. Once Hayley lost her footing completely, and Frosya dragged her a couple of steps before she managed to pull her hand free and scramble up.

The church's main entrance faced the river, a ribbed archway filled with a heavy, studded door. Frosya shook her head at it and pulled Hayley further on, round the corner of the building. Halfway along the far side, she let go of Hayley's hand suddenly and lowered herself on to her knees, scrabbling in the snow, scooping it away until she located a big, flat stone.

The key was underneath the stone. It had lain in the earth so long that its shape was etched into the ground, a long dent with a looped top at one end and complicated, jagged shapes at the other. Frosya worked away at it with her fingers, levering it free.

When she had it in her hand, she looked up. Hayley held out a hand and pulled her to her feet.

'All right,' she said. 'Let's see this church.'

Still holding on, Frosya hauled her back round the corner, to the big front door. She pushed the key into the black metal keyhole, just below the ring handle, and let go of Hayley so that she could use both hands to turn it.

The lock squealed and grated. Releasing the key, Frosya stepped back and waved her hand, inviting Hayley to go in first. Hayley pulled out the key and dropped it into her pocket. Then she twisted the ring handle, pushed the door open and stepped into the church.

Inside, it was bare and dim, with four arches making a square under a central dome. There was a faint scent, as though incense had seeped into the stones. Apart from that scent, there was nothing at all inside. No seats, no altar, not even a candle end. Just the walls, rising like cliffs, and the massive round arches.

And the paintings.

Every surface was covered in painting. Saints and angels stood sentinel on the pillars and hung on the walls, high above Hayley's head. Complicated multi-coloured patterns stretched along the undersides of the arches and twined into a stiff, formal border round the lower part of the walls. From the windows round the dome, light fell on to haloes and trees, clouds and rocks and strong, feathered wings. And in the darkness above the windows, gold glinted round the tall shape of a mother holding a child.

'Oh, how nice!' Hayley said. 'That's lovely!' She turned back to Frosya, smiling to show that she liked the place. Expecting to meet a smile in return.

But Frosya was totally solemn, staring up at the ceiling with wide eyes. It took her a moment to realize that Hayley was looking at her, and when she did realize, she still didn't smile. Instead, she walked forward, towards the middle of the church, beckoning Hayley to follow her. Sweeping her hand in a great gesture that took in all the pictures, she started to babble. The words were incomprehensible, but the message was plain.

Come and see.

24

I t was early morning when the men came to Grigory's flat.

That was the time he liked best, when the first light slanted between the buildings and the colours began to grow out of nothing. In that light he sat at his window every morning, turning the colours in the stillness of his mind.

When he first came to Petrovsk 9, he hadn't been able to see anything except a uniform, barren grey. Everywhere. Everything. In those days, he had a job, and money in his pocket, but he thought of it as his time of utter poverty. A time without hope, when he was restless and unhappy.

Then he lost his job. And one morning, his restlessness had woken him just before dawn. The sky was still grey, but it was grey like a pigeon's wing, changing every instant, revealing tiny glints of colour wherever he looked. A pair of red curtains at someone's window. A pot of yellow flowers on a balcony, and a blue van on the road. Light on a girl's ginger hair as she hurried to work.

The town was transformed for him. Everywhere he went—looking for work, visiting people, doing his frugal bits of shopping—he saw the small, singing patches of colour that had come out of darkness. Every morning, sitting still at his window before the sun rose, he tuned in to them.

But that morning, what he noticed most was something grey against the snow. A grey van was dawdling past the

202

blocks of flats, pausing as the driver peered at each building in turn to see its number. He was coming for Ivan's visitor. Grigory knew that without knowing how he knew.

Five minutes, he thought.

He longed to be the kind of man whose stillness doesn't falter for anything on earth, but he knew he wasn't good enough for that. He left the window quickly, trying not to panic, and went to shake the man on the mattress.

Last night, he had shown him what to do if anyone came, trusting that he would understand, even though they had no words in common. Now, when Grigory shook his arm, the man was instantly awake and on his feet, fully dressed except for his boots. Grigory picked those up and gave them to him, and the two of them tiptoed across the room to the cupboard by the sink.

It was a long time since Grigory had used that space under the cupboard floor. When he had money—in the grey time—he'd made the hiding place to save himself from being burgled, cutting a hole in the floorboards and fixing the cut boards together so that they could be lifted in a single piece. The space underneath, between the floorboards and the joists, was big enough for a hi-fi system and a microwave. It had fooled three burglars before he stopped caring about burglaries and gave the things away.

The man slid in, feet first, on his back. He squeezed along the space until he could wriggle his shoulders in— just—and lie flat. Grigory pushed in the boots, one on each side of his head. The last thing he saw, as he put the boards back, was the gleam of wide eyes, staring.

When he had tightened the screws, he put back the shelf and arranged packets of food on top of it and the tools underneath. As he shut the cupboard door, he heard the van pull up. There was a sound of doors closing and men talking.

One minute, he thought.

He knew he should pray, but his mind refused to be still, and he wouldn't pretend, so he tidied the mattress instead, straightening the pillow and smoothing the worn quilt. By the time the knock came on the door, his flat looked as bare and peaceful as it always did.

He opened the door.

There were six men outside, one carrying a small handgun and the others with knuckle-dusters and clenched fists. They barged in, pushing Grigory backwards so that he almost fell.

There was no introduction or explanation. They just hit the flat like a hurricane. Five of them attacked the furniture, pulling clothes out of drawers, turning the bed upside down, emptying the bookcase. The sixth man prodded at Grigory's chest with the gun, growling threats.

'Don't waste our time with lies. We want the man you're hiding and we'll twist it out of you if we have to. We know he's here.'

'Search where you like,' Grigory said. 'You can see how little there is.'

He was trying not to glance at the cupboard, but it was impossible. The other men had just reached it—and stopped. They glanced at each other and Grigory held himself very still, out of fear. Was there something out of place?

Then one of the men barked with laughter and swept his hand along the top of the cupboard. The icons slid off the end and crashed to the floor and all the men laughed together. They wrenched the cupboard doors open and began to pull out the packets of food. One of them found the tools and they used the screwdriver and the claws of the hammer to punch holes in the packets. Rice and buckwheat and lentils showered on to the floor and Grigory heard the mess crunching under their feet.

The gun prodded his chest again. 'We're busy men!' the leader barked, shaking lentils off his shoes. 'Not idiots with time for icons. We know who was here, and you're going to tell us where he's gone.'

He nodded briskly at the others and they abandoned the cupboard, turning with eager, wolfish faces. Grigory understood that in half an hour he would be injured. Maybe dead.

He closed his eyes and thought of silence. Stillness and silence and the colours that grew out of darkness.

When they gave up at last, the leader turned away impatiently. 'He's no use to us. Sew him up.'

The men hesitated, looking at his gun. Bad-temperedly, he pushed it at one of them.

'Use this, then, if you're too much of a coward to do it with your hands. But let the rest of us get clear before the noise.'

The others jeered as they followed him out of the flat, taunting him for their own hesitation. Grigory heard them clattering along the corridor, and felt the gun's nozzle pressed to the side of his head. He moved very slightly, to see the face of the man who was holding it, and felt the gun jerk nervously.

The man wasn't old. Twenty, perhaps, or even less. He still had soft, unformed features.

And he was still inexperienced enough to let their eyes meet. Grigory saw that he was aware of the moment, aware of himself, poised on the edge of pulling the trigger. No use trying to say anything to him. Any word, any more movement, would set off the trigger finger. All Grigory could do was look up, trying to keep his swollen eyes open. Trying to put into his face the words he couldn't say out loud. *If you pull the trigger, what then? What will it mean for you?*

It was a long moment. A space in both their lives. Then the young man's eyes went cold.

'I will do it!' he said, his voice rising. 'It's no use looking like that. I'm going to do it.'

Grigory knew he meant it. It was in his voice. A hysterical shrillness as he worked himself up to the shot.

'I'm going to kill you!'

He raised the gun—and at that second, the knocking started.

The noise was so loud, that it took Grigory a moment to work out what it was. He glanced across at the door, but the sound was closer than that. A steady, insistent rapping on wood, coming from the cupboard.

The man in the hiding place was knocking on the boards above his head.

The young man with the gun shifted suspiciously— and then realized what he was hearing. Keeping the gun trained on Grigory, he walked backwards to the cupboard and opened the door with his foot.

Now there was no mistake about the noise. And, even from where he was lying, Grigory could see the tell-tale marks on the screw heads. There were bright scratches in the metal where his screwdriver had slipped when he was hurrying.

The young man gestured with the gun, motioning Grigory towards the tools on the floor. 'Do it. Now.'

Dragging himself over the spilt grains, Grigory reached for the screwdriver, feeling the pain as he moved his fingers. The men had stamped on both his hands and he knew there was a bone broken in his right wrist. Maybe in the left thumb as well. He crawled across the floor and pulled the shelf out of the cupboard, working out how to shift it without moving his body too much.

The man in the hiding place was still knocking and now he was calling out as well. Loud, English words.

Grigory couldn't understand what he was saying, but the voice didn't sound panicky or afraid. Only determined.

He began to work at the screws, concentrating all his attention on manipulating the screwdriver. Gripping the handle was painful and exerting pressure on it made him feel sick and giddy, but he had no choice. He turned the screws, a twist at a time, resting his hands after each one. It was almost ten minutes before he could lift them out. He levered the boards out and peered into the space below.

The man came up instantly, pushing himself out of the hole with his feet and scrambling into the room. Getting to his feet, he glanced round, taking everything in. The splintered icons. The broken chair. The mark where the milk had hit the wall.

Grigory.

He registered it all, turning until he was facing the young man with the gun. He said something fierce, tapping himself on the chest, and then he turned to Grigory with his hands spread. Helplessly.

'We don't need words, my friend,' Grigory said. 'I was trying to save your life—but you have saved mine instead.'

He held out his hand.

'That's enough!' shouted the young man, waving his gun. 'He's coming with me!'

He grabbed at the man's arm, but before he could pull him away from Grigory there was a rush of feet along the corridor. The door of the flat was flung wide open, thumping back against the wall.

'What's keeping you?' said the leader's voice scornfully. 'Afraid to shoot?'

And then he saw the man he had come for—and the hole in the cupboard behind him. He stopped and caught his breath and a slow smile spread across his face.

'That's better. That's much better. Bring him!'

The man reached down quickly and touched Grigory's hand. He was still reaching for it as they grabbed him and dragged him away through the door.

The leader stayed for a moment, watching Grigory's face. Then he stepped forward and lashed out at him, knocking him backwards, into the cupboard.

'It's finished,' he said curtly. 'Kill him.'

He stayed just long enough to see the young man raise the gun and then turned away to follow his prisoner. Grigory stared up and thought, *Now. This is the moment. For me and for him too*. He closed his eyes, to make it easier for them both.

This time, the shots came without hesitation. Once. Then again. Grigory heard the wood of the cupboard splinter, right beside his head.

'Don't move,' the young man muttered roughly. 'Don't even open your eyes until the van's gone—or I *will* kill you.'

Grigory lay and listened to him hurrying along the corridor. He heard his feet hammer down the stairs and run across the concrete towards the van.

The engine was already running. The instant the door banged shut, they were off, screeching down the road and round the corner.

Grigory waited until the sound had died away completely. Then, slowly and painfully, he pulled himself out of the cupboard and on to his feet. He collected up the icons and brushed them clean with his hand.

When he had set them gently back in their places, he picked his old coat off the floor, where it had been thrown down into the pool of milk. Pulling it on, he limped out of the flat, closing the door on the mess behind him. There would be plenty of time to clear that up later.

First, he had to find someone who would drive him to the police station. Even if it was no use, he had to report that a crime had been committed. That a man had been carried off by force.

Then he had to telephone Ivan. Because, whatever had happened, however the secret had been given away, Ivan would need consoling.

Hobbling along the corridor, Grigory went to do the things that needed doing. As he went, he held in his mind the two men who had saved his life. And also those other men who had wrecked his flat and beaten him up.

He is lying trussed up on the floor of the van, with his arms wrenched behind him and his ankles lashed to his wrists. As the van lurches round corners, he rolls slightly from one side to the other and the men kick at him, almost casually, pushing him back towards the centre with their feet. They don't look at him. Their job is almost over. All they have to do is take him back to their boss.

Which one will it be? The Bear or the Wolf?

He lies with his eyes closed, wondering. Poised in that breathless, timeless moment between firing and blowdown, that moment just after the charges explode, when the building floats in air, still seemingly intact. Holding its shape, even though it is filled with the forces that are going to rip it apart

He can't remember what he holds inside his head that has such power. All he can do is snatch at glimpses . . . the Bear . . . the Wolf . . . Hotel Iksa. The words vibrate with danger, resonating in his memory even though he can't explain them. And he knows that the power is already loosed, already out of his control.

He can't stop it now.

25

W hat did Frosya want her to see? Hayley glanced round at the walls again. They'd been in the church for several minutes and she'd looked at everything already. What else could there be?

But she went along with Frosya, to be polite. Dragging her to the first pillar, Frosya put out an arm and began to chant in a steady, nonsense monotone, bending forward to touch first one part of the picture and then another. The shield. The wings. The great dark eyes.

Hayley nodded and smiled, not really paying attention. Looked at individually, the pictures seemed awkward and out of proportion. The faces were stiff and the paint was cracking and flaking. By the end of ten minutes, she was ready to scream with boredom.

'Thanks, Frosya,' she muttered. 'That's really interesting.'

She started to turn away, but Frosya seized her shoulder and shook it angrily, as if she were a badly-behaved child. She didn't stop shaking until Hayley turned back to the picture. Then the monotonous chanting began again.

And somehow, following the pointing finger, listening to the rise and fall of Frosya's voice, Hayley realized that she was being told a story.

Whether it was the story that really belonged with the picture, she had no idea. She didn't know who the winged figure was, any more than she knew what Frosya was saying. But it came to her, suddenly, that the pictures weren't just decorations. They signified something. As

Frosya's finger pointed and moved and pointed again, she began to look at them properly.

And she started to see the details of the drawing and the rich variety of the colours. The way the feathers overlapped, each one on its neighbour, each slightly differently, so that there was a shifting pattern of angles. The strong downward lines of the angel's shield, echoing the verticals in his face. The shaded contours of the cloud behind him.

When Frosya moved on, she moved with her, to see if the next picture would come alive in the same way. They didn't move directly from pillar to pillar, across empty space. Instead, Frosya reached up, following the underside of the arch. Her finger traced the twisting red lines of the tendril pattern as though it made a road from one figure to another. From the stern, militant angel to the man dressed in shaggy animal skins. And then on, to a woman covered only by her own long, thick fair hair.

Every figure was different. Every face, every finger, every line. The technique was amateur and irregular, but that didn't make the paintings dull. It filled them with an irresistible sense of actual, blundering life. Hayley could almost see the real hands that had held the paintbrushes. The real foreheads, frowning as the painters struggled with shapes and meanings and the irregularities of a real building.

Frosya led her round the whole building, inch by inch, and she felt her eyes opening. She felt her mind expand, blown apart by the vigour of the pictures and the richness of their unknown stories.

She never thought about the time. When they set out, they'd had ten hours for the round trip. The walk had taken four hours, which left plenty of time to study every millimetre of the walls before they needed to start back.

When Frosya finished the long recital at last, the

211

two of them stood together under the dome, looking round at the space that her incomprehensible words had transformed.

When Hayley walked in, all she had seen was flat walls, decorated with pretty shapes and colours. Now she knew that she was surrounded by a stillness that vibrated with energy and meaning. It was rich and strange—and homely. Busy with every kind of shape and colour imaginable—and utterly still.

She didn't understand any of it, but the stillness and the silence folded round her. She felt her pulse slow, and her mind unknot itself. *Yes,* she thought. *Yes.*

It was Frosya who started to worry first. She began to pull Hayley's sleeve, pointing up at the high, narrow windows and muttering fretfully. Hayley was suddenly aware that the sunlight had gone. The church was even dimmer than before.

Had they stayed too long?

She looked down at her watch and relaxed again. 'It's all right, Frosya. It's only one o'clock. There's lots of time. If we eat our lunch now, we've got four or five hours to walk back before it's dark.' She tapped the watch face, smiling and nodding, to show what she meant.

But Frosya didn't smile back. She began to pull at the sleeve, urging Hayley towards the door, mumbling and frowning.

'All right,' Hayley said, resigning herself. 'Don't worry. We can leave now if you like.'

She shook her arm free and marched up to the door, turning the handle and tugging at it. They could always eat their lunch while they were walking, if that would keep Frosya quiet. It would have been better to sit and rest for another hour or so, but there wouldn't be much rest if—

She didn't even hear the noise. Not until the door opened. The thick walls of the church shut out everything and she was expecting to see what they had left when they walked in. The bright, smooth surface of the snow, with no marks except their own footprints. And, beyond it, the grey river and the delicate winter forest.

Instead, there was half-darkness and the roar of a gale blowing straight at the church. Opening the door wider, she was caught by the full force of it.

The gale was thick with snowflakes, driving out of an almost invisible sky. They filled the air so that the river and everything beyond it were obliterated. They swirled into Hayley's face and over her clothes, stinging her skin and knocking her breath away. By the time she managed to wrestle the door shut again, she was panting and panicky, her coat crusted with snow, her nose and hair and eyelashes covered with clinging flakes.

You see now? Frosya's babble said, unmistakably. *You see what I meant?*

'What are we going to do?' Hayley said. 'How are we going to get back?'

She heard a shrill, hysterical note in her own voice. Abruptly she realized that she was tired and hungry and stranded in the middle of a blizzard—in the middle of a forest in the middle of Siberia in the middle of Russia. Her heart was thudding from the effort of pushing the door shut and she began to shiver.

Then Frosya patted her arm. Not a big, dramatic gesture. Just a red, roughened hand, patting the worn surface of the sleeve. A middle-aged Russian woman shrugging with resignation and shaking her head. That was all.

But the world righted itself.

Hayley didn't understand Frosya's babble, but she understood her rueful smile. *What a pain. There's a snowstorm. We can't go out.*

213

And that was all it was, after all. Just a snowstorm. Hayley looked up and smiled and Frosya beamed at her and patted her cheek as if she were a small child. Then she went through a slow, careful pantomime, stopping after each movement to work out the next one.

She pointed at the door, and shivered.

She walked her fingers across the back of her hand and shook her head, looking horrified. Shivering much harder.

She pointed at herself, then at Hayley, and then at the floor of the church, smiling again and nodding approvingly.

Finally, she pillowed her head on her hands and closed her eyes.

And Hayley got it. The whole thing. Frosya meant that they were immensely lucky to be still in the church. If they had set out, as they'd planned, they would have been trapped in the snow, half the way back to the village. As it was, what had they got to worry about? They would just have to spend the night in the church.

It was so simple. Hayley smiled again and started to giggle with relief. Frosya giggled too, pulling at her arm and beckoning her down the church, away from the door.

At the far end, the building divided into three. There was a wide central section bounded by two short walls, running parallel to the main side walls. The separated areas to left and right were like narrow, open-fronted chapels. Frosya headed for the right hand one. As she went, she pulled off her thick outer coat.

Putting it down on the floor, in one corner of the chapel, she sat on it and signed to Hayley to join her. Then she took off her headscarf and spread it on the floor beside her. Methodically, she started to go through her pockets, laying out food on the scarf.

A couple of pieces of bread in a bag made of knotted

string. Some salt in a twist of paper. Two hard-boiled eggs and a piece of smoked sausage.

She looked at them for a moment and then cocked her head sideways and glanced up at Hayley.

'What do you—? Oh, of course. Sorry.' Hayley sat down too, and felt in her own pockets. 'I don't suppose I've got anything useful.'

She felt in her pockets and added what she could to Frosya's collection. The key to the church. A chocolate bar. John's notebook and Annie's camera. An empty crisp bag.

She nearly took back the crisp bag, but Frosya shook her head fiercely and grabbed it. When Hayley looked puzzled, she motioned to her to stay where she was and headed for the church door, with the bag in her hand. She came back with it crammed full of snow, signalling that Hayley should hold it and wait for the snow to melt.

They ate the food. Because there was a lot of time to use up, they ate slowly, filling the minutes with the texture of the bread and the sweetness of the chocolate, the strong, greasy taste of the sausage and the cold plainness of the melted snow.

Frosya peeled Hayley's egg as well as her own, splitting it apart and sprinkling salt on it without asking permission. For a moment, Hayley was annoyed.

Then she realized that this was what Frosya did, all the time. She looked after everyone else. It was the only way of living that she knew. Taking the egg, Hayley bit into it, smiling and nodding to show that it was good.

They saved some of the bread and a small piece of chocolate. Frosya bundled those up and put them into her pocket. Then she looked at Hayley. Waiting. Expecting something.

Hayley tried to think of a way to pass the time. What could the two of them possibly do together? They couldn't talk or tell stories, because they had no language in common. They couldn't go for a walk outside because of the snowstorm. What was left?

She looked round. Annie's camera was still lying on the headscarf, with the key and John's notebook. Putting the other things into her pocket, she picked up the camera. She had promised to take photographs, after all. Slowly she stood up, deciding how to do it.

It was a digital camera with a spare storage card. That gave her around forty pictures to play with. Enough to cover the whole church, if she planned it out carefully. She walked across to the first angel picture—where Frosya had started—and lined it up in the viewfinder.

Frosya stood up too, and followed her. It was obvious that she didn't know what to expect. The first flash startled her so much that she screamed loudly, and Hayley nearly dropped the camera.

But after that, she was enchanted. She trailed round behind Hayley, burbling and jigging from foot to foot. Once the first shock was over, she didn't take any notice of the camera itself. It was the light she wanted.

As Hayley pointed the camera, trying to make sure that she didn't miss anything out, Frosya hovered at her elbow, holding her breath and gazing at the wall. Each flash lit up a separate section. Figures jumped out of the shadows, bright and vivid, and Frosya squealed with delight. Then it was dark again, and there was a moment of total, satisfied silence before the whole process started up afresh.

Hayley took all forty pictures, working it out carefully. Recording every inch of the walls to take back to Annie. By the time she had finished, she was completely exhausted. She yawned and stretched, to show Frosya what she meant to do, and then headed back to the side chapel, hoping she could sleep with only a coat to cushion the hard, cold floor. She wondered how low the temperature would drop in the middle of the night.

She took off the old fur coat, laid it on the floor and sat down. Immediately, Frosya sat down too, right next to her.

'No,' Hayley said gently. 'I was going to lie down. I need to—'

Frosya nodded and put an arm round her, pulling her sideways.

It was so simple that she couldn't believe she hadn't thought of it herself. The obvious way to deal with the cold. She leaned against Frosya's shoulder, catching the smell of woodsmoke and sweat from her coat. It was a strong, unfamiliar smell, but comforting too. So was Frosya's heavy, solid body. It was easy to lean against her. There was no risk of knocking her over.

Hayley relaxed, feeling herself float into sleep. *This is all it takes*, she thought. *Things are really simple, after all.* Tonight she would sleep, leaning against Frosya's shoulder. Tomorrow, when the blizzard had stopped, they would walk back along the river bank. Everything was going to be all right . . .

26

Viktor Orlov was reading his e-mails when they phoned him about the Englishman.

Click Kiev:

Kolya looks like cracking. Give me another couple of days . . .

Click St Petersburg:

We've had a moonwalker driving around here for three days now. Could be the garbage are getting ready to poke their noses in. Maybe we ought to apply a bit of pressure to their bosses . . . ?

Click Nizhny Novgorod:

It's time to settle accounts with the bitches. Osip is sewn up already. OK to take out Igor next?

All the messages were read, memorized, and deleted. They were fitted into the network of contacts and projects that he kept in his head. He could do three or four deals at a time, speaking to one contact on the phone while he tapped out an e-mail to another and ran his eyes over a note from a third.

He never wrote anything down on paper. Never let anyone else have the complete picture. The threads that held his business together linked a dozen different cities, but he was the only person who knew how they were woven together. If he let go of them, whole systems would crumble, whole cities would collapse into gang warfare.

Everything was controlled by instinct and memory—and a nose for danger. He slept on a knife edge. Ready. Always ready. He could pick up the stink of treachery while the thoughts were still forming in the *sooka*'s mind. No one ever put one over on him.

No one.

The phone call about the Englishman came through while he was reading the last e-mail. His eyes went on scanning the screen as he answered.

'Viktor Orlov.'

(And *click* the suspicions from his contact in Yekaterinburg were wiped off the computer and filed in his mind.)

'We've found the foreigner,' said the man on the other end of the phone. He didn't bother to identify himself. His voice was recognized.

'Alive?' Viktor said sharply.

'Of course, Viktor Mikhailich.'

'You're sure it's the right man?'

'Certain. Yevgeny met him once, in Tomsk. It's the Englishman all right.'

Viktor closed his eyes and allowed himself a split second of triumph.

He'd always known that Leonid was lying about the explosion in Tomsk. From the very first phone call, all his instincts had told him there was something rotten there. Something that threatened his own position.

He would have had anyone else sewn up straight away, the moment he began to suspect. But he couldn't take a risk like that with Leonid. The organization ran on loyalty to the two of them and any quarrel between them—any suspicion of treachery—would jeopardize the whole business.

He had to prove that Leonid was the traitor and he had to do it cleanly, in a single swoop.

That meant patience. Hundreds of contacts put on alert, in a dozen towns, with the constant danger that Leonid would find out what he was doing. And all the time—

219

nothing to go on. Just the same message coming back from everywhere.

The Englishman's dead. He blew himself up in Tomsk.

Whatever had happened out there in Siberia, Leonid had covered his tracks perfectly. The death certificate was good and there were half a dozen witnesses, all saying the same.

The Englishman blew himself up. He was lousy with vodka and he ran straight back into the building. Blown to bits.

The cover story was unbreakable—but it made Viktor's skin itch. He was certain Leonid was plotting something. So he went on watching and waiting, waiting and watching—until the first, uncertain rumour came from Krasny Yar. And then the message from the three trusted contacts who were shadowing Leonid.

He has been to see the Englishwomen in their hotel. Now he's looking for a boat to take three cars into the forest. Looks as if he's going north-west in a hurry. Should we follow?

Following Leonid would have been the obvious, clod-hopping move. But Viktor distrusted the obvious. He'd taken a gamble and kept his shadows in Tomsk and Petrovsk instead, watching Leonid's men there.

And the gamble had paid off. When Leonid's men got the message, they dashed for the taxi rank at Petrovsk station—and *his* shadows were right behind them. Ready to seize their chance.

He'd got the Englishman.

Viktor opened his eyes again and was instantly focused. 'What about the opposition?' he said into the phone. 'Are they far behind?'

There was a hoarse chuckle from the other end of the line. 'They're right off the clock! They went chasing after the taxi and lost it, and now they're hunting round in Novosibirsk. They didn't have the wit to stay in Petrovsk and work on the taxi driver's family instead.'

'You got the family to co-operate?'

Another chuckle. Harsher. 'No problem. They sent us straight to him.'

Viktor considered his plans.

He had enough evidence to fix Leonid now. All it needed was a single phone call to the police in Tomsk. *You know that Englishman who's supposed to be dead? Well, he's sitting in a hotel in Petrovsk. If you don't want to look like idiots, you'd better question a few people in your pathology lab. There's going to be a stink about faking evidence . . .* The police wouldn't risk a cover-up—not with a foreigner involved.

But just fixing Leonid wasn't good enough. If he was a traitor, the whole organization had to know. They had to hear exactly what he'd been plotting.

Viktor spoke sharply into the phone. 'What have you got out of the Englishman?'

There was an apologetic growl from the other end. 'No joy there. He won't sing a note. Lost his memory.'

Viktor made a scornful, disbelieving noise.

The voice on the phone rose slightly, sounding injured. 'No, it seems to be real. We've . . . applied pressure, but it doesn't make any difference.'

'He can't remember anything?'

'Only the last few weeks. Says he was found in the forest, with a fever, and before that—pfff! Everything's a blank.'

Viktor hunted for something to work on. '*Where* was he found? Does he know that?'

'We've worked it out from what he says.'

'And?' Viktor said impatiently.

There was an even more apologetic noise. 'It's . . . nowhere, Viktor Mikhailich. Away in the forest, north-west of Petrovsk. There's not even a village on the map. It's useless.'

It wasn't useless to Viktor. His brain made the

221

connection instantly, slotting in another piece of the puzzle.

. . . he's looking for a boat to take three cars into the forest. Looks as if he's going north-west in a hurry . . .

So that was why Leonid had raced off into the forest. He'd discovered something to link the Englishman to that nowhere place—and whatever he found there had sent his men scurrying off to Petrovsk station.

Viktor chewed his lip. It was time he went to Siberia anyway. Leonid had had a free hand there far too long. *He* needed to show his face in Tomsk and Petrovsk, to remind them who was the elder brother. And a trip to the forest might be a good way to start.

It might even restore the Englishman's memory.

For a moment Viktor revolved the idea in his mind, estimating the risks. Then he looked at his watch. Petrovsk was four hours' flight away. That would take it to something like two o'clock in the afternoon there. He made the decision and gave his orders crisply down the phone.

'I'll be flying in around two. I want you at the airport, with the Englishman. Lay on a room for us to talk and a helicopter, to go into the forest.'

'A helicopter?'

Viktor was amused by the gulp at the other end of the line, but his voice didn't give that away. 'I'll need a helicopter to take six people. You have a problem with that?'

'Of course not, of course not. We'll be there, Viktor Mikhailich. Two o'clock.'

'Do it discreetly. Without speaking to anyone else in the network.'

'Naturally. Of course, Viktor Mikhailich. Two o'clock.'

Viktor rang off, not wasting time by saying goodbye, and dialled again. Twice. The first call was quickly done.

Yes, there would be a seat on the Petrovsk plane for him, even if someone else had to go without. Yes, it was at the front. *You're checked in already, Viktor Mikhailich. And shall I book the usual hotels? The Iksa in Tomsk and the Tsentralnaya in Petrovsk . . . ?*

The second call was more delicate. An almost-ignorant contact at the University. Viktor breathed deeply while the phone was ringing, getting rid of the urgency in his voice. Letting the Professor go on with his game of innocence. When he spoke again, he sounded relaxed and genial.

'Professor? It's Viktor Orlov here . . . your family well? . . . we must have lunch again . . . yes . . . but just now I could do with a little help . . . I need some information about loss of memory and how to treat it . . . '

It was Leonid's Englishman all right. Viktor recognized him instantly.

The man had lost weight, and he had a black eye and a split lip, but it was unmistakably the same person. The one Frank Walsh had brought in three months ago. *Our electrician's mate,* Frank had called him.

The man was sitting in a corner of the little interview room at the airport. He looked up quickly when the door opened, and his eyes widened.

'You know me?' Viktor said, in Russian.

He spoke reasonable English, but he liked the cushion that translation gave him. A few more moments to take in the reaction to his words. Also a way of lulling the English speakers into a false sense of security, so that they babbled to each other.

When the Englishman understood the question, he shrugged. 'Are you the one who's going to kill me?'

His voice was level. *Resigned to it,* Viktor thought, annoyed and admiring. They'd told him the story of the knocking on the cupboard floor. How the Englishman had allowed himself to be taken when the danger was over. Fools like that were hard to negotiate with. Accepting their own death gave them a kind of power.

Viktor waited for the translation. Then he said, 'I'm not going to kill you.' He matched his own voice to the Englishman's flat, emotionless tones. 'I'm going to help you. Will you come into the forest with me?'

He watched, steady and unblinking, to see how the translated words were received. The Englishman met his gaze with an ironic lift of the eyebrows. 'I have a choice?'

He recognizes me, Viktor thought. *But he doesn't know who I am. And he doesn't trust me.* He weighed up the situation, looking for the right handle to turn. What would he want most, himself, if he had lost his memory?

When he had the answer, he took the other chair in the room and sat down, facing the Englishman. That enclosed them in a kind of intimacy that excluded the others. Even the translator, whispering over Viktor's shoulder, was not really a part of the conversation.

'You have forgotten your name?' Viktor said easily.

The Englishman nodded when he understood.

Viktor smiled and spread his hands. 'I know who you are. You are called John Cox and you are an electrician's mate.'

He spoke the name as clearly as he could and he saw the Englishman recognize it. But when the second part of the sentence was translated, he shook his head.

'I'm not an electrician.'

Viktor kept his face a blank, until the words came to him in Russian. Then he smiled. 'You see? You remember this now. I have helped you already, and in the forest, you will remember more things. Shall we go to the helicopter?'

224

He stood up and walked towards the door. The Englishman followed, but only with his eyes. He didn't speak until Viktor reached the door.

Then he said, 'I will come with you if you tell me one more thing.'

Does he think he can bargain? said the translator's face as he passed on the words. Viktor frowned him into silence and then raised his eyebrows, waiting for the Englishman to go on.

He asked the obvious question, of course. 'What's in this for you? Why do you want me to get my memory back?'

Viktor was expecting that. He had the reply ready.

'I think we have the same enemy, you and I. He planned your death and he has planned mine too. And he will plan them again and again, until he succeeds. I need your lost memories, John Cox, as much as you do.'

It is death that links him to the Wolf. Death that links him to the Bear.

That's the answer he's been dreading. The answer that confirms all his shreds of memory. From the moment the Wolf walked in, he's been waiting for it.

. . . I need your lost memories . . .

He's tangled in the steel teeth. Trapped in the struggle that locks two enemies together, as much a part of it as they are themselves. He holds the knowledge that will blow the whole thing, and he can feel it moving just below the surface of his mind, like a dragon moving in its egg. Ready to hatch.

As he follows the Wolf across the snow-covered tarmac, towards the helicopter, words jangle together in his brain.

Hotel Iksa.

The Bear.

His own name, newly-found. John Cox.

And the other name that dances beside it. Annie Glasgow.

Does he want to remember? How can he know? How can he tell? He's torn between longing and terror. Desperate to find his way back into the self he's lost—and terrified of what he will discover if he does.

I was only a consultant, says the voice in his mind. *I was only doing my job.*

But it doesn't work this time.

27

Frosya heard the helicopter first.

She and Hayley were almost back at the cottages. They were wading through the last few yards of snow on the river bank before they hit the track up through the forest. Both of them were giggling slightly, out of relief that they had nearly made it. The blizzard hadn't stopped until midday, and the return journey had taken longer, because of the extra snow. But they were going to be safely indoors before dark.

Suddenly Frosya stopped and turned round, throwing back her head to peer up at the sky. Now that the blizzard had gone, it was a bright ice blue and the helicopter showed like a black smudge, working its way up the river.

Frosya laughed and waved, tugging at Hayley's arm. Hayley waved too, even though the helicopter was much too far away for the pilot to see them. Then she tapped her watch.

'We ought to keep going.'

Frosya beamed benignly at her and patted her arm. Then she began to wade forward again, heaving one leg after another. She was sweating from the effort, but she hadn't flagged once, all the way.

Hayley grinned and followed, trying not to complain to herself. The snow was way over the top of her boots and her feet were wet and freezing cold, but she knew she could get there.

Loitering to let her catch up, Frosya waved at the

helicopter again, and Hayley saw that it was closer now. The whirl of the rotors was clearly visible and the colours showed against the pale sky. Red and white and black. It was a big helicopter and the sound it made drowned out the small noises of the forest.

They reached the clear track and turned away from the river, into the trees. Hayley was still trying to watch the helicopter, but Frosya barged at her to attract her attention.

'What's the matter?' Hayley tried not to sound annoyed, but it wasn't easy. Frosya's solid bulk—so comfortable and comforting in the church—was enough to make her stagger.

Frosya jabbered, pointing at wheel marks on the track.

'Of course there are wheel marks,' Hayley said impatiently. She didn't bother to make signs so that Frosya would understand. It was too difficult. 'There were wheel marks when we went out too. It was Leonid Orlov's cars.'

More barging and jabbering.

Hayley couldn't work out what the fuss was all about, so she smiled and nodded, just to be free of the barging.

They came up the slope to the village—and suddenly she realized what all the jabbering had been about. Of *course* those weren't yesterday's wheel marks on the track. The blizzard had covered those. Frosya had been trying to tell her that someone had driven up from the river since the snow stopped. Only she'd been too stupid to understand.

Until she saw the cars.

Leonid Orlov's Range Rover was parked close to Irina Petrovna's cottage. The two Nivas were lower down, on the other side of the clearing.

Hayley started to shake, and a voice set up a chant in her brain, repeating the same thing over and over. *He's*

228

killed John and now he's come back to kill us. He's killed John and now he's come back . . . The words tangled themselves into the noise of the helicopter overhead, beating like a pulse.

She stopped and stared at the cars, full of wild ideas about running off and hiding in the forest. But how could she? She was very tired and beginning to feel cold. And Frosya was chivvying her towards Irina Petrovna's cottage, pulling her hand and clucking her tongue disapprovingly at the delay.

There was no real chance to escape. Someone must have been watching them through the crack in the shutters, because the cottage door opened suddenly and Yuri looked out, smiling.

'Hayley, you are back!' He sounded genuinely pleased. 'We were worried when we came and you weren't here—'

He broke off because he caught the sound of the helicopter. He glanced up, past Hayley, and all at once his expression changed. The smile vanished and he darted back into the cottage.

Looking over her shoulder, Hayley saw why.

The helicopter was much closer now. It was coming up from the river, following the line of the track. As she watched, it reached the clearing and stopped, hovering overhead.

Then, very slowly, it started to come down.

The noise of its engines was deafening. The wind from the rotor blades disturbed the loose snow, stirring up a miniature blizzard and stripping the tree branches around the clearing, so that they stood bare and dark against the rest of the forest. Hayley backed away, catching hold of Frosya's hand to pull her back as well.

Out of the corner of her eye, she saw people crowding into the doorway of Irina Petrovna's cottage. Leonid Orlov, with Yuri at his elbow. And behind them, in the shadows,

229

the shape of the wheelchair and the pale glimmer of Annie's weasel-face.

The helicopter sank until it touched the surface of the snow. It rose a little way, to alter its position, and then settled. The rotor blades slowed and stopped and the door opened. Hayley held her breath as she saw a figure climbing out. He was wearing a thick jacket and a hat with flaps, but she recognized him instantly, as soon as he turned to face the cottage.

It was Leonid Orlov's brother, Viktor. The man who had been in the restaurant with Frank Walsh.

Frosya was tugging at her sleeve, pointing at the helicopter and babbling. Hayley shook her head.

'Ssh! Wait.'

Someone else was getting out of the helicopter. Jumping down lightly and landing on both feet, as neat and balanced as a cat. Hayley recognized the movement and her heart thudded and stopped.

No, it's not. It can't be—

But she knew it was. This time he was real. This time she could run across the space between them and he wouldn't vanish. Her arms would go round solid flesh and bone. She would hear his voice and see him grin.

He straightened, and she saw his face. It was thinner than before, and there was a bruise on his right cheek, but it was John. Himself. Away on her left, she heard Annie shout his name and it triggered her into motion. She started to run towards him, forgetting how tired she was and how many miles she'd walked. All she could think of was crossing the space that separated them.

She was almost there, almost near enough to touch him—when she met his eyes. And the look in them stopped her dead.

He doesn't recognize me, she thought. *He doesn't know who I am.*

230

His face was confused and puzzled and apprehensive. Without realizing it, he had put up a hand to hold her off and the movement paralysed her. All at once, he was more unreal than the dissolving illusions she had seen before.

He doesn't know who I am . . .

28

Irina Petrovna was in the shadows, standing beside Annie-in-the-wheelchair. When she heard the shout, and the sound of feet running, she bent her head and peered between Leonid Orlov and his son, looking to see who had come in the helicopter.

It was the lost man. The man that Frosya had found in the forest. He was standing motionless, facing the English girl, and she was staring back at him. Not saying a word.

They really were brother and sister. That was clear to any fool who saw them together. But whether that meant love or fighting was anyone's guess. Irina Petrovna had lived a long time, not always in the forest, and she knew what happened when blood went sour. She held her breath as she watched them, waiting for the silence to break.

But neither of them broke it. It was someone else who did that. A bulky figure came barging past the English girl, laughing and jabbering and scattering snow everywhere. She flung herself straight at the lost man, throwing her arms round him in a suffocating hug.

Oh Frosya, dear Frosya, Irina Petrovna thought. *Why do you never know how to be careful? Why have you never learnt about danger?* Frosya was beaming at the lost man, babbling into his ear and patting his hair as if he were her son, come back after twenty years away. What would she do if he didn't recognize her either?

But he did recognize her. His face brightened suddenly and he hugged her in return. She stroked his cheek, clicking her tongue at the bruises, and he smiled and shook his head.

The tension was broken and other people started to move. Three more men jumped out of the helicopter. They glanced sideways, looking for orders towards the man who had jumped out first. The man with the steady, calculating eyes.

So we have two bosses, Irina Petrovna thought. The breath in her lungs was suddenly like ice. She looked up sideways, first at Leonid Orlov and then at his son. The father's eyes were darting about, trying to watch everyone at once. But the boy was watching his father, waiting to see what he would do.

The new boss made a small movement with his hand. Immediately, the other three began to hustle the lost man and his sister towards the cottage.

'Please let me through,' Irina Petrovna said, raising her voice just enough to be heard. Not meek or pleading, but dignified. It was her house, and she meant to give the strangers a proper welcome.

Annie-in-the-wheelchair said something too. She manoeuvred her chair forward, bumping the boy and his father so that they stepped aside automatically. Then she shouted for a second time, hunching forward as far as she could in her seat and calling to the lost man.

His eyes found her face and fixed on it, but he didn't walk faster. He came into the cottage at a slow, dreamlike pace, with Frosya hanging on to his hand and the English girl a few steps behind. As he came through the door, he stopped and stared down at Annie, biting his lip. Hunting for something.

'He's forgotten her?' Irina Petrovna said to the next person who came in. It was the man with the steady eyes.

For a split second he looked shrewdly at her, summing

233

her up. 'He's forgotten a lot of things,' he said. 'But he's going to remember. That's why he's come here.'

There was the ghost of a threat in his voice, but Irina Petrovna knew that it wasn't aimed at her. It was meant for one of the others to overhear. He turned away from her, towards the wheelchair, and spoke to Annie, in Russian.

'He'll know who you are soon enough. He just needs something to jolt his memory. Have you got anything with you? Something that belongs to him, maybe. That he can hold in his hands.'

Annie glanced round at Leonid Orlov's son, waiting for a translation. But Frosya had understood the Russian words already and she didn't give the boy a chance to begin. She started jabbering excitedly, nudging the lost man's sister and pulling at her coat. Irina Petrovna could usually make a guess at what Frosya wanted, but not this time. She had no idea.

Frosya was too impatient to wait. Suddenly she moved, thrusting a hand into the English girl's pocket. She pulled out the black notebook they'd made all the fuss about. Bending her head, she started to flick through the pages, searching for something. But she was in too much of a hurry and her fingers were awkward. She couldn't find it, and she began to mumble angrily.

'Let me do it,' Irina Petrovna said.

She knew, now, what Frosya wanted. The drawing of the old church of Saint Peter and Saint Paul, beside the river. Taking the book, she turned the pages and found it.

The poor, empty Peter and Paul church.

Sixty years ago, she had helped to strip it bare. That was the thing to do with churches when she was young. She had come to Siberia with the Komsomol, all of them eager to sweep away the ancient darkness and build something new.

They had forced the old priest to unlock the church and then they had made him watch while they threw out

234

everything movable, and ripped the wooden fittings off the walls. The altar was pitched into the river and the icons and the iconostasis were broken up and burnt. The walls had survived, but only because they were solid and there was no bulldozer to knock them down.

That was what they did in those days. They thought it was the way to make a new world. Now, things had changed. There was another new world and different things were being pulled to pieces.

Everyone in the cottage was watching her now, waiting to see what would happen when she gave the book to the lost man. She held it out, and he bent closer, peering at it in the dim light.

He takes the book out of Irina Petrovna's hands and looks down at the drawing.

'Isn't it lovely?' says the girl standing beside him. The one who ran and then stopped. 'Did you draw it just because it was so beautiful?'

He can't tell her she's wrong. He can't say anything, because memory has exploded suddenly in his brain, cascading outwards from the image of the church. He is caught in the instant when he peered through those high, narrow windows and saw everything—his whole life, his whole self—in its true colours.

He remembers it all now. Everything.

In his mind, he is standing on the river bank, in the autumn light. The wind is cold, but he needs a reason to stop for a while. Three days on the run have exhausted him, mentally and physically. The church gives him the excuse he wants. It's a puzzle, standing there on its own, on the river bank. The sort of structure he's never worked on yet.

He lets his mind play with the idea of it, relaxing out of danger for a few minutes. When he's walked all the way round the building, he begins to draw it, trying to work out how it's constructed. His pen makes the shape, and his brain grapples with the problem that fascinates him, over and over again, every time he starts a job.

How would I blow this one?

I'll just solve this, he tells himself, *and then I'll go on to Strezevoy.*

It's like a talisman. If he can work it out, he'll know that luck is on his side. He'll make it north through the forest, to the airport at Strezevoy. Outside the Orlovs' territory. He'll find a plane and slip through their fingers, to Moscow and back to England. Then they can blow each other up all they want. He'll be well out of it. All he needs is a bit of luck.

But the luck eludes him. He looks down at his drawing and he can't see how to blow the church.

Most buildings give up their secrets easily. He's been inside dozens of grey Russian blocks, and he can decode them just by looking now. From the outside. But this church is different. He doesn't know how the dome is supported or where he would be able to wire in his charges. He can't guess how many pillars there are. He can't solve it without seeing the inside.

He looks for a window. But the only windows are high up in the walls, way above his head. The sensible thing to do is give up and keep on heading north, to Strezevoy. He ought to put his notebook away and leave.

But he can't. Because he needs the luck.

He walks round the walls again, looking at them differently now, with a rock climber's eyes. And suddenly it seems so easy that he laughs out loud. The building is covered with ledges and carvings and blind arches. He can be up at a window in five minutes.

Sitting down, he takes off his clumsy shoes and thick socks. In his bare feet, he begins to climb, not rushing but checking every foothold carefully. He expects to find loose stones and crumbling mortar, but the walls are sound and strong. He reaches a window and presses himself against the clear glass, peering down into the shadowy interior.

And he sees—not brick and stone, but faces. They line the walls and stare out from every surface of the pillars. Human faces, each one different, with great dark eyes . . .

29

Hayley was watching John as he stared down at the page. They were all watching him, gazing at his bent head and his clenched hands, gripping the notebook.

He's remembering, Hayley thought. *In a moment, he'll look up at me and smile. Everything will be all right. Everything will be exactly the same as it was—before all this began.* She held her breath, waiting. *Any moment now . . .*

But he didn't look at her. Instead, he began talking in a rough voice, as if the words hurt. Holding up the drawing of the church in front of him.

'You see this? Every building in Siberia is like that. Every building in the whole world. Just a block. You don't have to worry about all the extra stuff—curtains and windows and paint. Any fool could strip those out. It's the structure that's interesting if you want to blow it. The way it's put together.' He stopped, breathing harshly.

'What's the matter?' Annie said. Her face was white and tense.

John didn't even look at her. He shook the notebook savagely, rattling the pages. 'All the things people chose— the carpets and the furniture and the pictures—they're not important any more. And getting the people out of the building—the people who lived there—you don't have to worry about that. It's just a block—'

He was forcing the words out now, almost choking. Annie pushed her chair forward and put a hand on his arm.

237

'You don't have to worry about the people because someone *else* does that,' she said. 'It's not your job.'

Fiercely John rounded on her, shaking her hand away. 'My job? Not my job? You think it's all right to draw lines like that? *I was only doing my job. That's not my responsibility. I was only the consultant*—so it's not my fault if a hundred people die. Even though I didn't think. Even though I pretended to myself—'

'What are you talking about?' Hayley said, shouting because she had to stop him somehow. Because she couldn't bear that voice any longer. 'You'd never blow up a building with people in it! No one would do that.'

Behind her, she heard Leonid ask a muttered question. She heard Yuri's voice translating what she'd said. And she felt her words fall into a deep silence.

It was John who broke the silence. In a different, duller voice he said, 'Oh, but they do, Halo. It's a *mafiya* thing. And if you destroy the block where your rival lives, you don't just get rid of an enemy. Everyone else in the building gets blown up too. And that makes other people—*respectful*. Careful not to get in your way.'

'But *you* wouldn't do that,' Annie said. And then, when he didn't answer, 'John? That block of flats in Tomsk—?'

He shook his head. 'That one was all right. Just an ordinary job. Leonid's bought the site to develop it.'

And the other one? The next one in the notebook? Hayley didn't say it. Couldn't say it. And she could see from Annie's face that the same words were frozen inside her head as well.

It was Viktor Orlov who asked the question. He broke in suddenly, speaking clear English, with a strong Russian accent.

'So what other job did Leonid give you to do?'

John bent his head, staring at the ground, still silent.

The only sound was Yuri's voice, keeping the translation going. And a sudden, protesting grunt from his father.

Viktor ignored that, concentrating on John. 'Tell us,' he said. His voice was mild, but when there was no answer he repeated the words more forcefully. *'Tell us.'*

As if the words were a signal, his three heavies moved closer, surrounding John. Annie caught her breath and Hayley shrank back, but neither of them spoke.

It was Frosya who reacted fiercely. All the time John was talking, she had been watching him with a broad smile, obviously not understanding a word he said, but pleased to be listening to him. When the men moved, she stepped forward, chattering crossly. Snatching at their arms, she tried to drag them away from John.

Viktor made a small gesture. Two of the men picked her up and the third man opened the door. With a shout, they flung her through it, sending her sprawling in the snow.

Frosya heaved herself up, yelling and waving her arms. She started heading back into the cottage, but one of the men made a threatening movement and she scuttled off towards her own cottage instead.

Viktor went on as if there had been no interruption. 'Tell us about the other job, John Cox.'

John looked down at the floor. 'It was only a plan. That was all Leonid wanted. *To see what it would take to bring the building down.* But it had to be a secret, because he was thinking of buying the place and he didn't want the owners to know he was interested.'

Viktor arched one eyebrow. 'And this place. Was it another block of flats?'

John shook his head.

Viktor nodded. 'Offices, maybe?' His voice was spiky with irony.

'It was a hotel,' John muttered. 'In Tomsk.'

239

The room was very still now. Breathless. Viktor waited a moment, letting them all feel the tension before he said anything else. When he did, he spoke very lightly. Without any emphasis.

'So my brother told you that he was planning to buy the Hotel Iksa. Yes? And you believed him, of course.'

John shook his head angrily. 'I don't know *what* I believed. I was trying not to think too much.'

'Did you know that this is where I always stay in Tomsk? The Iksa?' Viktor's voice was icy. 'Maybe you thought that it was kind of my brother to buy my favourite hotel?'

Hayley glanced at Leonid. He didn't react at all when Yuri muttered the translation. His heavy face was expressionless, the small eyes fixed on John. The whole room was very still except for Annie's fingers, tapping at the arm of her chair.

'I was trying to work out how to stay alive.' John's voice was hardly louder than a whisper now. 'I knew Leonid would kill me anyway, once he knew where to put the charges. He didn't want anything to link him to the explosion.'

'Of course not,' Viktor murmured. 'It would be necessary to blame another gang for that. How else could he take over the organization? It is built on loyalty to the Orlov family. The men would not let my murderer take it over.'

Yuri began to translate that, but Leonid growled sharply, obviously ordering him to stop. Viktor said something scornful in Russian and nodded to Misha to take over. Hayley watched the men's faces as they took in what Viktor had said.

When it was clear that they'd all understood, Viktor turned back to John. 'You gave the explosion plan to my brother—so that he could kill me. And then you found a chance to escape. Yes? Is that how it was?'

240

The air was electric. Hayley felt the hairs rise, all along her arms. She saw Yuri look up at his father, drawing away, almost imperceptibly. They were all waiting for John to reply.

He lifted his head. 'I—'

But he didn't get the chance to finish. Leonid moved suddenly, stepping forward to grab Annie's chair. Swinging it round, he pushed it hard towards Viktor and his men, sending them staggering sideways.

One of the men stumbled into the wood heap. It collapsed and a cascade of logs rolled down, thundering across the floor. Hayley jumped out of the way and Yuri caught hold of Irina Petrovna, to save her from falling.

In the middle of the chaos, Leonid seized John round the neck, dragging him backwards.

Hayley was looking wildly in all directions. At Annie, thrown forward and almost pitched out of her chair; at Yuri, with his mouth tight and miserable; at Irina Petrovna, struggling to keep on her feet. She even noticed that Leonid Orlov was sweating heavily and that his face was ugly and urgent.

But she didn't see the gun.

Not until Leonid moved it up, pressing it to the side of John's head.

It looked like the old toy guns that John had had when he was six or seven. Hayley had played with them herself sometimes, when she was small. It was hard to believe this one was real.

Annie didn't seem to believe it either. 'Put that away!' she said scathingly. Even half out of her chair, she wanted to be in control. 'Yuri, tell your father—'

It was Viktor who brought them into the chill of reality. He spoke very quietly, hardly moving his mouth.

'Be quiet, Annie Glasgow. If you startle Leonid, he will

241

shoot. John Cox will die. We shall all die. Be quiet and do not move.'

Hayley froze, holding her breath. Scared even to blink, in case the movement of her eyelids was too disruptive. *If you startle Leonid, he will shoot.*

Leonid's arm was round John's neck and the gun— the real, deadly gun—was pressed hard against flesh and bone. That was what John had been talking about. Killing people. But Hayley hadn't understood properly. You don't believe it at first, even when you see the gun. Even when you have worked out, yourself, where to put the charges. The words are just toys. *Mafiya. Explosion. Death.*

No one moved. No one spoke. The gun stayed pressed to John's temple.

It was timeless. A frozen terror that went on and on, without measure. But it couldn't have lasted more than a few seconds.

Then the men in the doorway said something sharply, in Russian. They all began to move—Leonid's men and Viktor's together—shoving further into the cottage to get away from the door.

Frosya was standing in the doorway, red-faced and glaring. The men parted, left and right, and the moment she saw Leonid Orlov properly she began to yell, screaming nonsense words.

Against her shoulder, aimed straight at him, was her father's heavy old hunting rifle.

30

John sees her too. He sees her in the doorway, with the big rifle up against her shoulder, and she's yelling her usual nonsense. But suddenly it's terrifying nonsense, with the rifle's double eye staring through it.

He sees Irina Petrovna start forward, trying to grab at Frosya's arm. The rifle jerks erratically and the Wolf mutters a warning. The Bear's gun is pressing harder now, jammed against his skull. Glancing sideways, John sees that, for once, Leonid's small eyes are completely still. He's watching Frosya.

Everyone is watching Frosya.

She is standing in the doorway, silhouetted against the light. Every time anyone speaks or moves, she jerks round in that direction and her finger tenses on the trigger. Poor Frosya. Poor dear, simple Frosya. She doesn't know she's a sitting target. She thinks she's in control. She thinks she's going to save him.

'For heaven's sake,' Annie mutters under her breath. 'Can't anyone get that thing away from her?'

All the men are waiting for a signal. Whispering to each other, without moving their mouths. John can't understand what they're saying, but he knows that Leonid isn't the only one with a gun. Any moment now, one of the men will make a move, to distract Frosya's attention. And as she turns, another man will fire. It's bound to happen. Unless—

Unless he does something.

He's the one who has to do it. Frosya won't shoot him. He's the person she's come to rescue, the one person who's safe. If he's going to save her, he's got to persuade her to put down the rifle.

He pushes at Leonid's arm, knocking it away from around his neck. Then he steps sideways and spreads his hands to show that he's free.

'It's OK, Frosya,' he says gently. 'There's no need to be angry. Look. I'm all right.'

Frosya smiles at him and babbles a few words, but she doesn't put the rifle down. Instead, she waves it impatiently, towards Leonid Orlov.

'She wants his gun!' Annie says. 'She wants you to take the gun, John. Yuri, tell your father—'

Miserably the boy mutters a few Russian words, and everyone looks at Leonid. He scowls and raises his arm slowly, holding out the gun. For a moment, they all believe that he's going to give it up. That he'll drop it into John's outstretched hands without a struggle.

But at the last moment, John sees the small eyes flicker—and he doesn't wait for any other warning. He takes a guess and flings himself forward, so that Leonid's action and his reaction come together, in the same split second.

Leonid moves, swinging his gun round towards Frosya—

John moves, throwing his body against the gun, to knock it out of the way—

Frosya's reactions are slower, but she moves too. As Leonid's gun clatters to the ground she lowers her head and fires without taking aim, like a hunter faced with a charging bear.

And the rifle explodes in her face.

It throws her backwards, out of the cottage and down the steps into the snow. She sprawls there, spread-eagled, exactly as she did when the men threw

244

her out a few minutes before. But this time she doesn't scramble up again.

There was never any chance that she would live. John went racing out after her, dropping on to his knees beside her body. Leonid pushed through to check it out for himself. Viktor rapped out orders in Russian, in a low, urgent voice. But none of that made any difference. From the moment the rifle went off, Frosya was dead, and they all knew it.

Irina Petrovna began to wail. It was a thin noise, almost too shrill to be human. Hayley put an arm round her shoulders, but she shook it off and hobbled outside, leaning heavily on her sticks.

The rest of the old people were coming out of their cottages too, drawn by the noise. The old woman with the chickens. The two old men, one on crutches and the other with a tin mug in his hand. Even Frosya's father came to the door, holding himself up against the side of the frame. He started to call out to her in his crazy, cracked voice.

'Frosya! Frosya!' And then a tumble of Russian.

Hayley stood and watched them, completely numb until she felt the tears on her face. Then she went out too, to be with Frosya.

They were still standing there, in the bloody, trampled snow, when the car came bumping up the track from the river. Hayley thought for a moment that Viktor had planned it that way. That he had contacted the police before he set off in the helicopter.

But it turned out that they had come with Boris and Aleksandr, the river traders. Boris and Aleksandr brought candles and sugar and tea—and this time they'd brought

245

the police as well. To investigate the stranger from out of the forest.

The policemen ran across the clearing towards the body, shouting as they came. Viktor said something and his men moved suddenly, clustering round Leonid.

'What is it?' Hayley whispered to Yuri. 'What's happening?'

Yuri's face was white. 'My uncle . . . my father—' The English words failed him and he held up a hand, telling her to wait. His eyes were fixed on his father and the muscles of his jaw were tight and tense.

Leonid didn't wait for the police to ask questions. The moment they were near enough, he launched into a long speech, bombarding them with words. He pointed at Viktor, at Frosya's body, back into the cottage, waving his arms fiercely for emphasis. There was no space for anyone else to speak. Leonid's voice rolled on and on, like thunder, getting louder all the time.

Even Hayley could tell that he was desperate.

Viktor didn't try to interrupt. He just stood beside Frosya's body, waiting for the tirade to finish.

Gradually, the torrent of words rose to its climax. Leonid flung an arm up into the air and turned to the men who'd come with him, calling on them to back him up.

No one said a word.

There was a long, horrible silence, while Leonid's face grew red and angry. Once Yuri opened his mouth, as though he might say something, but Viktor put a hand on his arm and he shut it again, hanging his head.

When it was obvious that no one else was going to speak, Viktor began to talk at last. His voice was level and sensible and the policemen took out their notebooks to write down what he said.

It didn't take long. When he'd finished, they took a

few more statements and talked to John for a while, with Misha as interpreter. Then they ushered Leonid off to their car.

As he left, one of the men called scornfully after him. *'Sooka!'*

And Misha spat sideways, into the snow.

Yuri's face was wretched. Hayley laid a hand on his arm. 'Are you all right?'

He answered very softly, without looking at her. Softly and bitterly. 'Oh, my uncle Viktor will look after me. He can be kind, because he has the whole business in his hands. Tomsk and Petrovsk as well. There is no one to stand up to him now.'

'Does that matter?' Hayley said. 'Is one *mafiya* boss so different from another?'

Yuri spread his beautiful, long-fingered hands. 'It will be worse now, I think.'

'It's never going to be good while there are gangs like his. Someone ought to end it. Break it up.' Hayley meant it, but she said it easily. Like someone who knows she is going away soon.

She looked across the clearing. John had carried Annie over to the cars and they were sitting in one of the Nivas, talking quietly. Suddenly she was overcome with relief. It was all finished. They were going to take John home—and everything would be back to normal.

If Yuri hadn't been watching her, she would have smiled.

John wasn't smiling.

'I wanted to die,' he said. 'When I looked through that window, into the church, I just wanted to die.'

Annie studied his bent head. *He's different. He's changed.*

247

Aloud, she said, 'But it's only a building. How could it make you feel like that?'

'It was the *faces*.' John leaned forward, resting his head on the steering wheel. 'I thought it would be empty in there. But there were dozens of faces. And I suddenly realized—'

He stopped, catching his breath. Annie sat very still, watching and waiting.

'When we went round that hotel, it was the middle of the day.' John's head was still down and his voice was muffled. 'So there was no one about. And anyway I was concentrating on the job. Thinking about the building, not the people in it.'

'You hadn't guessed what Leonid was up to?'

'Oh, I don't know. I don't *know*!' John ran his hands through his hair. 'Well, yes, I suppose I guessed in a way. But I thought, *Why should I take sides? One of them's bound to kill the other in the end. Does it matter which one gets control of the organization? They're as bad as each other.* I was shutting everything else out of my mind. I just wanted to escape and get back to you.'

'That's why you hitched a ride in that lorry?' Annie said.

'It was the quickest way to get right out of Petrovsk. I thought I could find a lift north and then walk through the forest, so that Leonid didn't track me down. I was planning to pick up a plane at Strezevoy.'

Annie tried to piece the journey together in her mind. 'You hitched the lift and then you disappeared into the forest. Yes? And that's where you saw the church. But the fever stopped you getting to Strezevoy and you landed up here instead. Is that right?'

'Not exactly,' John lifted his head and stared through the windscreen. 'It wasn't the fever that stopped me getting to Strezevoy. I was already on my way back to Tomsk by then.'

'*You were going back?*' That was the last thing Annie had expected.

'I had to.' John closed his eyes. 'Do you know the first thing they teach you about explosives? The very first thing? *Before any explosion, it's your responsibility to count the people out. You must never let the charges be fired until you know the building's completely empty.* I saw all those faces—and I realized what I'd done. When Leonid blew up the hotel, it was going to be full of people—and they were all my responsibility. I had to go back. If I hadn't been ill—'

'If you hadn't been ill, you'd be dead yourself by now!' Annie was fierce. 'What did you want to be? Some kind of martyr?'

'You don't understand!' John whipped round to look at her and their eyes clashed. He was as fierce as she was. 'It was all my fault and I've got to make up for it somehow. How can I live with myself if I get off scot free?'

'But nothing *happened*! There *wasn't* an explosion. Nobody died!'

Annie shouted the words—and the moment they were out, she realized what she'd said. She put a hand over her mouth.

'You see?' John said gently. 'It's all my fault. If I'd done the right thing in the first place—if I'd stood up to Leonid—Frosya would still be alive.'

'But you can't do anything about that now. You can't bring her back.'

'I can't wipe everything out and start again. But there is *something* I can do.'

Picking up Annie's hand, he started to explain it to her. She watched his mouth making the words—and thought of all the effort that had brought her there. Of the energy she'd used up, and the money she'd spent and the

249

pain she'd suffered. Her mind and her body were both bruised and aching and exhausted.

And now he was asking her to go through something else. For one split second, she thought, *I can't. I can't bear any more* . . .

Then she took a long, determined breath and braced herself. Ready for whatever he needed her to do.

'What do you mean you're not coming home with us?' Hayley said. She'd been waiting for John to get into the Niva with them. They were all about to leave. 'You can't just stay here! What are we going to tell Mum and Dad?'

John shook his head at her. Smiling. 'I can't go anywhere, Halo. Not until my papers are sorted out. I don't exist.'

'But it won't take long to sort out the papers. Not if you come back to Moscow with us.' Hayley leaned forward and put a hand on Annie's shoulder. 'He's mad. Can't you make him see sense?'

But John didn't look mad. He looked—still. Tranquil.

'He's made his mind up,' Annie said. 'It's pretty important to him.'

John nodded at the cottages. 'What do you think they're all going to do this winter, without Frosya? They're going to need a lot of help.'

'You're going to be here *all the winter*?' Hayley was horrified. 'But we've come such a long way—and we thought you were dead—and Mum's going crazy without you. How *can* you stay here?'

Annie reached back, patting Hayley's arm. 'Cheer up,' she said briskly. 'He won't be here for ever. They'll fling him out of the country in the end.'

She sounded her usual self, unsentimental and businesslike. But her other hand had tightened on the edge of the window. The ends of the fingers showed through the glass, white-tipped.

'I thought it was all over.' Hayley was angry. 'I thought everything was going to be normal again.'

'But that's not how life is,' Annie said. 'We can't wipe out the bits we don't like and pretend they never happened. Things change all the time, don't they?'

She looked up at John, through the window, and Hayley saw her expression for the first time. *She's frightened*, she thought. *John's different, and Annie's afraid.*

And then she saw that the fear made Annie different too. Just as she was different herself. Just as Yuri and Viktor and Leonid were all different, all changed by what had happened. They were all changing, all the time. There was no going back.

And Frosya was the most changed of all.

'*Some* things stay the same!' she said desperately. 'You two are still getting married, aren't you?'

'I hope so.' John looked down at Annie. 'What do you think?'

'Buy me a ring and I'll tell you,' Annie said lightly. 'You were going to bring one home. Remember? Made of Siberian gold.'

John smiled ruefully. 'I did buy one, but I haven't got a clue where it is. I left it behind when I ran away from Petrovsk.'

'Well, maybe you'd better find another one. Unless you've changed so much that you don't keep your promises.' It could have been a joke, but Annie's voice was very brittle.

Like someone in a dream, Hayley put her hand down into the pocket of the coat she was wearing. Her own, old coat that Chris had forced her to bring. She found the little lump of metal she had pulled out of the bonfire, still there at the bottom of the pocket.

'Is this the ring?' she said.

It was too distorted to fit on to anyone's finger. John took it from her and held it up for Annie to see.

'Well, it's still gold,' he said. 'But I don't know if it's any use like this.'

Annie reached out and he put it carefully into the palm of her hand. Her fingers closed round it, holding it tight. 'I suppose I'll just have to manage,' she said. Her voice was shaking slightly. 'But I haven't got one to give *you*. Shall I buy you something when I get back to England?'

Hayley couldn't see why it mattered, but John laughed suddenly, bending in through the window. Grinning in the cheerful, delighted way that Hayley had known since she was very small.

'As a matter of fact, there *is* something you can buy me . . .'

Hayley has printed out the photographs and stuck them up, all over her bedroom walls. She looks round at them now, before she starts her letter. John the Baptist. St Sergius. Mary the Egyptian and the Archangel Michael. Dozens of faces looking down at her. Angels and bishops and kings. Prophets and priests and prostitutes. A tax gatherer at his stall and a hermit huddled in a rocky cave. Each one with a different story. Unique.

She is trying to learn their stories. Some of them aren't easy to find, but she's determined to do it. It's her way of remembering Frosya. She thinks of that for a moment, imagining how she will tell the stories to John when he comes home. Wondering what he will be like when he does.

Then she picks up her pen and begins to write to him.

Dear John,

I hope you are well, and the old people too. Thank you for your letter. We all laughed a lot—especially Mum. She and Dad have sent you some fantastic thermal underwear, which should arrive before the river freezes.

Annie has bought the bicycle . . .